A Limited Lawyer:

The unlikely rise and foreseeable trials of a corporate lawyer

Peter Fairchild

A catalogue record for this book is available from the National Library of Australia

Publisher:
ASPG (Australian Self-Publishing Group)
P.O. Box 159, Calwell, ACT Australia 2905
Email: publishaspg@gmail.com
http://www.inspiringpublishers.com

National Library of Australia Cataloguing-in-Publication entry

Author: Fairchild, Peter

Title: **A Limited Lawyer:** The unlikely rise and foreseeable trials of a corporate lawyer

ISBN 978-1-922618-65-8 (pbk)
ISBN 978-1-922618-66-5 (eBook)

For Dr Rod Settle

My brother from another mother

Acknowledgments

This book would not have been possible without the inspiring input and guidance of my editor, Dannielle Jackman. Thanks also to my friends and former colleagues, especially to Blair, Judy, Lorna, Russell, Tanya and Tony, for their suggestions and corrections, and to the past and present patrons of the 'Ascot Vale Hilton' for their support and quintessential humour. Best thanks of all to my wife, Leng, for her expertise in child protection legislation and many kindnesses. And to the late Rod Settle, to whom this book is dedicated, for his years of mentorship and encouragement.

Preface

The distance from my home to the local public house is three hundred and eighty-five steps or three minutes at a brisk military pace. I well know, as that journey has become a daily occurrence. Invariably, the return trip takes longer. Over recent years, that pub has become my refuge and Carlton Draught my saviour. Once there, I can forget who I am, what I once was and, more importantly, what I did. Neither the Geordie barman nor the assortment of patrons that serve as my retirement friends particularly care about my past; they have their problems, and I would not have it any other way. I once claimed that I found their presence cathartic. I should have kept my trap shut.

'An emotional state that arises from downing a dozen schooners is hardly therapeutic,' retorted the bush academic on the corner barstool. 'You're just a pommy fuckwit that doesn't know when to hang his stubbie holder up for the night.'

The response was more insightful than my beer buddy could ever have known. I confess I am now a hopeless alcoholic, and without any hint of false modesty, I have probably always been a pommy fuckwit. Yet, the response from the public bar did stir me into action. I hoped that in reducing my story to writing that I would experience some liberating relief; some limited amends for past failings. Sadly, that experience remains to be experienced.

This book chronicles the mistakes that destroyed my career, self-confidence, and the life of a friend. Mine is a story of false starts, compromises and improbable aspirations that began in childhood. Long, long ago, I dreamed of a legal career. Those were wild-childish thoughts in which law, or rather legal characters, played centre-stage. Throughout my formative years, I eagerly followed the exploits of Perry Mason and, later, Horace Rumpole in glorious BBC monochrome. I recall a feeling of pride when I first realised I shared my family name with the American character. Perhaps that realisation stirred my initial interest in matters legal.

The writings of Dickens, Mortimer, Harper Lee, Dostoevsky, and Kafka filled my adolescent bookshelf, just next to that iconic poster of a swim-suit clad Farrah Fawcett-Majors. I was an avid reader, but my English language skills were weak, and my mind would often wander from the text. I spent the daytime dreaming, playing out make-believe narratives, with myself centre-stage and with Farrah as an admiring witness.

My hero authors created genuinely great characters. Yet, whatever their nationality, they were all attorneys. My boyhood world of lawyers was small. It was a make-believe world that contained criminal barristers, district attorneys, and family law specialists, each with unparalleled eloquence and style in their defeat of injustice. Oh, how I longed to emulate my heroes. Oh, how I dreamed of extracting court-room confessions from rapists or corrupt corporate high-flyers. No seasoned copper could match my quick wit or cross-examination. These, of course, were just the fantasies of an impressionable middle-class underachiever. Unquestionably, I mistook justice for law, and, of course, I would never practise in such areas.

Half a century later, those dreams appear foolish. My English secondary modern education was not designed to cultivate the ranks of the professions. The grammar schools would develop generations of accountants, architects, surveyors, and lawyers. However, the crème de la crème of the elite occupations would emerge from the likes of Eton, Harrow, Charterhouse, and Marlborough.

I should have listened to my teachers. As passionate believers in the English class system, they had questioned my social fibre from the start. I simply was not destined for a legal career. Unsurprisingly, therefore, along life's way there would be times, even years, where legal ambitions would lay dormant. Indeed, thoughts of rising above my station in life had been stifled at a young age. In truth, therefore, I was so proud the first day I donned the wig and gown. I had a real feeling that my teachers were wrong and that even an average English boy's legal dreams could be realised.

In reality, my achievements would hardly scratch the surface of a privileged profession, let alone challenge the English class system. My admission to practice was in the Banco Court in the Supreme Court of Victoria, Australia. It was the only day I ever wore a lawyer's trademark attire. Indeed, both were borrowed from a barrister friend of a solicitor acquaintance. The gown was partially ripped and in need of a lengthy appointment with a dry cleaner. The horsehair wig both stank and itched. Given my subsequent ordeals, that wig and gown were remarkably appropriate.

My area of legal practice, for what it was worth, was far removed from the daily experiences of high-flying silks or the prestigious equity partners of the top-tier law firms. I was merely an employee that provided services within the confines of a commercial business. The provision of legal services was often just a small component of a role that included compliance, risk management, company secretarial, and, above all, administration. I was, as the name suggests, an in-house lawyer.

Nonetheless, throughout the Western world and now through much of the Eastern one, there is an ever-increasing body of lawyers whose hearts and souls are tied to a single entity or corporate group. A modern form of indenture arises that, in practice, plays havoc with the ethical and professional responsibilities imposed on practising lawyers as a whole. But more of that particular problem later.

You may know of famous lawyers who have practised as employees of private corporations or institutions, but I do not. I have conducted Google searches, spoken with former practitioners, and rummaged through many of the Melbourne libraries. I have even reviewed the membership list of the Association of Corporate Counsel Australia. There are no prominent household names there. Quite simply, the lot of an in-house lawyer is of little public interest and a lifetime of her trials and tribulations would scarcely rank as anything more than a passing scene in *LA Law* or *Boston Legal*. However, we do have our moments, and I hope that in the pages that follow that you will read them with an open mind.

You may be inclined to judge me harshly or dismiss this publication as self-serving nonsense. If you do, then please stop reading, and avoid the pubs in Melbourne's western suburbs. I'm sorry, Dear Reader, but this book is of more interest to me than a meagre royalty stream. My storytelling is designed to heal old wounds; my old wounds. So, Dear Reader, please don't bugger that process up.

x

$$\Diamondsuit$$

Chapter One
The Introductions

The Lee Family Office had its headquarters, indeed its only quarters, in one of Melbourne's iconic landmarks. It was on the thirty-fifth level of Nauru House at the Paris end of Melbourne's Collins Street. I was nearly forty years old when I walked through the sliding glass doors on a chilly winter morning in my new off-the-peg grey pinstriped suit. The suits were always grey or dark blue. I had joined the army of faceless accountants, lawyers, brokers, fund managers, and bureaucrats who mingled around the cheap sandwich bars or Doc Martin's Tavern. By then, I had had fifteen years' experience as a generally diligent but largely ignored public servant.

It had been a long and rather uninspiring journey into corporate Australia. As the south-westerly wind breezed through the piazza adjacent to St Michael's Church and generally played havoc with my smartly combed hair, I stood tall and proud. I had never had a business card before. Yet, there was my name and position, in embossed lettering:

Greg Mason - Legal Counsel
Lee Family Office
Level 35, 80 Collins Street
Melbourne VIC 3000

Not bad for a reject from the English education system. I draw an index finger over the embossed words. It felt good, and I felt good; really good.

The Lee family had historical links to the East India Company and had grown fat in the period between the two Opium Wars. In the old days, they had properties from Canton to Madras before their offspring descended on the Ballarat, Bendigo, and Castlemaine goldfields of country Victoria. While their businesses had evolved from many a murky deal, at least in Australia, the family interests focussed on legitimate real property and freight. I was, however, far more interested in the two restaurants and nightclub that they still operated in Chinatown.

In those early days, shortly before the concerted war on drink driving, the Lee family restaurants hosted our long and alcoholic Friday lunchtime banquets. A former colleague once suggested that this was the family's way of redirecting our hard-earned salaries back to our employer. Yet, the reality was more complex and far more selfless.

Frequently, one or two generations of the Lee family would attend the Friday soirees and, more often than not, staff contributions towards the invariably large bills were mere tokenism. The Lee family and its representatives that served on the board of the Lee Family Office viewed their staff as part of their extended family. In time-honoured Chinese fashion, family cohesion was best nurtured and protected around the dining table. Five generations of Australian-born Lees had not influenced that dynamic.

You could make a case that those Friday lunches had an informative purpose, or at least until 2:30 pm when the effects of too many Tsingtao beers and whisky chasers would invariably kick in. I learnt as much about Chinese culture and values as I did of the fascinating dishes that appeared on the laminated menus. Unfortunately, all that ceased one Friday afternoon a few years later when Winston Lee drove his convertible Mercedes at speed into a suburban lamp post and regurgitated the remains of a sesame chicken and bottle of XO brandy over the arresting police officer.

Winston's father, Alfred, was then the patriarch, a fatherly figure in his early fifties although he looked and acted a decade or two older. He was a kind and gracious man and set a fine example for his extended family. I learnt to say, 'Neih hou ma?' (pronounced *ney ho ma*)—literally, 'how are you?' It was one of the few snippets of Cantonese I learnt. I was hopeless at foreign languages and the tonal nature of Chinese dialects exacerbated my language learning difficulties.

The Lee Family Office had been founded in the late 1980s primarily to serve the accounting and investment needs of Alfred's limb of the Lee family tree. A couple of brothers and a few cousins formed the backbone of the client-base, although their respective spouses and offspring were welcome additions. From the early 1990s, the client base had expanded to include several wealthy entrepreneurs. It was true that many of them were of Chinese descent or involved in Chinese affairs. Restaurant owners and hoteliers, retailers, and property tycoons were readily accepted. However, the clients were not restricted to the wealthy Chinese community, or at least, not for long.

Over time, the Lee Family Office employed more Caucasian staff and clients. That was not a conscious decision, and it was never clear to me who came first. As the company took on more non-Chinese client advisers, the pipeline of potential clients increased. As the client-base enlarged, the need to engage suitable professional and administration staff also grew. Despite the rise of Melbourne as an educational hub for Asian students, the market for suitably trained staff was always tight. The Lee Family Office could not, even if it had wanted to, afford to limit its personnel to one ethnic group.

The business model of the Lee Family Office had been moulded by an appreciation of charitable and religious endeavours. We would provide tax and accounting services at discount rates, and to many of the philanthropic clients, those services were provided pro bono. So, the Lee family's name became synonymous with charity as well as entrepreneurialism, although outside of Victoria's Chinese community, the name had little standing. The Baillieus, Besens, Lews, Myers, Pratts, and Smorgons, amongst many others, had more substantial and better-known family offices. In contrast, Alfred Lee was never one for public attention. Indeed, he eschewed the media with a passion.

The firm had a strict media-relations policy. No one was to speak publicly on Lee Family Office matters without Alfred's or Winston's prior approval. Indeed, that permission was rarely granted. The result, of course, was that the Lee Family Office enjoyed a high level of anonymity, well at least until recent events soured the family's reputation. If you went back twenty years ago and surveyed a random sample of the average Melbourne business community about what they thought of the Lee Family Office, I suspect many of that sample would never have heard of it.

While Alfred never fully articulated his passion for privacy, there were a couple of explanations. First, Alfred would always go about his business in a quiet, calculated manner.

'Stay in the shadows,' Alfred once remarked. 'If you don't, the taxman will be after you.'

Alfred seemed to espouse the belief that you would not get caught unless you drew attention to yourself. In that regard, he clearly underestimated the resources available to the Australian Tax Office and other regulatory agencies.

The second explanation focussed on the 'tall poppy syndrome.' Stick your head up in the open and someone would take delight in cutting it off. I always thought that that explanation was more insightful. Still, I was never sure if Alfred's fear of being a tall poppy developed as a consequence of being born Chinese or having imbued the well-known Australian complex over time. Perhaps it was both. It was undoubtedly true that in both cultures there was a fascination in 'bringing down' the prominent and influential. I suspect though, that the general brutality of Mao's rule and the specific purges undertaken by the Gang of Four had more of a lasting impact on a young, impressionable Alfred than any Australian expression of the syndrome. Indeed, aside from the taxman, Alfred did not care what anyone thought of him.

By the time I joined the Lee Family Office, Winston Lee, Alfred's oldest son, had taken over the business reins as chief executive officer. In chronological terms, I was quite a few years his senior, but in terms of position and public standing, I was many years his junior. As a young boy, he was simply known to his family as 'eldest son,' while his peers referred to him by his Chinese name, Win Sun. Over the years, that name had become anglicised either by design or mispronunciation to Winston. Just like his father, he never formally changed his name. However, both agreed that it was easier to deal with white Australians by adopting British-sounding names. It never dawned on either of them that their selected names were more suited to an older generation.

Chapter Two
The Kinsmen

Despite being born and raised in the affluent suburb of Toorak and attending the prestigious Scotch College, Winston was, like his father, a Hong Kong boy at heart and immensely proud of the colony and its economic and social achievements. For the Lees, Hong Kong was more than just four hundred square miles of the world's most densely populated land. It was a shining monument to the triumph and virtue of capitalism. Indeed, the shanty towns and sampan cities would mostly be cleared during Winston's Hong Kong days, and that label 'made in Hong Kong,' and the cheap connotations that went with it, would slowly disappear with the awakening of the economic dragon to the colony's north.

Winston was highly amused that I appeared at the Lee Family Office the day after the Prince of Wales and Governor Patten sailed out of Hong Kong Harbour.

'It's ironic. We get rid of British rule, and I immediately get to rule an Englishman,' he laughed. I laughed with him the first few times he said it, but Winston was never one to let a good joke go without numerous repetitions. 'It's ironic,' he would repeat, just in case we had not heard him the first time.

Yet, the date of my arrival was not ironic. Call it coincidence, call it chance, but despite his Scotch College education, an honours degree in economics from Monash University, and a Masters in something esoteric from the University of Hong Kong, he never could use that word correctly.

I immediately thought of Alanis Morissette's classic song from her *Jagged Little Pill* album and whenever Winston would use the word 'ironic' I would, silently, recall her contentious illustrations of the term. A downpour ruining a special occasion is both unfortunate and disappointing. It is not ironic, or at least not identifiably ironic. Nonetheless, I would chuckle as I was never quite sure myself what the word meant. Perhaps any inaccurate use of the word ironic was itself ironic. It is funny how the brain can conjure up associations from the most trivial of matters. To this day, whenever I see a Morissette video or hear her voice, Winston's face with his wry smile immediately comes to mind. If you read further, Dear Reader, you will not be surprised to learn that there are no Alanis Morissette albums in my music collection.

To merely characterise Alfred and Winston as Hong Kong boys would be misleading. Hong Kong itself was a colony of disparities. The bright, fresh expanses of The Peak stood in contrast to the cramped concrete boxes of the back streets of Wan Chai and the Walled City that functioned as both homes and abattoirs. The deafening racket emanating from the mahjong parlours or the drunken shouts of sailors in Lockhart Road was a world away from the solitude of the Sai Kung Peninsula.

Winston was Tsim Sha Tsui through and through. He was brash and ruthless. The tip of Kowloon represented everything good and bad. You could find cheap love in the Waltzing Matilda Inn,

Bottoms Up or Club Tasogare, and within an hour, be ripped off in some jade jewellery store. There were no pervading morals to regulate behaviour. No one would pass judgement on you. The bright colours, the neon lights and the ready supply of San Miguel and Carlsberg were overwhelming.

When Winston was in Tsimsy, as the locals call it, his afternoons would be spent in the foyer of his luxury hotel taking tea and British scones and generally annoying others with his raucous laugh and gregarious manner. If he needed a companion, it would be efficiently arranged through the concierge and without any evidentiary trail on his credit card statements. He once claimed that he had one responsibility in life, only one, and that was to ensure that his wife never knew who he had been with the night before. It was said in such a way you could not help but smile, albeit in an uncomfortable way. However, I later discovered he had plagiarised the line from one of Barry Humphries' more morally challenged characters. Winston, I reasoned, was more invective than inventive.

Alfred would not be seen dead in the Peninsula Hotel. For him, pleasure was a simple bowl of chicken rice in a linoleum tabled cafe in Chung King Mansions, a dilapidated nearby high-rise. Yet, it was not just the food. The background whirring of the fans, the smell of fresh and stale cigarettes and dust through the louvred windows, churned by the parade of red double-decker buses along Nathan Road, made the experience real. That was Alfred's reality. He was three hundred metres and a world away from the starched tablecloths and Oxbridge accents of the Peninsula.

For the Star Ferry sailors, the bar girls, and hotel cleaners, Alfred was just the quiet, normal man at the corner table. None of them knew that he was guardian to the Lee family fortune and an acclaimed businessman in his own right, and even if they had known, it would not have mattered. Alfred was as comfortable in that tiny downtrodden cafe as he was in any board of directors meeting or Liberal Party convention.

'You'd love Chung King Mansions, Mr Mason,' he'd say. 'Full of Indian restaurants. All illegal, you know?' I did not know.

There was a general misconception back then, as there is today, that all Englishman love Indian curries. It is true that until the influx of immigrants from sub-continental Asia, fish and chips and baked beans on toast had been the staple English diet. In fairness, every town, mine included, had a Chinese restaurant, but each served chop suey, egg foo young, and a whole range of other bland and unadventurous dishes more suited to an English than Asian palate. I suspect my love of such food developed in reaction to Mother's excessive reliance on tins of Heinz protein and Campbell's soup.

I first met Alfred on my first day at the office. To be precise, it was lunchtime, and I was steadily devouring a plastic container of takeaway sweet-and-sour pork with a broken plastic fork.

Alfred politely knocked on my door, entered, smiled and said, 'It's Mr Mason, isn't it? I'm Alfred Lee.' I immediately stood up and shook his outstretched hand. It was a firm shake. He immediately beckoned me to sit down and to continue eating.

'It's a pleasure to meet you, Mr Mason. You come highly recommended,' he said.

'I'll try not to let you down, sir,' was my instant reply.

'Just do your best, that's all we ask.'

He followed this polite introduction with a strange comment: 'I see,' he said.

'Gwai lo yuk,' he said, looking down at my container of sweet-and-sour pork. Gwai lo yuk? I had no idea what Alfred was talking about, although given his broad smile, I could tell he was joking and at my expense. 'You're a gwai lo, right?' I was still perplexed. 'You're a gwai lo, a foreign devil, and all foreign devils like gwoo lo yuk, sweet-and-sour pork. So, gwai lo yuk! Get it?'

It was a pure play on Cantonese words with a bit of English, which would have been familiar to any sweet-and-sour pork-loving Hong Kong expatriate. I smiled to falsely indicate that I did get his meaning, but later sought clarification from one of the Chinese office workers. She explained that Alfred was not mean or derogatory, and that while 'gwai lo' did mean 'foreign devil,' it was a term of endearment, a bit like being called a 'pommy bastard,' and gwoo lo yuk was simply the Cantonese name for sweet-and-sour pork. In fact, Alfred's observation that gwai lo's like gwoo lo yuk was pretty accurate. I saved the expression in my memory bank—'gwai lo yuk.'

However, I digress. Unlike his son, Alfred's Hong Kong was a quieter and more reflective place. He had a favourite hotel a short way up Chatham Road opposite the army barracks, but away from the neon lights and hustle of Nathan Road. Chatham Road was but a quick trip to the Walled City and high-rise tenements that lined the arterial road to the airport and island tunnel. For Alfred, Hong Kong life was a combination of high-finance and social responsibility. When his time was done at the offices of Admiralty and the Connaught Centre, Alfred was invariably on the road to one of many charitable projects. He supported the Lions Club and Rotary as well as numerous Chinese friendship societies, or triads, if you believed Winston.

'Ever been to Chai Wan, Mr Mason?' Alfred once asked. I looked puzzled. 'It's at the end of Hong Kong Island, just up from beautiful Shek O beach; it's a poor part of town.' I still appeared puzzled.

'Why the hell would he go there?' interjected Winston. 'It's just a concrete ghetto in the middle of a bloody graveyard,' he exclaimed.

It would be fair to say that Winston presented a far less favourable mental image of the former colony than his father.

'I haven't been to Hong Kong,' was all I muttered.

'You should,' said Alfred with a broad smile. 'Lots of gwai lo yuk.'

We all loved Alfred's sense of humour, particularly Winston, who frequently sought to match his father's wit and repartee. Yet, taxation was the one topic of conversation guaranteed to remove even the faintest smile from Winston's face.

For Winston, tax amounted to state-sponsored theft. 'How dare those dole bludgers and irresponsible bogans with eight kids and countless fathers have a claim to what's mine,' he would complain.

Even though it would be fair to say that, over the years, my politics have been more aligned with Thatcherism than socialism, Winston's protestations were just plain offensive.

'If that's your view,' I remarked, 'who pays for the police, schools and health services?' It could have been a rhetorical question. The look of annoyance on Winston's face said it all. My comment did not elicit a verbal response.

Alfred, like his son, articulated the virtues of smaller government. However, for Alfred, smaller government necessarily demanded personal responsibility.

'Charity doesn't begin at home,' Alfred would say. 'It begins in each one of us. We all must give, but those with the most must give more.'

I never heard Winston utter those words or anything like them. Alfred would resent the Medicare levy but donate generously and anonymously to the Royal Children's Hospital Good Friday appeal. I figured his son would not give ten dollars unless the donation was tax-deductible, and his generosity rewarded by a prominent plaque in his honour. Yet, there was more to Alfred's moral principles than anonymous charity. Alfred demanded hard work. It was not good enough to give a fortune away. He believed he had a personal obligation to create more wealth through his own sheer hard work. By contrast, his son Winston's mid-week visits to his favourite golf course or his biannual visits to the Caribbean hardly fell into the hard work category. Even Blind Freddie could see that these were very different men.

Over the years, I tried to understand the politics of this generous patriarch. I once mentioned my support for liberal democracy and was treated with a barrage of polite rebukes.

'Simplistic Western idealism,' was Alfred's initial response. 'Didn't you once ask who pays for the police? Well, that's right. We need strong laws and strong police. How many were killed at Port Arthur? Thirty? Thirty-five? Well, that's thirty-five too many.'

I was initially surprised that Alfred would support strong gun controls. He was also a firm advocate of a strong defence force, and I soon learnt that, despite being a card-carrying member of the Liberal Party, he was only a lukewarm supporter of parliamentary democracy and freedom of speech. In the end, I reasoned that his primary interests were to make money and use that money in his personally-favoured social endeavours. So long as the government did not interfere with those processes, he was happy.

One early morning, years later, I found Alfred in his office with Winston by his side. Alfred had bloodshot eyes and was clearly a mess. 'Three thousand New Yorkers killed by terrorists and the world changes forever. Devastating earthquakes in Sichuan and no one cares. Seventy thousand dead and five million homeless.' He had a point. 'Look,' he said, 'a small article on page six of *The Age*.'

'Yeah, it's ironic,' said Winston.

I said nothing as I looked into the face of the sad, grieving man. It was not just that so many of Alfred's kinfolk had died under horrific circumstances. He was struggling with his own conscience. He loved America and everything the 'American Dream' stood for. He despised Maoism and barely tolerated the Hu Jintao regime that then ruled. For Alfred, that did not, or rather should not, make Americans more important or newsworthy. Still, in the unfair Caucasian world that the Lee Family had chosen to live, American lives were valued more highly than those of Alfred's Chinese brethren.

Later that morning, Alfred was gone. He had boarded a flight to Chengdu. Alfred would return two weeks later, five kilograms and a couple of million dollars lighter. Along that journey, he would pick up a couple of extra lines on his brow. They would remain until his untimely death.

'Sir. I'm pleased to see you back,' was all I said upon Alfred's return. I meant it.

'Good to be back, Mr Mason,' was his only response. He would never mention what he saw or did in Sichuan.

The Lee Family Office would employ me for nearly half of my working life. Ultimately, premature retirement would be thrust upon me, but that was not Alfred's doing. This compassionate older man would always have a special place in my heart. I just could not say the same about his son.

✦

Chapter Three
The Childhood

Despite distinct racial differences, Alfred bore a striking resemblance to Tich Allen. They were small, rotund men whose lack of height was no physical barrier. They dominated their respective audiences. On occasions, I feared them both but respected only Alfred.

Tich was an uncompromising man with few friends even amongst his peers. I first met Tich pre-puberty. He was the Deputy Headmaster and an English teacher at my secondary modern school in rural England. Schoolyard rumours floated around that he led a cult. In truth, he was an evangelical Christian with firm and unsophisticated views on the institutions of life. He was also a lonely, drunk of a man who held no theological objections to the consumption of alcohol. Tich was often seen with a bottle at his desk and on the dashboard of his car. Lucky for Tich, those were the days before the war on drink-driving.

Over the years, I have always endeavoured to respect the dead. Tich, though, is an exception. He was a hard, uncompromising disciplinarian, where our obedience was fashioned by the fear of physical harm. Only Christ knows how he reconciled his cruel behaviour with Christian doctrine. Perhaps he was merely following Headmaster's orders. Maybe he was compensating for his lack of height. The reasons for his actions did not concern me, although the consequences did.

In fairness, Tich's actual violence was far rarer than it seemed. We all lived in a continual environment of fear but, for many of us, physical harm was infrequent. The constant threat of Tich's ruler was sufficient. Further, where violence was employed, it was done openly and to maximum effect. The most notable forum was morning assembly. Those daily gatherings of the whole school were the usual setting for Tich's laissez-faire use of the twelve-inch ruler.

The spectacle was complemented by a repetitive cry of 'Watch it, laddie.' He always started with 'Watch it, laddie.' 'Heh you boy, up here, against the wall,' he would screech in a high-pitched voice whenever a boy was talking or standing out of line.

The poor culprit would spend the next thirty minutes on a podium with his back to the five-hundred-strong assembly and with his face six inches from the wall. If he moved, Tich's ruler would be planted firmly and squarely at the back of the knees. Smaller and slighter boys stood no chance of remaining upright. Others, many of them nearly men, would be reduced to tears. Needless to say, the vast majority of offenders stood frozen like statues. Obedience was achieved through the threat of violence and public shaming. I talked out of line once, only once, but was haunted by the incident for a long time after. I had learnt a valuable lesson. Do not mess with Tich.

Yet, Tich would mess with us. It would also be fair to remark that Tich lacked considerable imagination. Our English lessons followed a routine format. A ten-word spelling test would invariably follow a few passages from a Chaucer or Eliot novel that none of us understood. Half an hour of detention for every spelling mistake. Every other week he would set us an essay, with riveting topics such as *'Why are the Ten Commandments so important?* or *'What profession inspires you?'* I responded to the latter with relish and provided a five-page treatise on my imagined daily routine as a proficient barrister. I believed I was on firm ground. I figured Tich would not have read John Mortimer, so I plagiarised at will. The response was both immediate and calculated.

'I was expecting a critique of a profession, not a fanciful first-person narrative. Let me remind you, Mason, why you're here,' Tich said, building up to one of his lectures. 'You have poor English skills and intelligence, and the best you can hope for is a job with the Thames Valley ouses or a position on the Ford assembly line.' I was dumbstruck, but Tich was on a roll. 'If you behave yourself and work hard, you may even make a policeman. But laddie, you'll never make a lawyer or,' as he added with a knowing smirk, 'a BBC scriptwriter.'

I'm in real trouble now, I thought, as I shuddered to myself, fully conscious of my face turning a deep shade of red. Tich, however, refrained from further criticism of my plagiarised homework. He probably believed that his response had succeeded in crushing my ambition. For him, that would have been pleasure enough.

Tich, of course, did have a point. The subjects we were taught were only marginally academic. For those of us that failed the 'eleven-plus' examinations, there would be no chemistry, biology or foreign languages; but for Tich to deride the intelligence of bus drivers and car workers was as unnecessary as it was pathetic. He was, of course, a snob. I vowed I would never follow in his footsteps, even if I were capable of doing so.

My inability to pass the eleven-plus was one of those character-defining moments. Over fifty years on, I still recall the exact moment I heard the news of my failure. In my class, there were thirty junior school students. I was the fourth and last to be ushered into the headmaster's office and informed that my dreams of a grammar school education had evaporated. Like so many secondary modern students, I felt that my future had been ripped apart from under me. I was more than an academic failure. I was an embarrassment that would never be appreciated for anything intellectual.

Still, there was one person that did not care about my results, or at least seemed not to care. My mother, who had witnessed my tears and sullen reaction, spent hours gently caring for her only son.

'Think on the bright side. You won't get to wear the colours of Catholicism,' Mother consoled. 'I'll make a Rangers supporter of you yet. Look, even your new school colours are blue.'

To be honest, at the time, I did not fully grasp what Mother was talking about. I knew she was Scottish and, along with ten siblings, had been raised a Catholic. I also knew that her childhood had been desperate. There was no joy in being raised in Garngad, Glasgow and the Catholic Church did its bit to ensure social harmony by suppressing any form of social disobedience. The good folk of what is now Roystonhill stuck to their lowly life stations. However, as soon as Hitler invaded Poland, Mother and a fellow fifteen-year-old female friend were packed. When Churchill declared war on Germany, they were gone, both physically and theologically. Neither would return to Glasgow nor ever again partake of the sacrament.

The pair hitchhiked to London and found jobs in armament factories, slept in cheap boarding houses, and slowly and deliberately learnt to speak with Oxbridge accents. Later, Mother learnt touch typing and Pitman's shorthand, only resorting to a Glaswegian drawl when excited or stressed. She had achieved English lower-middle-class respectability. That was her new lot in life, and she was happy with it. Yet, one mention of the Catholic Church and her mild manner would quickly evaporate. Shortly after I failed the eleven-plus, I learnt that the Catholic Glasgow Celtic football team wore shirts of green and white hoops—the same sporting colours of the local boys' grammar school. No wonder Mother had looked on the bright side.

My secondary modern school stood at the top of a hill on the main road south from town. Travellers, even then, would stop at the old pubs on either side of the road. The scenery was almost picture postcard, and many a tourist would pose for a photograph next to the memorial for a seventeenth-century battle (analysed, no doubt, in some History Channel documentary). Unfortunately, the tranquility of this English rural scene had been interrupted by the development of uninspired low-cost housing estates to the east and west. Identical square cream-coloured boxes with brown tiled roofs littered the side roads down the valley.

The semi-detached dwellings were the product of 1960s architecture. Today, you would not let the architect behind those homes design a family kitchen, let alone a housing estate. Although, if you ventured down the valley toward the canal that dissected the town centre, an older, more aesthetically pleasing, town plan emerged. Circling the main streets and the market square was a rich design of late Victorian and Edwardian homes that initially housed the canal and railway workers. Now, those same dwellings are home to the young and upwardly mobile commuters that fill the floors of London's accounting and legal firms. Even back then, the town had an unmistakable aura of wealth and development that contributed to my daily angst. Put simply, the town was on the road to success, while I was travelling a path to nowhere.

There was no way one could ignore or block out the life around. Even though I increasingly retreated to a private, fantasy world, there was still a social life to live involving school, scouts, and church choir. So, I was an active participant in a world that increasingly alienated me. What I did see and experience each weekday morning, for five long years, were the grammar schoolboys and girls, on foot, bikes, and buses on their way down the hill to their prestigious seats of learning. Each weekday afternoon the procession was reversed. The look of disdain on the passing faces of my intelligent contemporaries said it all. We secondary modern kids were just too dumb to elicit any iota of respect.

There would be no mistaking them and no mistaking us. The green and white rugby shirts and matching scarfs were clear visual statements. It was though the wearers were with one voice exclaiming: 'I passed the eleven-plus; therefore, I wear the Celtic strip.'

Of course, there was never an occasion where I actually heard those words. However, there was no misconstruing who I was. I was a secondary modern boy, a failed eleven-year-old, with my dark and light blue tie and matching school cap. Looking back now, I cannot remember if it was the attire of those self-righteous grammar school kids or Mother's contempt for the Catholic Church that led me to hate the Glasgow Celtic Football Club. In truth, both factors were important, and while my football-loving school friends would support Manchester United or Arsenal or Chelsea, I followed Mother's example and became a lifelong Glasgow Rangers fan.

I would not for one moment claim that my decision to support the blue half of the Old Firm was one of life's defining moments, but Tich's mockery of my legal aspirations was. I would never read a John Mortimer book again or see a Leo McKern performance. To this day, I cannot see the actor behind the character. Leo McKern was Rumpole of the Bailey. He could never be anything more. More importantly, Tich did stifle my ambitions. I would never make a lawyer, so there was no point of dreaming of being one. For the next two decades, such high-minded ambitions were way out of mind. I was not cut out for a life on the buses or at the Ford plant, but my legal career had been dealt a hammer blow.

I briefly thought that I should try to prove Tich wrong, but it was a fleeting thought. After all, whatever I felt about Tich, he was in a position of authority. He had not become Deputy Headmaster of a school of six hundred plus boys through ignorance or mere luck. Yes, he had failings, but he probably had an excellent appreciation of what happened to former secondary modern boys in adult life. So, I consciously chose to eliminate the idea of becoming a lawyer. However, there was nothing to replace that ambition. There were no substitutes. I would simply drift and take whatever chances life would offer.

✦

Chapter Four
The Farewell

A further character-defining event arose shortly after Tich Allen and I said our final goodbyes. In the year remembered for its Indian summer, Mother, with her body riddled with disease and inadequate morphine, departed. She was five months from diagnosis to grave. If there had ever been a God in my life, he or she left me that year. While temporally quick, in my adolescent mind, Mother's suffering seemed to endure an eternity. Any merciful supreme being would have ended her pain and screams of agony considerably earlier. Yet, that was not to be. A generation later, I still dreamt of her cries for help in her thick, piercing Glaswegian accent.

It would be the height of self-indulgence to dwell on our response to Mother's passing. Bowel and other forms of cancer are hardly the preserve of the Mason family. Suffice to say, we could have responded to our loss in one of two ways. We could have pulled together in that fine British, Dunkirk tradition and drawn on our collective experience to support and nurture each other. Alternatively, the family unit could implode. We chose the latter. Over the intervening years, the distance between us grew, first emotionally, and then geographically. While we never completely lost contact, in the end, family ties were limited to birthday and Christmas cards and once-in-a-blue-moon visits.

This book is not a biography or even a chronology of significant events that took me from Berkshire to discreditation. I was, and probably still am, too busy acting in my own self-indulgent private world to document or even adequately reflect on what was going on around me. Apartheid, the Vietnam War, three-day week, stagflation, Watergate, and Three Mile Island all passed me by without serious thought. Until Tich's intervention, I was stuck in a make-believe world of fictional lawyers. Before too long, such imaginings were pushed aside thanks to puberty and sexual awareness. Of course, like most teenage boys, sexual pleasure was one-sided and frequently hands-on. The emotions of my adolescent years were shaped by Farrah fantasies and a couple of neighbourhood girls who hadn't the faintest clue I existed.

In between childhood crushes, and despite Tich's discouragement, I did study. Yes, I was a slow learner and my results were mixed, but some glimpses of academic ability were at least noticeable to a couple of teachers. Somewhat controversially, those teachers promoted personal development and creativity as a basis for pedagogical endeavour. They constituted a small voice in an institution focussed on discipline and rote-learning. Thankfully, over the years their collective voice grew to an audible whisper.

With the help of a young teacher, I slowly managed to persuade the school that I was capable of completing O-levels. I started my penultimate school year with a commitment to nine subjects. Unfortunately, based on my science results, I was hardly a candidate for the nearby military research and atomic weapons facilities. The school itself cancelled my enrolment in Physics, Chemistry, and Biology. Come final exams, I scrapped through five of the remaining six subjects and flunked Geography. But, Dear Reader, I was no failure. I had my bundle of five O-levels, including Mathematics and a couple of English subjects, with a University of Oxford Department of Education and Science certificate to prove it.

Less than two years later, those five O-levels were supplemented by a couple of A-Levels from the town's sixth form college. For an impatient and immature juvenile, those months dragged. I knew that once I had finished, I would have my one-way ticket out of Berkshire. However, the months felt like a lifetime. I dreaded failure and an inevitable repeat year that Father would insist on. Thankfully, that was not to be. I studied reasonably hard and received positive feedback from my teachers. Having suffered Tich for five long years, I should have felt more appreciative. There was no violence, no public shaming. The curriculum was diverse and the college teachers were genuinely concerned with the needs and interests of students.

I am sure that, objectively, my time in sixth form college should warrant more than a couple of brief paragraphs. Those were the months where childhood was replaced with young adulthood. Coca Cola gave way to Courage ales and school lunches were traded for nutritionally bankrupt Wimpy burgers and packets of Benson and Hedges. However, by then, I was absorbed in my own fantasies; in a world divorced from sixth form reality. I had few friends and no student from the opposite sex displayed any interest in me. Despite the occasional beer and fags, my pocket money and pay from a Saturday job in a local hardware store were too stretched to finance a massive social life (even if Father had permitted me to do so). Indeed, most of my income I saved. It was saved for my escape.

I did not receive my A-Level results for some months. Those were the days before the internet and immediate electronic gratification. Days after my final exams, I said my goodbyes to my father and sister and caught a bus to Greece. I had left England, or at least my status as a resident, for good.

$$\diamond$$

Chapter Five
The Vocation

I never could get Tich Allen out of my head. Even today, I frequently reflect on that frightful little man. It is not the fear of violence that still stands out. Instead, it's the uninspiring nature of the man. Rote learning, coupled with the threat of physical force was hardly a recipe for success. It was an outdated approach, even then. In short, Tich lacked creativity. Where vision was required, he provided disillusionment. Where encouragement was needed, he responded with derision. Tich had the uncanny ability to literally throttle the creative imaginations of nearly three generations of secondary modern students. Little did I know it then, but Tich would have made an excellent in-house lawyer.

The problem was that my work as an in-house lawyer lacked imagination. The work was often routine, dull, and pointless. If there was one type of legal document that epitomised this state of affairs, it was the interminable confidentiality or non-disclosure agreement. This fancifully titled document detailed what information was precious, how it should be used, and to whom it could be disclosed. You knew that no one would provide information, whether confidential or not, without such a document but as soon as it was signed, it would be thrown in the bottom drawer and forgotten about. No one would query; no one would litigate. Drafting or settling a confidentiality agreement was an exercise in futility.

In truth, my services in negotiating such documents were limited. I would ensure the correct parties signed on the dotted line and that it landed on the correct parties' desks to review. Assuming the Lee Family Office was the information recipient, I would try to ensure there were no positive obligations to do anything, such as return or destroy documents at the end of the transaction. Those obligations were increasingly difficult to comply with, particularly in an electronic age with back-up storage and off-site disaster recovery. You just could not be sure that you had destroyed or returned everything confidential.

Finally, I would cross out the indemnities. Unfortunately, the word 'indemnity' creates an air of mystique, ruling out the possibility of any rational dialogue involving the term. The word is a communication stopper, as I soon discovered in my early years at the Lee Family Office; it is guaranteed to douse the interest of any reasonable conversationalist. But in its simplest form, an indemnity is just a protection against financial liability. Someone agrees to pay up for someone else's loss in agreed circumstances.

Indemnities are all too common in commercial arrangements. Typically, contracts have included indemnities for damage to property or personal injury, infringement of other persons' intellectual property rights, claims by other persons and for breach of contract. The idea of giving an indemnity, particularly one for a breach of contract, verges on the obscene. An indemnity for a breach of contract is akin to having your cake and eating it too. The indemnified cannot only sue for breach of contract but can seek to enforce payment under the indemnity. In short, the indemnifier is hit with a double whammy.

To this day, I have never fully understood the fundamental need for indemnities. Their presence seems to question the whole basis of compensation. They represent mistrust with the civil courts or assume that damages are an insufficient remedy. Perhaps less controversially, indemnities are a source of antagonism in contractual negotiations. Their presence flags an imbalance of power between the contracting parties. The powerful will seek broad non-negotiable indemnities in their favour. The powerless will unsuccessfully request their removal.

My first professional concern with indemnities followed a landmark High Court decision that had settled a legal stoush between a certain Mr and Mrs Amadio and a very certain Commercial Bank of Australia. Unfortunately, for the bank, the High Court took a very dim view on the blasé practice of requiring guarantees and indemnities from individuals with no knowledge of what they were signing up for. Mr and Mrs Amadio spoke little English and had no idea of what a mortgage and guarantee meant (provided in support of their son's business overdraft facility) until the bank attempted to foreclose on them. For the High Court, the bank should have required the Amadios to seek independent legal advice before signing the guarantee and indemnity documents.

Alas, for me, the financial services industry generally, and the Lee Family Office specifically, misinterpreted the High Court decision. I lost count of the times Winston or a client adviser required my attendance at client meetings to merely witness a client's signature on some guarantee and indemnity documents.

On each occasion, my frustration grew as I explained the real need for my attendance.

'Read the bloody document,' I once snapped at a client adviser. 'Your client needs legal advice, not a solicitor to just witness his signature.' This is not my job, I thought myself. Still, I lost count of the hours I spent reviewing relevant bank documentation, explaining the onerous obligations under the documents, and completing a solicitor's certificate as evidence that independent legal advice had been provided.

In my early days, I laboured on the legal distinction between a guarantee and indemnity, although the wall of glazed looks necessitated a more direct response. In the end, the simple observation that the client stood to lose the full loan amount, including future borrowings across all accounts in the client's name, plus interest and fees was usually sufficient. Generally, the clients appreciated my advice and refused to sign the guarantee and indemnity documents. However, the failure to sign necessarily resulted in renegotiated loan arrangements. For the most part, the task fell onto our somewhat unimpressed client advisers.

'Greg. Why do you have to stymie perfectly normal and low-risk loan arrangements,' was the usual retort, or rather, it was the typical response before the global financial crisis. Thanks to the GFC and a couple of over-extended clients, the word 'bankruptcy' entered the Lee Family Office vocabulary. It was only then that client advisers actively sought to limit the security arrangements placed on their clients by the large financial institutions.

Fortunately, my involvement with solicitor's certificates ceased when Winston's close barrister friend suggested that

I was probably in breach of my corporate practising certificate by providing legal advice directly to Lee Family Office clients. The barrister's son had recently established his own law firm, and 'for a very competitive fee,' was more than happy to provide certificates for all Lee Family Office clients.

Tich Allen, in all likelihood, would claim he was right. I was not a real lawyer, not even a real commercial lawyer. Negotiating confidentiality agreements or providing solicitor's certificates was hardly cutting-edge stuff. Such documents were on a par with basic website user agreements, privacy statements, memorandums of understanding and the versatile deed of release. Whenever we compensated a dissatisfied client, an aggrieved employee or provided a very generous and legally dubious redundancy package for one of Winston's favoured staff, I would be asked to roll out a deed of release.

While the purposes varied, deeds of release would follow a reasonably standard format. A comment that the Lee Family Office denied liability would follow brief details of the allegation or transaction. A condensed confidentiality requirement would follow details of the settlement sum, with a provision for 'GST.' Finally, I would include a clear statement that the payment was in full and final settlement of the relevant matter. In each case, Winston and the chief financial officer, Martin Flynn, would jointly execute the deed and Martin would arrange payment. The fully executed deed would either find its way to a bottom draw or undistinguished manila folder. Either way, it would never return to see the light of day.

Anything marginally complicated would be referred to our panel of out-house lawyers. What did I know of limited liability partnership agreements, capital raising, definitive merger agreements, master securities loan agreements or cross-guarantees? I was just the first link in the legal food chain. Anything more than the mundane was hand-balled to an external law firm, then counsel, then silk. In worst-case scenarios, the whole lot of us would be involved.

The bulk of my work was a mixture of regulatory compliance. Loose-leaf copies of the Corporations Act, Privacy Act and Financial Transaction Reports Act sat conspicuously on my bookshelf. However, my office library mainly consisted of forms, templates and draft policies and procedures that no one read or referred to. Such material was hardly enticing. Reviewing and completing a W-BEN 8 Inland Revenue Service form for some unfashionable investment in the USA or registering a security interest in personal property with the Insolvency and Trustee Service Australia, would hardly be at the forefront of an aspiring law student's mind.

In later years, after regulatory authorities became serious about the extent of white-collar crime and multi-national tax avoidance, a new body of acronyms entered our everyday compliance vocabulary. Yet, 'KYC' (know your client), 'CIP' (client identification program), 'AML/CTF' (anti-money laundering and counter-terrorism financing) became more than just common parlance. They introduced a new body of requirements designed to evidence identities, relationships, sources of funds and wealth. For those on the periphery of client identification, the new requirements merely restated the '100-point check.' For those of us charged with introducing AML/CTF programs, the requirements took on lives of their own. New processes, procedures, and records were all introduced in response to the numerous policy directions imposed by the regulator.

Sighting a copy of passport or driving licence was one minor piece in the AML/CTF regulatory jigsaw puzzle. Yet, the basic need to confirm someone's identity by reference to a name and photograph on government-sourced document was still the fundamental objective. Nothing of substance had changed. Our novel acronyms and procedures were merely the emperor's new clothes. To argue they curtailed money laundering, tax evasion or terrorism was nonsense.

More generally, compliance with each regulatory regime required documented policies and procedures. Much of my time was spent drafting marketing, client onboarding, securities dealing, and advisory documents at least to present the illusion of a consistent, accountable, and efficient compliance regime. Of course, the reality was different. At best, my policies and procedures facilitated the perception that we were good corporate citizens and helped justify my role at the Lee Family Office. For that, I should have been grateful, but this was dull and bureaucratic stuff.

Throughout my career, I always strove to make a positive contribution to the health and wellbeing of my employer. Compliance work provided no sense of contribution, particularly when approved procedures were routinely ignored in the name of commercial pragmatism.

'Greg, we're a hundred and ten per cent in support of your compliance framework,' Winston once remarked. 'Right up to the minute though, I choose to ignore it.'

The fact Winston spoke in a resolute and measured manner suggested that he could not be relied upon to install a healthy culture of compliance across the office. 'Compliance if we can be bothered' was the message from our leaders. Still, at least

Winston had read and remembered the compliance framework. That was more than many of our client advisers who seemed to spend considerable time actively avoiding me. In short, I was enmeshed in a culture of wilful blindness. One could disregard compliance by shunning the legal and compliance officer.

Of course, there were exceptions, and over the years numerous client advisers, particularly the senior accountants, took issue with my characterisation of our compliance culture.

'Stop acting like a bloody frustrated cop,' was a typical response from a client adviser commonly referred to as 'Winston's dutiful sycophant.' 'Just remember we deal with all kinds of tax legislation and accounting standards daily. I'm a chartered accountant bound by professional conduct rules, just like you. Don't think you've got the monopoly on regulatory compliance.'

The same client adviser would, like so many of his peers, conveniently forget that as a member of an esteemed profession he was authorised to witness statutory declarations and certify whether a copy of an original document was an exact copy. Invariably, those dull tasks would fall onto me.

'Looks more official if you witness the declaration,' was the standard retort. 'I haven't got a stamp, so can you do it?' was the other usual response.

I lost count of the times I was called by staff and clients to certify documents, witness statutory declarations or affidavits, often with highly spurious excuses. Did the dutiful wife really drive her husband's car through a red light after hubby had hit maximum demerit points? Was it really the pressure of running a business and not a lengthy Mediterranean cruise that justified the evasion of jury service?

I would often bite my tongue at the sheer audacity of many deponents. Early in my Lee Family Office career, I attended a seminar where the presenter referred to in-house counsel as the company's moral conscience or the guardian of moral capital. I'm not sure that biting my tongue was the obvious moral choice. Nonetheless, with one fatal exception, there was one demand that I resolutely shunned. Too many deponents called on me to witness pre-signed declarations. Worse, too many relatives of deponents handed up pre-signed declarations for my signature.

'Yes, I do need your wife to swear her affidavit in front of me, and the fact I supposedly know her signature is irrelevant,' was my all-too-familiar response.

Too often, I would be asked to certify original documents without sighting the original. Indeed, once I was requested to certify a copy of a passport because the original had been lost or stolen. I responded by stating that I needed to work on my clairvoyance skills before I could certify the copy. Apparently, my response was considered condescending and unhelpful. Yet, by the time I was called to account for my poor behaviour, Winston's dutiful sycophant had stepped in and certified the copy. I refrained from asking how his conduct squared with his professional conduct rules.

Perhaps I should have been more grateful. The burgeoning compliance burdens, at least in theory, helped my job security. Many of the various regulatory regimes required the appointment of specific personnel. At one stage, I was, in addition to my role as legal counsel, the AML/CTF Compliance Officer, Training Officer, Privacy Officer and Complaints Manager. Unfortunately, there was often a disconnect between what the relevant regulators expected from those roles and what the Lee Family Office practised.

As the Complaints Officer, I was responsible for responding to all forms of client displeasure. The regulator had taken a broad view of what constituted a complaint. Any expression of dissatisfaction related to our financial products or services where a response would be reasonably expected was sufficient to trigger my involvement as Complaints Officer. In theory, our need for a complaints handling procedure was limited to products and services regulated by the Australian Securities and Investments Commission (ASIC). However, the practical reality of providing an integrated wealth management service meant that it was illogical to divorce non-ASIC regulated products and services from our complaints handling processes.

Over the years, I dealt with a myriad of client gripes and grumbles. Allegations of late settlements, mislaid tax returns, inaccurate performance reports, wrong e-mail attachments, poor proxy voting practices and tardy record-keeping all landed on my desk. Many of them should have been too trite to remember, but at the centre of the process, was the requirement to keep complete and accurate records of all complaints. The other basic process requirements included the need to communicate with complainants, conduct investigations within specific time frames, and review complaints as part of process improvement.

The best that can be said of the Lee Family Office's complaints handling process was that it existed and, if scrutiny was limited to a cursory glance, it complied with the regulator's requirements, including the need to subscribe to an external dispute resolution scheme. The fact that no one was ever referred to the Financial Industry Complaints Service may suggest that complaints were few and far between. The reality though was that Lee Family Office would do anything to keep a client on-side. On various occasions, Winston would invariably take control of the complaints handling process. I was ignored, as were the regulatory obligations.

I recall one incident where a client from Winston's arm of the family had complained that the Lee Family Office had bought various parcels of shares through the firm's stockbroker. The relevant client adviser had been entrusted by the client to do so, and the instruction had been appropriately minuted. In what turned out to be an unfortunate series of events, the client himself instructed his personal assistant to place an identical order with the client's own broker. The result was that the shares were bought twice, and our custody team settled both orders. The team had assumed, quite reasonably, that the transaction had been deliberately split between two brokers.

Despite the minutes of meeting being personally signed by the client, both the client adviser and custody team were ultimately admonished for not adequately communicating with the client before both the purchase of shares and settlement. The Lee Family Office not only sold the duplicate shares but transferred over $20,000 from its own funds into the client's account. That transfer compensated the client for the capital loss incurred as a consequence of a declining market, along with the brokerage costs and foregone interest.

'The client is always right,' muttered the relevant client adviser. 'Particularly, when he has a narcissistic personality disorder.'

My claim that I remembered the incident is somewhat misleading. In fact, I only heard about it through the client adviser's grumblings, which occurred some weeks after the matter had been resolved. Winston had taken personal charge of the complaint. He had conducted his own investigations and determined the quantum of compensation. Of course, there were no notes, no records, no board notifications, and nothing to evidence the complaint in the first place.

With the benefit of hindsight, the case of the duplicate share purchases was just one of many disputes that never hit our formal complaints handling process. It appeared that my procedures were only relevant for minor whinges, and for complaints that did not involve certain clients.

'We treat all our clients equally,' a colleague once joked. 'Except some clients are more equal than others.'

In the context of client complaints, that colleague was right. He could also have added that I was an unwitting accomplice. The existence of my formal complaints handling procedures meant we had a documented process. That process included maintaining a complaints register and the minuting of board discussions to demonstrate complaints had been considered and addressed. However, the existence of the very same procedures provided Winston with the opportunity to ignore them. A few complaints dealt with outside the formal procedures, or 'workarounds' as Winston referred to them, would not comprise the perception of compliance. Of course, those 'workarounds' were limited to his immediate family and close friends. All thanks to me, Winston could readily engage in nepotism without challenging the perception of the professionalism of the Lee Family Office as a whole. In my view, that was ironic.

Chapter Six
The Romance

I first saw Lena across a crowded restaurant on the Greek island of Paros in the middle of a Fix beer and Gauloises cigarette. She was with friends engrossed in the politics of the day. There were ouzo toasts to the demise of the Greek Colonels, mutterings about Marshal Tito's health and concern over Yugoslavia's future. A young Canadian hippie with Rastafarian hair and Che Guevara T-shirt provided a lengthy discourse on America's support of the Mujahidin, while a quiet lass from Birmingham let out an audible hiss at the mention of Thatcher or Reagan. Lena was amongst a group of disparate leftist students and activists.

Some of the group were just middle-class, pseudo-intellectuals that lived off their university grants without ever personally experiencing oppression. I sat in quiet amusement as the Canadian hippie remarked on the 'global industrial complex' with frequent references to 'the reproduction of hegemony' and the 'dialectics of nature.' I had no idea what any of that meant, but it sounded incredibly pretentious.

Still, as I listened more, I started to appreciate their commitment and passion. These were generally selfless souls whose own material wants and needs were limited. It might sound somewhat trite, but they championed the poor, the helpless and the underdog. Many had real dirt under their fingernails. The eldest in the group was a quietly spoken Swede who had lost an eye in Paris during the May uprisings. The Brummie girl had spent months on the so-called Grunwick picket line. The Tito admirer was a Croatian and gripped the hand of her Serbian boyfriend. She had recently disowned her family following a violent beating of her partner at the hands of her siblings.

I was enthralled. Ethnic tension had hardly been rife in my part of Berkshire, where mention of Arthur Scargill and his union colleagues was considered blasphemy. It was true that I had lost a parent at a reasonably young age, and that Tich Allen had been an oppressive figure during my formative years. That, of course, was not real oppression and certainly no sacrifice on my part. While the philosophical and political messages were hardly convincing, the passion and zeal were. I wanted to be part of that group, and most preferably, with the one who proclaimed her eternal love for 'Gough.' At that time, I had no idea who Gough Whitlam was, and for a brief period, thought that he and I were in a battle for Lena's affection.

An Australian woman of Greek immigrants, Lena had worked for the best part of a decade as a primary school teacher before cashing in her long service leave and making the pilgrimage to the land of her forebears. It had been a long time coming. While she loved her young pupils, as she referred to her clientele of mainly six to seven-year-olds, she was generally overworked and underpaid. Teacher-student ratios were high, as were the stress levels of her peers. Seven years of classroom politics across three schools were enough. Unsupportive headmasters, uncompromising parents, and a lack of substitute teachers would eventually take their toll. By the time of her twenty-fifth birthday, she was burnt out.

Greece was more to Lena than a spiritual homecoming. It was a retreat. It was a place to recharge her batteries and rekindle her zest for life. At least that was her expectation as she boarded her first Olympic Airlines flight from Melbourne to Athens. Indeed, it was not only her first flight; it was her first trip outside of the State of Victoria. Ultimately, she would embrace that adventure with as much relish as her first day of teaching. She claimed she would never forget the faces, or indeed the bright smiles of her first students. I would be surprised if those students ever forgot Lena's.

I had never believed in love at first sight. I recall that a few months before Paros, I had been alone in some small taverna flipping through an old English woman's magazine. An article on a famous British actor took my eye. The article was a blatant attempt to present the actor as a master of versatility. Yet, whether he played a smooth playboy, disillusioned secret agent, sophisticated gentlemen or even a seasoned Luftwaffe commander, he always spoke with the same distinctive Cockney accent. I was no fan. However, a couple of paragraphs on his private life attracted my interest. The actor had fallen for a South American beauty he had seen in a commercial for some well-known brand of coffee, and had spent weeks effectively stalking her until she succumbed to his affable charms. I considered the story no more credible than the rest of the drivel that filled the pages of that magazine.

Yet, when I first saw Lena, I sort of understood. She had kind eyes and my mother's hair, all tightly curled and unkempt. A friend at that time remarked that she reminded him of Olivia Newton-John on a bad hair day. He had a point. Indeed, Lena and that

Aussie starlet were about the same age and a few years older than me.

I was captivated, and I was not particularly sure why. Lena was slim but not supermodel skinny. Her skin was fair but blemished by freckles and the occasional mole. She smiled frequently but did not beam. It was a sort of a contented smile. Upon considerable reflection, you just could not appreciate Lena by reference to her specific qualities. She was considerably greater than the sum of her parts. You had to love the whole package. I did, then, and I still do now.

For a few months, Lena called a rather dingy boarding house in a narrow Plaka backstreet home. But she had a restless spirit and Athens could only hold her attention for so long. There were just too many fascinating places to the north and west to justify a sedentary lifestyle. In the end, the Plaka became a base for numerous travels to Yugoslavia and beyond.

It was during her European forays that Lena met Steve Rogers, a loud and overweight Kiwi with an ego to match. I first encountered Lena shortly after she had left him for the third time. They had initially met while travelling on InterRail, a popular method for seeing Europe on a shoestring. The general aim was to visit a city during daylight and sleep on a train to the next destination. Neither Lena nor Steve were pioneers of that brand of popular travel, and they would not be the last. One day in one city would hardly develop cultural awareness, but InterRail was an exciting adventure for many a student and thrifty primary school teacher.

Lena and Steve bumped into each other whilst travelling from Munich to Innsbruck, igniting the beginning of a relationship that was forged over cheap beers and menthol cigarettes. Before this chance encounter, their trains must have crossed each other at least a dozen times. By the time they reached Zagreb, they were calling themselves a couple. Yet, their relationship was hardly balanced. The Kiwi was firmly in charge of all decision-making—where they went, what they saw, and who they socialised with. Lena's contribution was coughing up the money. Upon saying goodbye to the classroom, she had cashed in a healthy balance of annual and long service leave. Her payout would help support a nomadic couple whose daily staple diet consisted of a tin of processed meat, a dozen stubbies of cheap beer and a packet of Alpine cigarettes. Not much, but solely financed by Lena.

Along their mutual travels, Steve's behaviour changed. To begin with, it was the impromptu poker games that inevitably brought InterRail travellers together. Later, his diet of beer would be supplemented by a local spirit or moonshine. By the time they reached the Greek capital, Lena was underwriting alcohol-infused all-night gambling sessions. At first, she said little and supplemented her stipend by the occasional odd job as a waitress or cleaner. Later, as Lena's savings dwindled, the need for regular work became more pressing.

Lena and Steve had slipped into a daily routine where she worked while he nursed a hangover. When Lena slept, Steve would party. The cycle would start the following evening anew. Over the subsequent weeks, the only noticeable change to the routine was Lena's increasing frustration. As Steve's selfish endeavours intensified, the frequency and severity of Lena's complaints increased. Indeed, there was a direct correlation between the extent of Steve's partying and the level of Lena's dissatisfaction.

One morning before heading from Athens to Mykonos, Lena had had enough. By the time they reached Piraeus, they were both in a frenzy. Steve was still plastered from the night before and exhaled breath that reeked of an ashtray. He felt the anger in Lena's voice as though he had been blasted with a twelve-gauge shotgun. Steve had no money for a second mug of lukewarm coffee, and in his own words, he felt like shit.

'Shut the fuck up, you patronising bitch,' was Steve's final response. He probably did not intend to utter those words, or at least not in the aggressive way they were presented.

Steve's profanities should not have mattered to Lena as she had heard them all before. However, she had heard them too many times before. This time there would be no time for apologies. There would be no more opportunities for Steve to proclaim his undying love or make unrealistic promises to change his behaviour. As she finished the remnants of her own barely drinkable coffee, Steve felt the full force of her ceramic coffee mug smash across his forehead. Lena turned for the door. By the time Steve registered the pain and noticed the red stream running down his face, Lena had grabbed her purse and backpack and was halfway to the door.

'That's fucking gratitude,' was the last she would hear. Lena had had enough. She slammed the door, storming out of the taverna and her relationship with Steve Rogers.

Lena marched into the local ferry ticket office and bought the first available passage to anywhere but Mykonos. And that was how Lena came to Paros. Steve, I later found out, required half a dozen stitches and a tetanus jab. He would spend three days in bed with a packet of aspirin and a badly bruised ego.

The first time I spoke with Lena was in a crowded bar one humid summer's evening. It was no surprise that we were seated together, let alone in the same taverna. It did not take long to locate her hostel after first setting eyes on her from afar in the Paros restaurant. I quietly followed her around the island for several days; the odd restaurant here, the occasional beach there. The Paros roads were few and the locations for social interaction were even fewer. It was not hard to track a girl with frizzy hair.

At a small taverna just out of town, Lena was with a French girl sharing a half bottle of dangerously potent retsina. I positioned myself on the same table diagonally opposite. The table was of the bench variety and long enough to sit three or four small groups of patrons. The room was dimly lit, and the bench was covered with the remnants of a long and messy lunch. The space between us was littered with piles of crockery and cutlery, glasses, empty bottles of beer and cheap wine. I was not camouflaged as such, but I reckoned that the real reason for my presence in that taverna would go unnoticed. Needless to say, I was proven wrong.

'A Taurus is practical and responsible,' Lena explained to her French companion. 'I'm not being big-headed; it's just my natural astrological trait.' She then muttered something about Venus on the ascendant, which meant absolutely nothing to me.

Lena, I quickly discovered, had a pre-occupation with zodiac signs, and it was equally clear that her French friend did not share the same passion.

'I think I'm a Libra,' was about the most relevant response to Lena's suggestion that her friend was acting like a typical Aquarian.

'Close enough,' was Lena's reply, without as much as a hint of embarrassment. 'Both are air elements. Obviously, to be precise,

I would need your exact time and place of birth as well as your birthday.'

I smiled. It was certainly not obvious that anyone could determine behaviour by mere reference to the time and place of birth.

'And you! You must be a Cancer,' was Lena's following comment. Her words were said methodically and definitively. By then, she had turned her head forty-five degrees and was looking straight at me.

My smile instantly dissolved. I instinctively muttered something along the lines of 'How did you know?' although by then my heart was pounding and my mouth was as parched as the dirt road back to town. Oh, my God, she had not just acknowledged my existence; she was actually talking to me. To be sure, that was my 'JFK moment.' Four decades later, I recall every word, expression, and detail of that first interchange. I remember the pattern of the faded tablecloth, the smells of lavender and alcohol, the evening sunlight, even the faces of the drunken proprietor and Lena's bemused French pal. I will treasure that memory for the rest of my life.

'Well, Greg. Can I call your Greg?' Lena began. 'Cancers are careful planners who make the best of limited means.' She laughed. 'And you, you've been so resourceful following me around for the last two weeks, and look, you're embarrassed. Yes, you're a Cancer, alright.'

It was only later that I realised that Lena's last comment could be construed differently. I knew from her voice that she was not suggesting I was a disease or malignant scourge. I was struggling enough as it was without the complication of alternative meanings of the word 'cancer.'

'Sorry, I, um…How do you know who I am?' was the best I could reply.

'Come on, Greg, do you think I wouldn't check out my shadow?' My face must have turned an even deeper shade of red. She laughed even more. 'I mean, it's not every day some cute boy shows an interest. I wanted to know who you were. By the way, I'm Lena Kostakidis,' she said as she reached to shake my hand, 'and if you want to continue this conversation, you can buy us a drink.'

And that was it. Lena was now part of my life. Her French friend must have said her goodbyes shortly after I returned with a second or maybe third round of drinks. I cannot now recall. It might sound like a pathetic cliché, but by then my eyes were firmly fixed on the one that would shortly become my one and only true friend, companion, and lover.

We spent the next few days on a hired Vespa exploring every remote café and secluded beach. We discovered Parikia's atmospheric alleys and the historic church of a hundred doors. We sipped cheap lemonade through the same straw, munched on wild Kalamata olives, and on one occasion liberated a couple of goats by cutting the ropes that shackled their legs. In the following days, we explored each other, first with an 'accidental' brush of a hand and peck on a cheek. Remember that this was the 1970s, and I was with a liberated Aussie girl. Lena had already indulged in her fair share of sexual encounters. It was not long before this shy English virgin experienced the pleasures of the flesh.

Later, we investigated our emotional sides. This outwardly open, self-competent Aussie woman hid a vulnerable secret. Less than a couple of days into our relationship, I declared my undying love towards her. I remember blurting out how I always wanted to be with her. I immediately regretted opening my mouth. I was hardly playing it cool, and I feared my declaration of love would be interpreted as teenage melodrama. Still, Lena's response was unexpected.

'It will be what it will be, Greg. Destiny will decide. You can't worry about what neither of us can control.'

Initially, I was quite surprised by this rather simplistic view of human nature, but it was the way she uttered the sentence that concerned me. While her words were voiced in a soft and non-confrontational manner, they were said with real honesty. I had no comeback, even though her views defied rationality. After a couple of minutes of silence, I said:

'That's it. I'm going to track down this Destiny person and shake him or her around until they agree you can be mine.'

A faint, barely noticeable smile swept Lena's face.

'There's no way I'll be yours.'

I must have visually expressed my immediate angst at hearing those words.

'Greg, there's no way I'll be yours or anybody else's,' she quickly explained. 'I'll always be my own person. However, if fate has its way, you can be mine.'

That was good enough for me. Lena was not closing the door on a long-term relationship. I just had to ensure somehow that fate or destiny continued to smile on me. Yet, as the weeks went by, it became increasingly evident that Lena's approach to her own destiny was tinged with a sense of foreboding. I discovered that trait at some makeshift cinema during the screening of *The Poseidon Adventure*.

It turned out that she hated movies with violence, natural disasters or car chases. Her taste was for musicals, historical dramas, and romantic comedies. The sinking of an ocean liner with the protracted screen deaths of big-name movie stars hardly fell into those categories.

'It was just horrible the way Shelley Winters died. It was providence that she survived for so long before succumbing to a heart attack. It's just so heartbreaking.'

A rational discussion was impossible. The fact we were talking about a fictional movie with an actress who was very much alive and kicking was irrelevant.

'Of course, it's not real, I know that, and don't patronise me. But it could have been real. Just look at the Titanic. That was real. Hundreds drowned and what a horrible way to go. That could be us, Greg. Wasn't The Poseidon sunk in the Aegean?'

In those moments, it was wise just to shut up. There would be plenty of time to calm her down. It was strange. Here I was with a highly competent, self-assured partner, yet a simple movie about a fictitious sinking could throw her into a distraught emotional state. Her response was genuine. While she would joke about her obsession with star signs, deep down there was a real belief that fate would take control and that whatever fate had in store for her, it would be far from pleasant. I knew she was not crying for Shelley Winters. She was crying for herself.

Happily, over the weeks and months that followed, tears of sadness were replaced with cries of joy. As our relationship blossomed, Lena's melancholic moments became only noticeable by their absence. Still, I quickly learnt that the mere mention of Steve Rogers was sufficient to test her inner tranquility. Unfortunately, we did bump into him on a few occasions, although always in crowded bars. The first time he walked to our table and thumped a bottle of retsina in front of me.

'That's for you mate, you'll need it,' was all he said.

He did not even look at Lena who was, by then, silently fuming. She watched as he retreated to the back of the bar and theatrically placed his arm around some unknown woman's shoulders.

'Ignore him,' I said. 'He's just a tosser.'

'I know, I know,' she replied, but I could not help noticing that she would regularly glance across to his table. He must have deeply hurt her to warrant that kind of continued attention. On the couple of occasions that he noticed her gaze, he responded with an insolent grin. That Kiwi piece of shit, I thought. This wonderful woman could not possibly deserve that sort of juvenile crap.

On other occasions, Steve was more restrained; or rather, he did not get a chance to be anything else. He and Lena acknowledged each other's presence with cursory nods but, each time, Lena grabbed me by the arm and we marched off in the opposite direction. A sensible response, I thought. There was no need for her to relive those dark and painful memories.

Chapter Seven
The Legacy

The Corporations Act is poorly drafted and always has been. Even the numbering is confusing. In its wisdom, parliament has enacted a chapter 6CA but no chapters 3 or 4. More importantly, the Act is one-size-fits-all legislation. It has applied to the small incorporated milk bar as it has to the mighty Rio Tinto and Commonwealth Bank.

Not all the Corporations Act is relevant to all players at all times. Still, throughout my Lee Family Office career, it would be fair to say that the legal requirements I was grappling with as a single in-house lawyer were the same matters confronting the band of in-house and external lawyers engaged by Macquarie Bank. I, just as they, needed to appreciate financial services licensing and the obligations imposed on licensees. The licensing regime was a mechanism for ensuring that providers of financial services were restricted to a closed shop of competent and trustworthy participants. At least, that was the idea. In practice, investor protection has been limited. Licensing has failed to curtail the shenanigans of Opes Prime and Storm Financial and indeed the advisory divisions of many banks.

The real problem with the Corporations Act, however, lies with the principles underlying the legislation. Financial services are authorised by a regulatory authority, made clear through prescribed disclosure and subject to external scrutiny, primarily in the form of audits. Yet, you do not need a doctorate in corporate law history to appreciate that the regulatory approach is just a footnote to British Prime Minister William Gladstone and the legacy of the mid-nineteenth century corporate law reform movement. Registration, disclosure, and audit were the catch-cries of Victorian parliamentarians. Little has changed in nearly two centuries.

Half a decade into my Lee Office employment, a new financial services regulatory regime emerged. With great fanfare, the old terminology of securities dealers, investment advisers, and futures brokers gave way to an all-encompassing new Chapter 7 of the legislation. Funds managers, derivatives dealers, custodians, superannuation advisers, and insurance brokers were suddenly all jammed into the same regulatory basket. Australian Financial Services Licensing or simply 'AFSL' was presented as an advance in regulatory consistency and uniformity. Disparate financial products and industry participants could be governed within the same regulatory regime but tailored to their particular circumstances.

Underlying the language of consistency and uniformity was the philosophical claim that mums and dads could make informed and calculated decisions by reference to standardised documents. Put another way, they should have no grounds for complaint if they had read the relevant financial services guide, prospectus, and statement of advice. The trouble was no one I knew behaved like that. The fund managers and large institutions would pore over those documents, not the small investors. Yet, according to the legislature, those institutions were big and sophisticated enough not to rely on them. For the mums and dads of this world, investment decisions were more likely to be made following informal suggestions or comments in the tabloid press. Retail protection under AFSL was based on nonsense. I knew that, and so did Alfred and Winston.

Nonetheless, I made sure that we were seen to climb through the regulatory hoops and at least present the perception of a commitment to compliance. The day after I submitted a draft plan to manage the two-year transition to AFSL regulation, Winston called me to his office. Winston had, in the space of a couple of seconds serious thought, determined that my plan was unnecessary, expensive, and outrageously uncommercial, even by my own poor standards.

'Look,' he said, referring to the AFSL application. 'The form's pretty damn simple. Don't make a wave out of a regulatory molehill.'

Lena would have been impressed with Winston's muddled idiom, but I was in no mood to laugh, mainly as it was pretty damn clear that there was more to the licensing process than ticking a few boxes on a multiple-choice questionnaire. The application itself required various descriptions or 'proofs' (as the regulator referred to them) concerning operations and procedures. It was a reasonable assumption that any business handling large sums of client monies and assets would have documented policies and procedures. Further, the regulator demanded active checks and balances and record-keeping to ensure the security of client funds, and to nurture honest and efficient client-service delivery.

Unfortunately, the Lee Family Office mantra was along the lines of 'trust us—we employ good people.' Documented controls were few and dismissed by Winston as unnecessary on the grounds that each client demanded a unique service. Of course, that was merely an excuse. In practice, while the content of client service varied, the inputs and approaches were highly consistent. After all, our professional staff operated in defined teams with structured reporting lines. Someone would need to document those practices, and I knew from an early stage in the application process that the nominated scribe would be me. The question, however, was where to start. I must admit, I sat initially with a blank piece of paper before the little bird in my brain suggested I read the ASIC licensing application form and ASIC licensing kit in detail.

Buried in the documents were references to the need for compliance and risk management frameworks based on Australian standards, and a training regime for client advisers. I made an executive decision to establish a compliance manual with the first part dedicated to compliance, the second to risk management, and third to training. My approach was hardly sophisticated or academically challenging stuff. Yet, it was hard. It was hard because it was necessary to address broad motherhood statements in policy and professional standards by documenting the real, practical and often informal processes that had developed over many years without much thought.

I spent hours with Martin Flynn and some of the more conscientious client advisers drafting procedures for executing client share transactions and preparing the content and form of statements of advice. I designed checklists and templates, registers, and forms. I established a monthly training forum for senior advisers, and with the help of the IT manager, implemented an exceptions reporting module developed on the back of an Excel spreadsheet. There were formal regulatory documents to be drafted and various arrangements with third party services providers, such as sub-custodians and brokers, to be negotiated. Looking back, I am not sure that any of these contributions benefitted client service delivery or governance practices. At best, the many and varied documents supported the perception that the Lee Family Office valued compliance. At worst, they imposed an increased level of bureaucracy and expenditure that undermined the company's financial performance.

The regulatory requirements were akin to protecting a poorly attired motorcyclist hitting an oncoming vehicle at high speed. If the legislation only required the rider to wear a compliant helmet, then the legal requirements were largely pointless. In the absence of a leather jacket and pants, back support, protective gloves, and sturdy boots there would not be much left of the rider from the neck down.

The Corporations Act demanded that we protect our clients through product disclosure statements, financial services guides, advice warnings, and statements of advice. Those terms slowly became part of the office refrain. Collectively, they were just our regulatory crash helmet. Yet, in the absence of a culture that genuinely prioritised client interests through clear and transparent policies and procedures, client protection was limited.

Further, the strength of the Lee Family Office's regulatory crash helmet was weakened by a cute legal distinction between 'retail' and 'wholesale' clients. Under the legislation, only the former required the full scope of regulatory protection. The latter, being clients of monetary substance, required less disclosure.

With wholesale clients, there was no need for disclosure statements, guides, warnings or statements of advice. The dubious assumption here was that wealthy clients were savvy with their finances, while poorer mortals were less so. Nonetheless, the Lee Family Office loved the retail-wholesale distinction, as it effectively provided an 'opt-out' mechanism for many of our products and services. Indeed, I spent considerable time ensuring that as many clients as possible were class fied as 'wholesale,' including those whose wealth was solely based on accidents of birth.

There were several ways of achieving 'wholesale' status, but, as Winston's attention to detail was limited, I kept matters simple. We either ensured that each client had at least $500,000 to invest in each of our products or was subject to a 'wealthy investor certificate' issued by an accountant. Obtaining certificates was not a hard task as the Lee Family Office accountants invariably prepared the financial accounts of our clients.

Most clients readily satisfied the definition of a 'wealthy investor' insofar as they had a gross income of $250,000 in the past two financial years or had net assets of $2.5 million. If a client did not satisfy the criteria, we could often rely on a carve-out. Personal offers of a financial product could be made up to twenty retail clients without the need for full regulatory protection, provided those retail clients did not collectively invest more than $2 million in the product over the previous year.

However, the Lee Family Office's financial services offering suffered from a fundamental flaw that even my policies and procedures and record-keeping could not overcome. Winston may have been right that we employed good accountants, but it was never quite clear that they were good enough. In particular, our investment advisory services were always going to be a problem despite sending half a dozen senior accountants to the Securities Institute for crash courses in financial products and markets. Our client advisers were proficient in tax and accounting matters, but they were no investment gurus. They had no practical experience as financial planners or investment advisers, and, indeed, trivialised the process of producing quality recommendations tailored to the needs of the clients.

Client expectations compounded the questionable competence of our advisers. Most clients were simply not interested in receiving a professional document detailing their personal circumstances, risk profile, and investment objectives. Instead, many clients were solely interested in receiving 'good tips.'

In a client complaints folder, long since archived in some off-site storage facility, are details of one such 'good tip' that turned out to be anything but. The relevant adviser, who I will refrain from naming, 'suggested' to one of his clients that he may 'wish' to invest in an ASX listed penny dreadful. Apparently, a strip of gold had recently been discovered in a Pilbara mine owned and controlled by that entity. The client adviser was aware of that information, as a friend of one his other clients held a position on the entity's board.

Following the client's investment, the entity's share price collapsed. The truth of the matter was that somewhere the story had got muddled. There was a strip of gold, but it was located in a mine owned and controlled by a competitor. Needless to say, the client was somewhat dismayed and demanded compensation. Winston and Martin handled the restitution, while I dealt with the client adviser. The latter was dumbstruck by what he called 'my absurd' claim that he had committed insider trading, particularly as the share price had tanked and that he had merely 'passed on' a comment. Further, he questioned my interpretation that a mere suggestion or wish could possibly amount to 'advice' within the meaning of the Corporations Act.

My interchange with the adviser was promptly reported to Winston, who took exception to my behaviour.

'Greg, we're one big family here. As a senior staff member, your job is to lead by example and deal with our advisers, in fact, all staff, in a professional and supportive manner. Quoting the law and suggesting an adviser has committed a criminal act is simply unacceptable. It just makes you look like a know-all.'

I must have muttered something about how I only had the Lee Family Office's best interests at heart, and that both the wording of insider trading rules and the definition of advice were broad.

'If that's the case,' Winston continued, 'I suggest you put together a training program covering those matters and present it to all staff. That is the way to be professional and constructive.'

A few weeks later, I delivered a couple of identical ninety-minute seminars on insider trading prohibitions. My presentation incorporated relevant court cases documented by ASIC, and I deliberately refrained from quoting sections of the Corporations Act. Only fifty per cent of client advisers showed up. The relevant client adviser and Winston were only noticeable by their absence.

'That's typical, not ironic,' I muttered to Martin Flynn, the only senior staff member to attend.

Chapter Eight
The Marriage

Lena and I married on a Paros back beach near the small town of Santa Maria and in the presence of four temporary friends and an Orthodox minister. The priest took pleasure in supplementing his meagre salary by offering quick (and I mean very quick) marriage ceremonies. Still, we had planned the setting. We chose a remote beach with panoramic views to the north and east.

We wore simple attire, nothing fancy. Despite Lena's travels, she had preserved a light cotton dress. All it needed was a rinse and an iron. Unfortunately, my mauve shirt and brown corduroy pants were, even by the low standards of the day, a sight for sore eyes. I would have been more at home on the set of *Saturday Night Fever* than at a wedding. At least the boss of our local taverna had lent me a black tie.

Our marriage vows were in keeping with local tradition and said in Greek. Lena, whose parents had been born in Thessaloniki, was able to translate, albeit poorly. The Greek that Lena had grown up with was from a different era and location. Her Greek was not the language of modern-day Paros. Yet, all I had to remember was 'nei,' which simply meant 'yes.'

Just before the priest handed me the twenty-drachma ring that I had purchased, he nodded, which was my queue to interject: 'I do,' I said enthusiastically. 'I mean, nei.'

Lena just smiled, but her attention had been side-tracked. Throughout the ceremony, thick black clouds had rolled in, the wind had gathered strength and the swell of the waves had grown momentum. It sounded like a hundred-piece orchestra in warm-up mode. The sea crashed and the wind howled. We were not in for a shower; we were in for a storm. Despite the fact we were a stone's throw from Santa Maria beach, it was clear that the Blessed Virgin Mary had deserted us.

After the ceremony had concluded, we stood together hand in hand as the heavens opened. A quick-thinking temporary friend ran over and handed us an umbrella. I certainly appreciated the gesture.

Before I could say: 'Of all the days,' Lena, with a huge smile put a hand to my cheek and looking directly at me uttered: 'This is wonderful, so wonderful.'

I must have looked somewhat perplexed.

'Don't you see? We've got each other. Nature can do its worst, but we're stronger than that.'

I was not convinced of her logic, but it sounded good, and in a split second, she grabbed the umbrella from my hand and tossed it towards the sea. We just stood there on the beach with no protection from the elements with our faces only six inches apart.

'I love you so much,' I must have said over and over again.

'I do too, Greg. We're together; we're one.'

As we stood there, soaked from head to toe, the rain belted us from all directions. A jagged bolt of lightning flashed to the north.

That bolt was followed by the sound of distant thunder and many more lightning strikes. It was evident to both of us that a massive storm was centred near Mykonos.

She muttered, 'I hope that Kiwi arsehole is on the end of one of those strikes.'

I knew Lena did not mean any serious physical harm to Steve Rogers, but it was so clear, even in that moment of our mutual bliss, that he was not far from her mind. He must have truly hurt her. Lena was a woman who was strong and self-assured. Yet, he had damaged her. She deserved love, and all he had provided was spite and hurt.

I made a second vow that day. It was a vow made in the pouring rain with the woman of my dreams clasped in my arms. But it was a silent vow. It was a vow I made to myself that I would always be there for her, no matter what. Lena was so special. She deserved my unqualified emotional support.

However, our decision to remain on the beach in the pouring rain was ill-conceived. There would be plenty of moments for intimacy and romance in more conducive circumstances. Within a day, we were both snivelling. Lena would spend three days in bed, and I would temporally lose my voice.

Between the sniffles and the wipes of her nose, Lena managed a smile. 'No one would really know that you can't talk,' she observed. 'You don't say much at the best of times.'

It was not an insult. It was an accurate assessment. It had always been true that I have tended to shy away from conversations. I have never been confident with public speaking, and even in private communications, I would feel that my contributions were trite or superficial. Therefore, I often chose to say little. The majority of my conversations take place within the confines of my head. I can be witty and engage in meaningful repartee. But, in truth, you will not hear it from my lips. Spontaneity is hardly my forte.

Of course, we soon got over our coughs and splutters and settled back into daily life. We cooked lamb casseroles and drank more than our fair share of thick black coffee. We worked in the tavernas and off-beat cafes and took many a menial job. It would fair to say that we generally lived off the smell of a dirty Aegean rag. At night we would return to our beach, the beach where we exchanged our vows. We would lay there for hours sharing a cigarette or bottle of Fix beer. Even our disagreements (and there were few) were handled with quiet mutual affection and humour.

'Tell me something you don't like about me?' Lena once asked, almost demanding a provocative response.

'Your Olivia Newton-John bad hair,' was the best I could come up with. There was literally nothing I hated, although the obsession with her daily star signs was tiring. I chose not to mention that.

'What! That Pommy upstart. She's more at home in Utah singing and dancing with that twinkle-toed religious zealot than promoting my proud Aussie homeland. If you're going to make a comparison, then at least pick a real Aussie.'

Lena had a way of mixing up facts and places to make her point. She knew the difference between the Churches of Scientology and the Latter-day Saints and knew that Olivia's and John Travolta's appearance in *Grease* was just romantic play-acting.

Lena, though, would never let the facts get in the way of a good argument. There would be occasions when my misrepresentations of the facts would be disastrous. But not then, not on that back-beach in Paros.

'You can't discuss Olivia like that,' I said. 'It's rich coming from a first-generation Greek with her heart in the Motherland and her head in the astrological clouds.'

'Good call, Greg. How long did it take you to dream that one up?' She laughed as she replied, but her sub-text was accurate. It was true; my spontaneous response had been well-rehearsed. I had just needed the right moment to deliver it.

Those Paros days were blissful times, but they had to end. One day Lena started talking about her parents back in Victoria. They lived in a modest 1950s weatherboard house in an equally unassuming suburb in Melbourne's east. Like so many Hellenes, Lena's parents had jumped at the opportunity for a new life, away from Greece's war-torn cities, disease, and unemployment. They were part of a mass wave of post-World War II economic refugees that had descended on Sydney, Melbourne, and Adelaide.

Lena's father had worked in various jobs including stints as a wharfie at the Footscray docks and as a kitchen hand in a fish and chips shop. By the age of forty, he had saved enough to purchase a taxi licence and send his two sons to La Trobe University, in Melbourne's north. His wife dutifully tended to the family home with the help of his only daughter. Lena's domestic efforts were expected, and for the most part, willingly forthcoming. Sadly, despite her father's efforts, there was never enough income to satisfy the financial demands of a house-bound wife and two Holden petrol heads that spent more time at Calder Park Thunderdome than in a university lecture theatre. Something had to give, and that something was Lena's tertiary education. Instead of a University of Melbourne Arts Degree, she had to settle for a teaching diploma at a local college of advanced education.

Like so many of their fellow European refugees, the grass on the family's quarter-acre block had been replaced by a less aesthetically pleasing substance. As Lena often remarked, there was enough reinforced cement in their Melbourne front yard to land a Boeing 747. To Lena, this was a source of amusement.

'Us wogs,' she would say, 'we came, we saw, we concreted.'

Lena's mother would spend much of her day hosing her front yard in much the same way as Lena's grandmother had washed her small Thessaloniki courtyard. But the garden hose was not all that her mother clung to. Like so many of their fellow refugees, Lena's parents cherished their former way of life. Thessaloniki of the 1940s had been lovingly transported to a remote town half a world away.

Lena's parents barely spoke English, and never to themselves or their children. Lena, like so many of her first-generation born contemporaries, was caught between the habits and expectations of two worlds. The old traditional ways of a pre-Nazi occupied Greece had little in common with an increasingly vibrant, hedonistic Australia. Her parents were too old and entrenched to embrace rock 'n' roll, 1960s counter-culture and student activism. Lena was born too late to fully appreciate the plight of her parents and the values that they continued to live and espouse.

It would be fair to say that Lena was often bemused by the behaviour of her parents, but she coped with the inevitable disagreements and dealt stoically with the laundry list of her failures as a 'good Greek daughter.' Her father's favouritism towards her brothers was a different matter. It was crystal clear that her brothers enjoyed a charmed and lazy existence. Unlike Lena, they contributed little in terms of time and effort to the family unit, and the filthy state of their respective bedroom suites stood in stark contrast to the pristine cubby hole that Lena occupied. Further, the souped-up Torana and Monaro in the driveway were constant reminders that her father's hard-earned income had been misused. For that, she blamed her brothers, and despite her parents' best efforts, by the time she left for Greece, her relationship with her siblings had been irreparably damaged. However, Lena would remain emotionally close to her parents and particularly her mother. Indeed, Lena's concerns and feelings for her mother crept into our daily discussions.

Those conversations became more frequent until one day, on an isolated Paros beach, I simply said, 'Let's go.'

'Could we?' she responded happily. 'I thought you never wanted to leave Greece!'

I said something like it did not matter where we were, and that was true. I would have followed Lena to Timbuktu or the Arctic Circle. By comparison, Melbourne seemed a more appealing destination. If I had known then of the ordeals that I would later face, then I may well have been less accommodating. The truth though was that I was hopelessly smitten and totally at Lena's mercy. I had no home, no money, and no prospects, but everything I wanted or needed was wrapped up in a bundle called 'Lena Kostakidis.'

Lying on the Paros sand gazing alternately between the deep blue sky and Lena's deep brown eyes were the happiest days of my life. I knew then that I could literally kill for her. It would take me years to realise that I had a more general propensity for serious violence.

Chapter Nine
The Instructions

There was one aspect of my in-house legal role that truly grated. It concerned the quality of my instructions, particularly from Winston.

'For your review, Greg,' or, 'any issues?' was the usual extent of Winston's communications as he passed me some contract, deed or written communication.

I often wondered where I could buy that 'crystal ball' that I was evidently lacking. Initially, I mistook the terseness of Winston's instructions as a compliment. He could rely on me to dissect the legal issues and provide an appropriate response. But the truth was less gratifying. For Winston, the 'legals' were just a necessary evil.

On the one hand, he certainly would not waste any of his precious time on them. On the other hand, the service agreement, trust deed or statutory declaration was irrelevant. It was though the commercial or business arrangements were somehow separated from the legal documents that gave effect to them.

'Remember, Greg,' Winston would often say, 'a good contract is one that is thrown in the bottom of a drawer and forgotten about.'

I could not have disagreed more, but my argument that a good contract would continually provide a mutually constructive framework fell on deaf eyes.

One day I tried a more direct approach. 'Winston,' I implored, 'if you think a good contract is one that will never see the light of day, then it needs to be properly drafted, negotiated and reviewed before it's thrown into your bottom draw. Getting it right may well necessitate considerable upfront legal and other costs.'

Winston's response was cutting, but surprisingly articulate. 'We need to get things right with minimal upfront legal and other costs. A good contract should not involve considerable costs,' he maintained. 'There are always risks in any commercial arrangement, but we are not going to spend decades delaying a deal for every little roadblock dreamed up by the self-servicing legal profession. You need to start thinking more commercially.'

I started to respond by saying that he was confusing two separate issues. One issue was the merits of the bottom draw and the other the need for detailed instructions. However, I stopped mid-sentence, as it was clear that my unhelpful insights had well and truly tested Winston's attention span.

To be fair, Winston was hardly the first person to claim that a good contract should neither be seen nor heard. Further, lack of clear instructions is the bane of many a lawyer's life. Yet, I suspect that in-house lawyers suffer disproportionately. If an external lawyer is charging you $400 or $500 an hour, there is a financial incentive to reduce costs. In part, cost savings can be achieved by ensuring the lawyer is well focussed on the tasks at hand. The same does not apply to the in-house, salaried variety of lawyer.

Over many years I fought against Winston's one-liners and his general lack of interest in communicating with me.

'Tell me what's going on, Winston,' I would say. 'What is this IT contract for?' 'What's the problem with Martin's banking arrangement?'

Sure, you could glean intent from the documents themselves, but what a complete waste of energy. A simple briefing would have saved an excessive amount of time.

'Surely, Winston, you would want to know if the rights and obligations presented in the agreement are what was agreed?'

'Of course,' would be the terse response. 'That's why we pay you big bucks.'

'But how would I know if I am always left out of negotiations?'

It was that question that highlighted my second but related concern. It was one thing not to receive a full briefing when required, but that concern could have been overcome if I had been granted a seat at the negotiation table in the first place. I envisaged myself as a sort of 'Miss Marple' sitting in a quiet corner of a meeting room taking everything in but saying little. The only difference between Miss Marple and myself, as I saw it, would be the absence of knitting needles. I considered that a pen and notepad would be more appropriate for my role.

Unfortunately, Winston did not share my Agatha Christie view of contractual negotiation. He believed that any extended involvement on my part would undermine commerciality and efficiency.

'Christ, if I had you next to me at every meeting, you and other side's lawyer would turn it into a six-month talk-fest. Nothing would get done or agreed.'

Winston's apathy towards legal matters crossed numerous boundaries, including funds management, property, intellectual property, trade practices, and financial regulation. However, that attitude was most forthright in discussions on tax. I would often see Martin shaking his head in disbelief at Winston's dismissive rhetoric.

'Never let tax rule a commercial decision,' or, 'let's do the deal and worry about tax afterwards,' Winston would often declare.

Martin never understood that approach and even Alfred with his own aversion to taxation was less forthright.

'Come on, Winston,' I once heard Alfred say, 'we have to know the tax consequences.'

Martin expressed the sentiment far more eloquently than either Alfred or I. 'Tax considerations should not determine commercial decision-making,' he reasoned with Winston, 'but they should inform them.'

The fact that Martin openly engaged with Winston over tax matters was reassuring. I was not the only victim of Winston's dismissive attitude. Nonetheless, over time, my brief instructions would be replaced with no explanations at all. E-mails with attachments headed *terms and conditions* would simply just appear. I was left to work out the missing instructions as best I could.

Nonetheless, the lack of instructions was preferable to another of Winston's favourite sayings: 'Don't waste time on this; just do a high-level review.' The instruction, though, was just a euphemism for 'tell me all the legal issues but do it quickly.' I was never quite sure what 'high level' actually meant. They never taught me that phrase at law school.

I recall that in one trust matter, I failed to adequately advise on the desired effect of income and capital distributions to different classes of unitholders. It was not a deliberate omission and I had put in a whole lot of work reviewing the relevant sections of the trust deed. In part, I never really understood Winston's instructions and was too hesitant to seek clarification.

The matter was ultimately settled in the Supreme Court of Victoria. It may have only taken one day, but the Lee Family Office was hit with invoices totalling over $250,000. Those funds were primarily shared between three senior counsel, six junior barristers and a couple of instructing law firms. Thankfully I was never singled out as the primary cause, but for weeks I heard Tich Allen's high-pitched scream inside my head: 'Heh you laddie, you will never make a lawyer. I told you so!'

The absence of clear instructions was, however, a mere source of annoyance. In fairness, my experience with Winston was probably no different from the majority of in-house lawyers. Still, there was one particularly galling incident. For Winston, January and February were decidedly enjoyable months, sandwiched between the solar and lunar New Years. These were celebratory times when Winston partied hard and worked little. The period before the Year of the Dog was especially festive, as Winston turned thirty-six that year. His usual trip to Hong Kong was supplemented by excursions to China, Macau and beyond. On a personal level, I was pleased and able to catch up on a backlog of semi-completed compliance policies and procedures without interruption.

Shortly after the Chinese New Year, I received a curt e-mail from Winston with a standard corporate loan facility agreement. *For your urgent review*, was the total extent of Winston's instructions. As I scrolled down the e-mail chain, I noticed that there had been prior communication between Winston and the relevant bank, and that the facility agreement had first been sent to Winston in November of the previous year. The e-mail chain also revealed that on the morning Winston had forwarded the document to me, the bank had sent through a gentle reminder for feedback. Buried in the communication was Winston's explanation for the delay—*Holiday hangover in legal.* I was the scapegoat for Winston's inaction.

'Stop being so precious,' was Martyn Flynn's response. 'Come on, Greg,' he laughed. 'You should only start worrying when such comments cease. It shows you're being taken seriously.'

Martin's logic did not convince me, but I felt better talking to him, and I wisely refrained from marching into Winston's office. I do not doubt that any complaint on my part would have been dismissed by Winston as overreacting.

Chapter Ten
The Reality

Lena and I moved into a rented 1960s orange brick veneer house somewhere along the Sandringham train line and in proximity to the big mansions of Brighton and Hampton along Port Phillip Bay. Those stately beachside homes seemed a world away, while we were just scrapping enough for rent, utilities, and essential provisions. In weeks when we had money left over, it would be blown on Carlton Draughts and West Coast Coolers at the Devonshire Hotel, a gleaming white building in the heart of affluent middle Brighton. But those visits were few, and most weekends were spent poring through the employment classifieds.

Lena got a position as a primary school teacher, albeit miles from the train line. After all, she had tertiary qualifications. Her role principally concerned the establishment and supervision of a children's library. With limited funds, she relied heavily on donations, supplemented by the occasional fundraiser in the form of a fete or morning tea. As the books flowed in, her primary concern was to ensure they were properly labelled and filed. However, as the Dewey Decimal System was hardly rocket science, the task was more physical than intellectual.

In many respects, a school librarian was an ideal position; she was somewhat removed from most of the teaching and support staff, and their demands and gripes. She also relished the direct involvement of the children in their beloved school library, and there was no shortage of volunteers eager to assist Miss Kostakidis.

One day, a ten-year-old child offered to help with the filing. Lena had known the child since her first week and was impressed with his enthusiasm and spirit for learning. She was aware he came from one of the poorer neighbourhoods, but there was no doubt in her mind that the child was destined for a place at a top tier university. Lena readily accepted his offer of help and effectively left him unattended for the next three hours.

Upon Lena's return to her growing library, she was, at first, delighted that all unfiled books had found their way to a place on the shelves. She quickly observed though, that the entire library collection had been re-filed. Over three thousand books had, in the space of three hours, been rearranged into a sequence that bore no resemblance to a Dewey Decimal Classification. The child had unilaterally decided that the most sensible way to file a book was by reference to its physical size. The smaller books were positioned on the top shelf with bigger ones on the lower shelves. Fiction was mixed in with non-fiction, foreign language with English, reading books with colouring books and other teaching aids.

'Me Dad always tells me to put the big books at the bottom, so the bookcase won't fall over,' explained a very proud ten-year-old.

There was undoubtedly a logic to child's explanation, and for fear of dampening his enthusiasm, Lena refrained from any criticism. She thanked the child for his efforts and then spent much of the following weekend sorting out the mess the child had inadvertently created.

'It's entirely my fault,' she chuckled. 'It was so funny. Where the books were of a similar size, he had dutifully batched them according to the colour of the book cover. It was so aesthetically pleasing to see all the red books together at one end leading to all the blues at the other. The kid plainly knows the spectrum,' and with that, she burst into a fit of laughter.

For Lena, the waste of a weekend was of little consequence. I could see in her eyes and on the expression of her face that children exhilarated her. How could she be angry or frustrated with a child that had been a love and joy? I recall thinking how wonderful our lives would be if Lena and I had children of our own.

Unfortunately, Lena's enthusiasm for her new role slowly waned. Over the next few months, her old concerns about classroom politics resurfaced. While the smiles on the children's face were ever-present, she was increasingly distracted by the conduct of her colleagues and by parental interference. Over time, the fuse on her temper became noticeably shorter.

One evening, when I arrived home, Lena was crying on the couch. Apparently, the Deputy Principal had suggested to her that the library was lacking in appropriate geography books. It seemed to me that this was hardly a cause for tears and that it was fitting the Deputy Principal should show an interest in the library. For fear of upsetting Lena any further, I said nothing, but I just wondered how long her job would last.

I got my employment break some months after arriving in Melbourne when I answered a small advertisement in *The Age* for a State Government position. At that time, Corporate

Affairs Victoria was the agency responsible in Victoria for the administration of laws relating to companies and the securities and futures industries. The various States and Territories handled the main bulk of prosecutions for corporate offences. Yet, in the 1970s there had been a recognition that greater uniformity in administration, and increased reciprocal arrangements and common standards across Australia, would be necessary to increase efficiency and enhance investor protection.

In its early years, Corporate Affairs Victoria mirrored its counterparts in Queensland and New South Wales. Over time, they were joined by corporate affairs offices in the other states and territories, but it would take a further few years before the Hawke-Keating Labor government effectively 'federalised' the regulation of Australian companies. It would be another decade, and long after my time, before the legislation became genuinely national.

I joined Corporate Affairs at an opportune time. The agency was in recruitment mode as it was about to assume responsibility for administering legislation for building societies, co-operatives societies, and friendly societies. I was in the right place at the right time, as many new administrative roles had been created.

Initially, I was assigned to assist complaints, mainly from liquidators, concerning criminal breaches of Victoria's Companies Act. But this was no fancy task. Effectively, my role was limited to collecting books and records, ordering stationery, and filing. However, my immediate boss was a kind soul and quickly arranged for me to undertake a part-time Bachelor of Business degree at the Royal Melbourne Institute of Technology (RMIT) majoring in accountancy. While daunted by the prospect of five years of part-time study, I was fully aware that RMIT presented an amazing opportunity. At the very least, the degree would propel me up the ranks of Corporate Affairs. I was genuinely exc ted by the prospect of one day matching Lena's financial contributions to the household.

'Wow! A business degree,' Lena remarked. 'To think a year ago we were washing dishes and sharing a filthy toilet with four others. You, I mean *we*, have come up in the world.'

I did not respond, as Lena's remarks uneased me. It was true that both of us now had a reasonable income and that our rented accommodation could hardly be called a squat. Still, even then I was not convinced that was progress. Physically, we had made a move to Melbourne, but I felt that we had left something of ourselves in Paros. I did not mind washing dishes for a pittance, and the unhygienic state of the communal washroom hardly bothered me. Lena's words left me with a sense of foreboding. Could we climb the social ladder and still blossom as we did in our Greek days? It would not take long to answer that quest on.

RMIT was a short walk from the Corporate Affairs offices in Little Bourke Street but studying part-time at a city campus meant there was no time to return home before class. The seminars and lecturers would finish by 8:30 pm, but the trains on the Sandringham train line were infrequent and slow. In the early days, I would rarely return home before 9:30 pm. Later, my socialisation with fellow students would further delay my return. Such socialisation invariably occurred in the many pubs or hotels that were in easy reach of RMIT. The old pub on the corner Swanston and A'Beckett streets was our favourite, and I suspect that, in its time, The Oxford Scholar Hotel had been the second home of many an RMIT undergraduate.

The drinking started innocently enough. After a particularly dull business finance class, a couple of mature aged students invited me for a drink. That became a regular occurrence. Two or three pots quickly became five or six. My arrival home became later and later.

At first, Lena was fully supportive.

'I'm pleased you've found some friends outside of that testosterone-laden institution,' which was how she referred to Corporate Affairs.

I was pleased too. Four days a week would comprise of nine hours at the office and a further two hours of on-campus study. The latter was hardly easy, and I was struggling even to understand the basics of accountancy. I knew that if the way I had approached my own finances were any indication, then I was headed for a big fat fail. But, rightly or wrongly, I felt that if I did fail then I would be letting both Lena and my boss down. So, The Oxford Scholar became more than a place for some quiet social relief; it became a further educational forum. I used that time to converse on matters economic and on the content of our student assignments. I would debate, ask and, more often than not, plagiarise from my more astute and intellectual drinking mates. At the end of each of those days, I was simply exhausted.

'Why can't you at least rinse your dinner plate even if you can't be bothered washing it?' Lena's question was more than rhetorical. Her tone indicated both frustration and disappointment. I mumbled a brief apology which, at least initially, appeared to appease her.

I certainly did not mean to upset her but, at the time, I had not appreciated how far my work and study had intruded on our relationship. It was not just full-time work and evening lectures.

The weekends were increasingly spent reading course materials, attending the RMIT library and drafting assignments. According to Lena, most of that study should have been done dur ng the week, after class and at home. Instead, I voluntarily elected to waste precious time with drunken students at the expense of my supportive wife.

'It's as though you don't want to be with me,' became a standard Lena catch-cry. That was not true, but it was true that our lives had changed. Lena would frequently harp on about my lack of interest in domestic chores. She also had a job, but at home she was the chief cook, cleaner, gardener, and shopper. Occasionally, I would clean the bathroom and attempt to mow the jungle that would appear on the nature strip. However, my efforts were all too little.

The main issue though was not about domestic responsibilities. My failings as a chef and cleaner were just symptomatic of a deeper problem. In Greece, we had been in each other's ccmpany almost twenty-four hours a day. We had not only slept together. Each day, we had worked together, ate together, laughed, and cried together. We had been inseparable both physically and emotionally. On the rare occasions we were apart, my whole demeanour changed. I became consumed with irrationa , often fanciful, thoughts about what she was doing or whom she was seeing. Even then, I knew such jealousy was pathetic. Perhaps the intense tightness in my chest and feelings of nausea that would invariably arise on those occasions was a just physical response to my juvenile emotions.

Lena felt likewise, or rather I believed she did. At the moment of being reunited, her face just seemed to shine. I would iterally fall into her arms. They were strong working-class arms. Once grasped, there was no way out. Lena would dictate how long we stayed entwined. Often our embrace would last considerably longer than normal social mores would condone. Afterwards, after reunification was complete, her smile would just ooze contentment.

Indeed, Lena's contented smile was infectious. On one such occasion in Paros, I heard the voice of a well-muscled, good-looking Cockney: 'You lucky, lucky bastard.' I had to look twice to realise he was talking to me. 'What have you got that a chick like that would go for?'

I did not have time to answer. It was probably the word 'chick' that did it. Lena's smile quickly evaporated.

'We're not listening to this dickhead's crap. We're out of here.'

With that, Lena released her embrace, grabbed me by the hand and almost frog-marched me to the small, dingy, room that then served as home. And I was pleased she moved so quickly. I caught a glimpse of the Cockney's face as it turned purple. He did not strike me as someone who was used to being called a 'dickhead.'

Those moments were never to be repeated in Melbourne. The appeal of a new home, half a world away from Berkshire, provided some brief excitement, and, for a few months or so, enriched our happy relationship. But then the reality of our new life began to sink in. The demands of work, study, the drudgery of routine Australian life and its daily pressures took their toll. In hindsight, it was all too obvious. We had been forced to grow up. We had not just arrived in Melbourne to be close to Lena's ageing parents. We had traded our simple idyllic existence in the Cyclades for a more socially conventional lifestyle.

To be sure, I had only taken my first steps on the corporate ladder, but it was in an environment that presented real concrete career opportunities. If we had stayed on Paros, or Syros or Milos, we would have grown old washing plates, chopping shrivelled tomatoes, swilling Fix beer, and sleeping in cheap, rented rooms. That is all we would have ever done. There were no alternatives, but I sure miss those hungry years.

In the process of growing up, we had become earnest, not just within ourselves but to each other. The fun and laughter that had once characterised our relationship had been displaced by discussions over finances, budgets, career ambitions, and domestic responsibilities. I am sure that change did not occur overnight, but it was undoubtedly quick. Now, many years later, I cannot recall any moment in Melbourne when we ever spontaneously fell into a state of helpless laughter. I cannot recollect a time when we passionately reached out for each other. Regrettably, I do remember times when our lovemaking seemed routine and emotionally distant.

Long before the end, it did feel that in our move from Greece to Australia, we had lost something precious. We had lost each other. Still, even that realisation did not adequately prepare me for the events that followed.

Chapter Eleven
The Office

The Lee Family Office was initially structured as a proprietary limited company, with a board of five family directors and approximately thirty shareholders. All shareholders were direct bloodline descendants of Alfred's father or corporate vehicles controlled by such descendants. Ownership and control were tight. As a matter of family policy, collateral descendants of Alfred's father (in other words, cousins, nieces, and nephews of Alfred's father), were expressly prohibited from owning shares in the Lee Family Office. Even more controversial was the decision to exclude the current spouses and de facto partners of bloodline descendants. Winston's wife, despite her wealthy Hong Kong Chinese origins and frequent requests, was consistently denied any shares of her own.

'My children hold shares,' she often grumbled, 'but you say their mother's not a worthy owner.'

Alfred's public response was to either ignore the criticism or merely point out that the company's constitution required shareholders to be adult lineal descendants. However, in private, or at least in his conversations with Winston, Alfred's angst was unmistakable. Alfred knew that such overt criticism had the potential to undermine family cohesion, which the shareholding restriction had been designed to promote. For Alfred, Winston's wife was a constant and vocal irritant, right up to the day that Winston appeared in the office with a Filipina model half his age and announced that Mrs Lee had departed Toorak for Toronto. Despite a costly divorce, I could tell Alfred secretly supported his philandering son.

So, while the Lee Family Office expanded its sphere and operations to include non-Lee family clients, the money, in the form of capital and biannual dividends, and power, through voting rights, remained tightly within the family. Later, when Alfred and Winston sought to invest in non-financial services businesses, a simple pyramid ownership structure was introduced. A shelf-company would be purchased with equity funding from the Lee Family office. The structure ensured bloodline family members ultimately controlled the new vehicle.

Control over ownership did more than protect and foster the family unit. It provided Lee family members with opportunities for gainful work and employment. The board of directors was solely comprised of family members, while the top executive positions were also reserved for the family. Like the Australian family office sector as a whole, I had arrived at a time when many such offices were primarily run by the first and second generations of the relevant wealth creators. Despite Winston's title as chief executive officer, Alfred, who on paper was merely the non-executive chairman, was clearly in charge. However, a clear succession plan had been articulated. Winston was effectively the apprentice. In time, he would inherit the chairmanship and pass the CEO baton to his eldest son.

Limiting succession was, though, a double-edged sword. Any family business that determines managerial appointments based on biology rather than merit compromises business competence and long-term survival. Alfred was acutely aware of the problem and often referred to an old Chinese saying: 'The first generation makes the wealth. The second holds it, and the third generation loses it.'

Alfred knew the statistics. Only three per cent of comparable American firms made it to the fourth generation and beyond. He had no reason to believe the Australian experience was any different. Alfred once admitted that he was delighted to employ a professional accountant in Martin Flynn and a qualified lawyer in me. He hoped that we would at least stall the demise of the Lee Family Office. Long-term issues aside, at the time of my arrival there was a compelling legal need to amend both the status of the Lee Family Office and to restructure one of its core products. Failure to do so would occasion considerable regulatory risk.

For a decade or so, the Lee Family Office had blissfully operated its cash management trust with total disregard for the Corporations Law. That had to be fixed. Known as the 'Lee Family Cash Fund' or simply the 'Lee Fund,' the fund became the hub of the business. The Lee Family Office, as trustee of the fund, had opened a cheque account with one of the major banks. Over the following twenty-odd years, ninety-nine per cent of monies in and out of the office flowed through that one bank account.

The Lee Fund was structured in a very traditional manner. One unit in the fund could be bought and sold for one dollar with the application monies pooled and invested mainly in short-term bank bills or term deposits. Returns from those investments were calculated daily and distributed pro-rata to unitholders at the end of each month. It was a basic investment vehicle, like those offered by the large banks and financial institutions.

Nonetheless, there were two features of the fund that require special mention. The first feature concerned the fund's functionality. A withdrawal of units could, at the direction of the relevant client, be used to pay third party bills. Clients would regularly avail themselves of that service. Withdrawal proceeds could be applied to invoices of a few dollars or to a few million dollars. The staff of the Lee Family Office would arrange payments to the nearby dry-cleaning service, BMW dealerships, and the local branch of Hong Kong and Shanghai Bank. Other payments would be made to Hong Kong, Shanghai and a world of airlines, hotels, and luxury department stores.

The bill-paying service did not merely provide administrative convenience to clients. The service, which was charged on top of the fund's management fee, was linked to accounting and tax. Each invoice would be reviewed and journalised in the appropriate client ledger. There was no need for clients to front up to the office each year at tax time with a shoebox full of receipts. All monies into and out of the Lee Fund had been recorded for tax purposes on the date the transactions occurred by one or two lowly paid bookkeepers. I suspect those bookkeepers never appreciated their real contribution to the organisational efficiency of the Lee Family Office.

The second feature of the Lee Fund concerned perception rather than reality. Unitholders viewed the Lee Fund as a bank account, although it was never a banking product. Until the end of the millennium, the fund was legally characterised as a prescribed interest. For those of you unfamiliar with financial product jargon, a prescribed interest was essentially an investment opportunity in anything other than shares or debentures. Strict rules governed such products. Unfortunately, the directors and management of the Lee Office Family were unaware of such requirements or had chosen to ignore them.

It took me some months before I understood the extent of the Lee Fund's non-compliance. At that time, the Howard Government had legislated to turn the regulation of prescribed interests on its head and created the concept of a 'single responsible entity.' The new rules imposed various requirements on responsible entities. The Lee Family Office met the financial obligations, but the amended Corporations Law required responsible entities to be public companies. I needed to transform the status of the Lee Family Office to a public company. I also needed to obtain a dealer's licence for the Lee Family Office and register the Lee Fund with ASIC under the then-new managed investment scheme provisions of the Corporations Law. Also, the fund required a prospectus in which to offer units to new clients.

It was a quadruple whammy. The Lee Family Office was a proprietary company with an investment adviser's licence. It needed to be a public company with a dealer's licence. The Lee Fund itself was not ASIC-registered and offers of units were made on the back of a three-page information memorandum drafted by Winston over a bottle of scotch and a can of dry ginger.

We tackled the problem in stages. Conversion to a public company required a simple form. However, the dealer's licence application required lengthy submissions to the regulator. In between ASIC requisitions, I established a due diligence committee. I also drafted a new 'constitution' to replace the old trust deed and a thirty-page 'prospectus' and application form as a substitute for Winston's drunken offering.

In all, the process took well over a year, and in truth, much of my legal drafting was copied. Constitutions of registered managed investment schemes including cash management trusts were lodged with ASIC, and, for a small fee, available to the public (or for free if you knew which ASIC employees to approach). Prospectuses were readily available at the branches of banks and large financial institutions. The lawyers of Deutsche, JB Were, and the Commonwealth and ANZ banks would have no appreciation of their pro bono contributions to the constituent documents of the Lee Fund.

Further, much of the content of the dealer's licence application was drafted in the confines of the Metropolitan Hotel in William Street with a couple of friends from ASIC's licensing team. Certainly, the Lee Family Office's Diners Club card took a hammering in those days. Still, the expense of entertaining ASIC staff was considerably cheaper than outsourcing the licence application to a law or compliance services firm.

Fortunately, other than my ASIC accomplices, the regulator never twigged the extent of the non-compliance or plagiarism, and the legalisation of the Lee Fund was achieved without adverse regulatory action.

Initially, Alfred had opposed any changes to the structure of the Lee Fund. He knew that the financial accounts of public companies were open to the public.

'Our balance sheets aren't going to be splattered across the *Financial Review*. What's more,' he added, almost as an afterthought, 'Arthur Andersen does well by us already. Why should we pay for the costs of another audit?'

Alfred's question was rhetorical and I intentionally refrained from comment, mainly as numerous companies and trusts within the broad Lee family group of companies were subject to audits. One more would hardly make a difference. Later, I approached a more relaxed Alfred and explained in detail the need for comprehensive reform.

Eventually, the Lee Fund would become a source of personal agitation and despair. Yet, back in my first couple of years of employment, it was an unlikely ally. What I had not appreciated was the firm's lack of awareness of regulatory compliance requirements. Other than accounting and tax, which had been for many years competently handled by Martin Flynn, neither Alfred nor Winston had more than a basic understanding of the regulatory environment. I quickly filled the void, and in so doing, ingratiated myself to Alfred. I would become his close if not trusted adviser.

'We're just a family, Mr Mason,' Alfred remarked when I first suggested the need to restructure both the Lee Family Office and Lee Fund. 'Surely there's no need for us to take on all this added expense and unnecessary regulation?'

I needed to make a point without sounding impolite: 'Unfortunately, Mr Lee, there are no exceptions for families in the Corporations Law. If we don't become a public company and get the Lee Fund registered, then we're taking on too much regulatory risk.'

'Mr Mason, that's what we pay you for. If you tell us we must do it, we will. But no more than the minimum.'

Except for Martin Flynn, who had spent many years dealing with the tax office, everyone in the Lee Family Office articulated the idea that one could readily identify or isolate the components of minimum compliance. The approach was like taking an exam with the express ambition of scraping a pass. I once tried explaining to Winston that regulations and regulatory enforcement were continually evolving. Ultimately, whether one passed or failed would be a matter for the courts to determine, and with the benefit of hindsight.

In fairness, Alfred's comments should not be taken literally. He understood that regulatory action was often ambiguous, often political, and invariably complicated. Always the businessman, all Alfred was saying was that he expected a cost-effective solution. I did not doubt that he believed that I was capable of delivering that result.

Winston, though, was less easily impressed. He had a love for nicknames and my shared secretary and I were christened with the acronym 'BPU,' the Lee Family Office's very own 'business prevention unit.' The first time I heard Winston use the expression was at a work function involving several clients. Winston was talking to a small group of like-minded individuals, and I was within earshot. It was clear that the assembled group had a collective disrespect for the legal profession.

I calmly walked over to Winston.

'I'm not the only business prevention unit in the place,' I threw back. 'Just remember, I don't take holidays for Chinese New Year,' which was the truth, 'and I don't have hangovers at work,' which was stretching the truth.

Before Winston could reply, I turned and quickly walked away. As I did, I heard one of the clients ask, 'What was all that about?'

'No idea. No idea at all,' said Winston.

Chapter Twelve
The Separation

My little domestic world would fall apart. Late one Friday night, shortly before the Black Monday financial crash, I returned home. While the furniture and kitchen utensils all remained, Lena and much of her clothes had gone. There was a note, a simple note.

Dearest Greg. Life separates those who are in love. You know as I know that we've drifted apart. I am sorry, but I have to go. I'm off to Sydney. Will be in contact. Love always, L xxx.

I later found out that Sydney was just a temporary stop on her travels east. Somehow, somewhere, she had rekindled her relationship with Steve Rogers, who was by then a television director with CTV, a regional station in Christchurch. He had done well. Later, after our divorce came through, Lena and Steve would marry and adopt two beautiful Vietnamese orphans. Still later, and much to their collective surprise, Lena, by then in her forties, gave birth to a baby girl of their own.

Steve, I heard, was a wonderful father and passionate husband. As a couple and as a family, they were inseparable. Lena retrained as a human resources officer, and just so she could be close to Steve during the working hours, accepted a junior HR position at CTV. In turn, he would do everything for her. Steve was the family cook, cleaner, gardener, and taxi driver. He had turned sober a few years before and had taken to Les Mills gyms as if he had found religion. He was healthy, trim, and simply revered Lena in a way I had only briefly done.

I never discovered how, when, and where Mr and Mrs Rogers renewed their relationship, although the answer to the 'why' was pretty damn obvious. I had failed that essential duty of care that I had vowed to uphold for eternity. Lena was more important than Corporate Affairs, RMIT and my drinking buddies combined. Yet, when she needed me, I was absent without leave.

Of course, I was angry. I was mad with myself. But I was also sad and embarrassed to have lost her. Dare I say that on occasions I even felt relieved. I was relieved from that self-imposed pressure to act and behave in my lover's best interests. I loved, adored, and worshipped her. Those were hard emotions to control each and every day.

Above all, there was one emotion that characterised and shaped my initial response to Lena's departure. I was gripped with jealousy, particularly when the ambiguity in Lena's farewell note slowly dawned on me. Perhaps, the problem with our relationship was not that we had drifted apart or that we had lost each other, or even that our life together had separated our love. That was not the problem. Instead, our time with each other had become unbearable for Lena precisely because it prevented her from being with Steve. For Lena, I was just a short or interim divergence. She had returned to her one true soulmate.

The sun in my life suddenly became hidden through deep black morose clouds. I became impatient at the slightest of provocations. I would snap at my workmates, and my boss openly referred to me as the 'pommy sook.' Apparently, he thought 'whinging pom' was a term of endearment that could not adequately describe my irritable and cantankerous behaviour. However, my boss had himself experienced a lengthy and acrimonious divorce. He provided considerable latitude.

Over the next few months, there would be bad days and bloody awful days. But thankfully, with time, the black clouds did lift. Light and laughter would slowly return, provided Lena was kept firmly at back of mind. Unfortunately, Lena never appreciated the impact she had on my mental state and would regularly telephone and write to check up on her 'favourite ex.' Indeed, as e-mail replaced *Australia Post*, the frequency of her communications increased. I must admit, in the early years I did not help myself. I answered the phone too often and responded to too many letters. Consequently, the Greek memories would come flooding back.

It was only later when I physically distanced myself from Lena that I was able to get a grip on my emotions. Lena would visit Melbourne regularly, mainly to see her mother or to attend one of those interminable human resource conferences. Those visits were the worst. She would jabber on in passionate defence about some bullshit staff engagement practice or insight. I would merely nod or mutter at the appropriate moments, while all the while wishing to hold her, and praying she would say something meaningful about us. She never did, and my resentment built. I hoped that Steve would die a horrible death and that she would fly back across the Tasman into my waiting arms. Alas, I knew that even if the worst did happen to Steve, it would not result in our reconciliation. Lena was a strong woman, both physically and mentally. If she were to lose her shining knight, there would be no replacement. She simply did not need one.

Our last meeting, in some swanky Southbank restaurant, was particularly difficult. Over a bottle of Moët & Chandon, and in between praise of Kurt Lewin's change management models, I felt increasingly uncomfortable. We were not conversing. I was simply her audience; there to listen to descriptions of her happy and contented life, her kids, her work with Rotary, and the culinary skills of her husband that put Jamie Oliver's to shame. It was too much. I felt my chest thumping as I fought to keep my tears internal.

'I love you,' I managed to mutter pathetically, deliberately out of her earshot, or so I had hoped.

'I love you too,' came the instant reply. It was not said flippantly or without feeling. Lena's response was genuine, but her voice was devoid of passion. She said the words as though they were a given. She did love me just as she loved that bottle of Moët, the Carlton footy team, Chanel No. 5, and a packet of Tim Tams. I was only one of many things she loved, but none of them would come close to that tosser at the top of the list. *What the hell do you see in him?* I felt like screaming, but no words came out.

'Are you okay? You're really sweating. I must get some water,' Lena asked with a sincerity that immediately triggered another emotion. I went from anger and jealousy to guilt in the time it took Lena to utter those few kind words.

It was too much. I cannot now remember my response. All I recall was thinking that we could not keep meeting like this. When she finally kissed my cheek and left for another meaningless HR seminar, I knew then that the meeting would be our last. I had made a resolution that I knew I would honour. After the tears and deep-numbing pain in my chest had ceased, I could reflect with some objectivity on that nature of that last meeting, although

I would invariably do so through the guise of a mock conversation: *'I'm more than just a fucking Tim Tam, Lena. You shouldn't treat me like this. That's why I can't see you.'*

Yet, whether I honoured my resolution through my own resolve is debatable. Real events, not hypothetical interactions, would interfere and would do so in the most unfair and extreme manner. Ultimately, Lena and Steve Rogers lived in the wrong place and at the wrong time. You see, Christchurch life is a lottery, a geological lottery that is, with no winners. The tension between the Pacific and Indo-Australia plates was a recurring nightmare for Cantabrians. The potential for desolation was just one earth tremor away. Innocently or negligently, the original architects of Christchurch had created a time bomb. Years later, that creation would explode with devastating consequences. But no one would lose more than Mr and Mrs Rogers.

In the first earthquake, Lena and Steve lost their home. Their semi-detached dwelling crumbled into a pile of bricks and debris. Bits of clothing, crockery, and furniture were pulled from the wreckage, but little was unbroken and even less was of use. The physical reminders of two decades of marital bliss had been shattered in ten seconds of pure hell. No dwelling in their street escaped intact. No resident in their suburb survived without physical or emotional pain.

Long before, in our Greek days, when liquidity was tight and the words 'rent' and 'arrears' were uttered in the same breath, we turned to humour for support. I recall that on one bad day, I was abruptly dumped as a kitchen hand from a local taverna. But that was just for starters. With nothing in our stomachs since breakfast, and a landlord's patience that had been well and truly tested, we discovered our scant belongings strewn unceremoniously across our street. Needless to say, the key to our pint-sized lodgings had been changed.

Lena, without so much as a sigh, let alone a curse, turned in my general direction. There was no anger, no tears, just a wry smile.

'Just remember, Greg, just remember,' she prophesied. 'As one door shuts, another slams in your face.'

Ten minutes later, when our tears of laughter had subsided, we would reflect more rationally on our financial plight and the pressing concerns of hunger and accommodation. But there would always be an odd job, a kind friend, or secluded shelter to satisfy our basic needs. Malaphors and misquoted idioms not only made us laugh, they helped us cope.

However, natura disasters, especially those of the magnitude experienced by Cantabrians, are not laughing matters. Indeed, Lena's words are now cruelly apposite. Five months after the Rogers' home was raised to rubble, a 6.3 magnitude aftershock ripped through the guts of New Zealand's oldest established city. It was in that second quake that Lena and Steve lost each other, along with one hundred and eighty-three other innocent souls.

For Lena and Steve Rogers, it would be death, not life, which would separate their love for each other. To this day, I often think about the couple's final moments and the sheer terror they must have experienced as the Canterbury Television Building collapsed around them. Had I truly, in my heart of hearts, wanted Steve dead? Had fate intervened and misread my desires? Did Lena and Steve even know what was happening to them in those horrific last seconds? What kind of life lay ahead for their orphaned children? I never did find out the answers to those questions.

Chapter Thirteen
The Regulator

For me, there would be other women.

'Man is not an island,' as one of my public bar drinking mates would say in jest. That phrase would often be followed by: 'I'd rather a pot than a poke,' and the public bar would laugh and pretend to agree.

Of course, this interaction was just typical Aussie banter. In truth, the sexual appeal of middle-aged men with thin grey hair and pronounced beer guts discussing the merits of gout or type two diabetes medication is questionable.

However, in my younger years, before age and alcohol wrecked my physical appearance, there would be opportunities to fancy and to be fancied. Sad to say, the relationships would be fleeting and shallow. There would be no one I could call special. No one compared to Lena. She had gone, but I would cherish her memory. Her photograph on my bedside table with that contented smile would be a constant reminder.

Lena had also given me something else—the chance to live in Australia. While I would have traded everything for a return to Paros with my beloved Lena, I knew the opportunity for an Australian life was also precious. I could never have passed the immigration hurdle by myself. Back then, with no tertiary qualifications or trade skills to my name, there was no way I could have cobbled together the required immigration points. But for Lena, I would never have dreamed of an Australian life. She had got me here and away from England and the likes of Tich Allen for good. I was determined to make the most of the opportunity.

The RMIT years came and went. The combination of full-time employment and part-time study was therapeutic. I had a renewed purpose in life that increasingly banished Lena to the back of my thoughts. Yet, progress was hardly linear. Student holidays were particularly hard, with no assignments to occupy my mind. In the evenings, I would still descend on The Oxford Scholar Hotel, but my fellow students were only noticeable by their absence. They were typical twenty-somethings with hectic family and social calendars. They had better things to do than hang out with a mature age student whose emotional state was anything but.

At the time, I was oblivious to my increasing reliance on alcohol. Drinking did not just soften the pain of losing Lena. Alcohol made me feel better about myself. I liked myself more when I was drunk, even admitting so once to my Corporate Affairs team leader, or 'the boss' as I called him.

'Yeah, you are a piss pot. Wake up to yourself,' he said thoughtfully, looking me in the eyes. 'You'll have a short life if you continue like this. And why the hell are you still living in that matrimonial home of yours? I'm no psychologist, but you need to move out.'

The boss was right. Hanging on to our shared home was preserving if not reinforcing Lena memories, and it was not just the rented house. The local shops and pubs, the beach and

Sandringham train line were all part of the mix. If I was serious about getting over Lena, I needed to move away.

In hindsight, my brief conversation with the boss did nothing to diminish my consumption of alcohol. In fact, it would be fair to say that even then my liver was on borrowed time. While I failed to exercise greater control over the quantity of alcohol I partook, I did manage perceptions. There would be no more daily lunchtime trips along King Street to the Great Western or Golden Age hotels. The boss would never see me drunk in office hours again.

The need for revision dominated the last few months of my business degree. Even I realised that homework was best done at home with textbooks and notes sprawled across the kitchen table. My trips to The Oxford Scholar became less frequent. Later, in my Lee Family Office days, I would keep my drinking relatively hidden. Dan Murphy's would become and remain my primary source of alcohol. Unless I were socialising with friends or colleagues, public bars were largely replaced by my lounge room as a preferred drinking destination.

I quickly moved out of the rented orange brick veneer abode and into a two-bedroomed Victorian terraced house in unfashionable Brunswick. A decade later, I would sell that same dwelling for a small fortune. The proceeds of that sale, together with a healthy Lee Family Office salary, would be sufficient to purchase a more expansive Edwardian property in stylish Fitzroy. The boss may only have been concerned with my emotional state, but he had instigated a chain of events that would ultimately lead to financial security. Unfortunately, that security would be undermined by a different chain of events.

Shortly after I graduated with an RMIT business degree, the federalisation of corporate regulation took a massive leap forward with the creation of the Australian Securities Commission (or ASC). The organisation was established as an independent government body with the primary purpose of regulating companies and the securities and futures industries across Australia. In subsequent years, it would be entrusted with more responsibilities for consumer, investor, and creditor protection.

Most of the Corporate Affairs staff, myself included, populated the ranks of the ASC. We were joined by National Securities Commission employees and several former Victoria police officers. There were even a couple of seconded Australian Federal Police (AFP) officers to undertake police record checks, execute search warrants and arrest offenders.

A single, well-resourced, nationally consistent institution had been created. However, the organisation was structurally schizophrenic due to the multiplicity of its roles. It was a regulator and business facilitator, as well as a corporate watchdog with its activities covering licensing, registration, public education, revenue collection, quasi-judicial decision-making, enforcement, and prosecution. An early chairman once remarked that he did not know if he should smile for the cameras or look serious. He was not sure if we were supposed to help or act as the corporate sheriff.

Unsurprisingly, tensions manifested themselves internally. Generally, many of the accountants were assigned to business facilitation activities, such as licensing and prospectus reviews, while the former coppers conducted criminal investigations. No one quite knew what the ASC lawyers did apart from stymieing the work of their colleagues.

Those were exciting times, and although I was transferred across on essentially the same employment salary and conditions, I had the grand title of 'Administrative Services Officer Class Four.' The title meant I was formally recognised as an assistant investigator. I was also delighted to know that my relationship with the boss would continue, albeit at a new location. In the process of transition, he had scored himself a corner office on an upper story level of the CGU Building, 485 La Trobe Street. I grabbed a nearby workstation with magnificent views across Spencer Street railway yards and Port Phillip Bay beyond.

In its establishment, the ASC had been given extensive powers to compel individuals to provide the regulator with all reasonable assistance in connection with its investigations, to appear before ASC officers for examinations on oath and to hand up company books and records. Most often, those evidence-gathering powers would be used by the ASC in civil or criminal proceedings brought against companies or their directors and officers. Or at least, that was the theory.

Over the next few years, I drafted notices for the production of company books and records and attendance at compulsory examinations, served such notices on company officers, employees and their advisers, took minutes of meetings, reviewed and documented exhibits, asked questions in formal examinations, interviewed potential witnesses and drafted their statements. I had reached the pinnacle of Tich Allen's expectations. I was a policeman, albeit a corporate one.

Yet, follow-up action in the form of criminal prosecutions or civil recovery action was a rarity. More often than not, our investigations would be curtailed with a short, sharp directive to close the relevant file. Still, it would be wrong to dismiss the ASC or its investigators as mere toothless tigers. The sheer volume of complaints, coupled with limited resources, meant that discretion was the name of the game. The organisation was necessarily selective in its decision-making. Unfortunately, when it came to the selection of enforcement action, the decision-making process was fundamentally flawed.

Too often, human resources were ploughed into large or complex investigations that were politically motivated. Investigations into those complaints would often require a principal investigator, a couple of senior investigators, numerous junior investigators, and half a dozen assistants, like me. Also, legal and accounting resources would be called upon where necessary. I recall one investigation that involved a twenty or so team from across Australia working from a separate floor in the CGU Tower. That investigation was headed by an external barrister on a $2,000-a-day retainer. After countless compulsory examinations, hundreds of notices and interviews, and even a couple of draft briefs of evidence to the Director of Public Prosecutions (DPP), the investigation collapsed. Two years of our lives and millions of taxpayers' dollars wasted.

If levelheadedness had prevailed, that investigation would have been shelved months before. However, as a high-profile businessman was the subject of the investigation, many stones were unnecessarily turned before someone at the DPP swallowed a healthy dose of common sense. Usually, the investigators would be gung-ho about the prospects of prosecution. In that case, though, it was the lawyers. The alarm bells should have gone off. The investigators uncovered mountains of allegations and innuendo. Even they knew that that did not constitute evidence.

Just as the ASC had a willingness to throw resources into questionable high-profile investigations, it also showed a reluctance to investigate the smaller, less politically charged variety. Indeed, the ASC never had much time for minor cases, which formed the bulk of complaints. The Complaints Handling Unit rejected most at source with a brief 'no further action' letter. Put simply, the ASC was structured to filter out most complaints. Yet, small ones would slip through the system. One such complaint found its way to the boss.

Early one morning, as I was barcoding a series of documents for some critical investigation that would be shelved six months later, the boss threw me a file.

'Take a look at this, Greg. If you want it, run with it. If not, piss it back to Complaints.' The boss had a way with words.

The big things in life often turn on the small stuff, and that complaint was one such small thing. Ultimately, the events that flowed from that complaint would change my life forever, if not for the better.

Chapter Fourteen
The Charity

James Powell was an English-born chartered accountant who had spent several years with Deloitte Touche Tohmatsu, in both London and Singapore. He arrived in Australia in the early part of the century, together with an Oxbridge educated wife and a trio of delightful private schoolboys.

James took positions with those divisions of accountarts who cater to the investment and taxation needs of the ultra-high net worth clients. Lucy Powell, his wife, went straight to the top as a funds manager and would be gainfully employed as a 'Mac Trader,' those Macquarie Bank elites on obscene remuneration packages. By all accounts, she was a damned good broker but hardly suffered fools gladly.

James arrived at the Lee Family Office one chilly July day and was immediately allocated ten client groups, including his namesake's family. Stephen Powell had made his fortune but was just sick of the ongoing administrative tasks that accompanied a personal nest egg worth more than $50 million.

Stephen Powell was a real rags to riches story. Born in a tough working-class inner suburb, his classmates had identified his homosexuality long before he had. As a consequence, he was a prime victim of classroom bullying. Leaving school at fifteen, he had worked as an apprentice mechanic and hid his sexuality. Fifty Victorian Football League games and a dozen triathlons later, he came out. Spurred on by an insatiable desire to succeed, he rose through the ranks of one of Australia's largest vehicle servicing outlets. Still, that was not enough. For almost a decade, he spent his evenings at Chisholm Institute and then Monash University. By the time he finished tertiary education, he held a master's degree in business studies. A decade later, he was executive chairman of his company and its largest shareholder.

Suddenly, at the age of fifty years, Stephen stopped work. A chance meeting with Alfred Lee at some high-brow function provided Stephen with his ticket to life as a yachtsman. The Lee Family Office would provide Stephen, his partner and adopted sons a comprehensive range of wealth management services, including custody and investment advisory services.

James Powell was assigned to provide Stephen with accounting, tax, and cash management services. Importantly, James was required to act as Stephen's client adviser. There was also an expectation that the Lee Family Office would provide Stephen, as with other wholesale clients, investment opportunities through its own pooled investment vehicles. These services effectively required James to understand the complexities of Stephen's financial affairs as well as the investments of his personal companies.

'If you don't know your clients' financial affairs better than the clients themselves, then it's time for you to move on,' Winston would often say to James and the other client advisers.

From my initial observations, James would not be heading out of the door in a hurry. He was well-educated and experienced, and in comparison to the bulk of client advisers, more passionate about the personal affairs of his clients. Client feedback was unequivocal. They appreciated his dedication and input. At each annual remuneration review, James would be rewarded with a healthy bonus.

I immediately took to James, although I quickly learnt that calling him Jim or Jimmy were absolute no-nos.

'Call yourself English?' were almost his first words to me. 'Glasgow Rangers, are you kidding me?'

Come on, Jim, what's with a Northampton boy sporting a Manchester United scarf?' Of course, that was not a particularly brilliant insight since half the world seems to barrack for the red half of Manchester.

'You're a Berkshire boy. What's wrong with Reading, or Queens Park Rangers or even Wycombe Wanderers?' he replied somewhat sarcastically, followed by, 'I see your point. No one supports Reading. Oh, and it's James by the way.'

James, who was never really a round ball football fan, hardly had the credentials to critique my football loyalties. Educated at Latymer College and the London School of Economics, he was a true rugby union tragic. Indeed, he once admitted that his main reason for moving to Australia was to be close to the 'Super 12s' as it was then. I am sure that over his lifetime James was often dismissed as just another stuck-up elite English schoolboy, with the obligatory plum in his mouth. However, the English upper classes are hardly renowned for their work ethic and sersitivity. James hailed from a different stock.

One of James Powell's early professional dealings concerned the structuring of Stephen Powell's philanthropic affairs. Specifically, James and Eileen, who was head of the Lee Family

Office's philanthropy team, helped Stephen, or rather Stephen's personal lawyer, establish a prescribed private fund or 'PPF' (later, private ancillary fund).

PPFs became available as a philanthropic structure during the Howard Government era, and knowledge of their existence and benefits, particularly for the ultra-rich, quickly widened. The Lee family were quick to respond, and within just a few years, the Lee Family Office helped establish over thirty PPFs for its clients or donors, to use the official PPF terminology.

Such funds were attractive for several related reasons, including tax deductions for funds donated to them, exemptions from income tax, no public fundraising requirements, and the ability, within limits, to accumulate funds. Not surprisingly, there were an array of regulatory obligations concerning the establishment and administration of a PPF. Each fund was governed by a model trust deed, required to undergo an annual audit, provide an annual return to the tax office, and have at least one external trustee or external director oversee the fund.

PPFs were also required to limit grants to eligible deductible gift recipient (DGR) organisations. However, a PPF provided its donor with the opportunity to accumulate far more significant amounts for charitable purposes than he or she might have otherwise considered for a single donation. In so doing, the PPF structure allowed donors to take greater control over their charitable activities.

To their supporters, PPFs have generated billions of additional dollars for non-profit endeavours and encouraged new participants into the sector. To their detractors, the PPF structure is a just lawful tax dodge. While mere mortals pay taxes, the ultra-rich can park their income away in a tax-free environment for causes of their own choosing. No one should be surprised that the bulk of donations to PPFs are made in the last few days of each financial year.

Stephen Powell's 'Powell Pride Foundation' was one of Australia's first PPFs. Its name was a deliberate play on words. Yet, there was an important social cause at stake. The Powell Pride Foundation was expressly founded to promote activities that challenged discrimination based on sexual orientation. For Stephen, 'gay pride' was not an empty slogan. He was a passionate campaigner and woe betide any vocal homophobe that stood in front of his right fist.

The Lee Family Office agreed to provide Stephen's foundation with investment opportunities and grant-making support, as well as ongoing accounting, tax, and cash management services. James and his team would provide all services other than grant-making. That role would fall onto Eileen who headed a small team dedicated to identifying, assessing, and recommending potential grant recipients. Until Stephen Powell's arrival, her team had worked exclusively for Lee family members. Stephen was her first non-family client, although he would not be her last. Indeed, Stephen Powell was so taken by the enthusiasm and professionalism of Eileen and her team that he would later involve his partner and children through the creation of further foundations.

My involvement with the Powell Pride Foundation was mainly limited to helping James and Eileen document their services. Unfortunately, at that time, Winston had been strongly opposed to introducing a standard client services agreement. His support would only be forthcoming with the commencement of the Australian financial services licence regime a couple of years later. Even then, it took Martin to persuade Winston of the merits of a standardised document. Until that time, client agreements, for what they were worth, were mainly a brief list of services and fees written on the back of a Chinese menu. Such arrangements were usually negotiated over a long lunch.

'We need flexibility,' Winston would say before reverting to his old chestnut that clients were all different and therefore demanded separate arrangements. Of course, what Winston really meant was that a standardised agreement would limit his flexibility to favour his side of the family and close mates. He knew full well that the scribbles on the various Chinese menus hardly amounted to legally enforceable contracts. They were never likely to restrict his nepotism.

Thankfully, whatever may have worked for Lee family members, was not going to work for non-family clients. James Powell and Eileen were far too professional for that. Indeed, so was Stephen Powell. He had expected and demanded a client services agreement for his non-philanthropic accounts and services. With James's help, I drafted, or rather plagiarised from a couple of stockbrokers, a standardised document that would later be rolled out for all clients. It was not a hard job to adapt that agreement to include grant-making administration and advice.

However, PPFs brought in little income, as did Eileen's team in general. In fact, the team's annual revenue barely covered costs. For Eileen, the Lee Family Office profit and loss statement were of little importance. She was there, at Alfred's instigation, to grow philanthropy and where better to start than with a strong, wealthy client base with the privileges of a substantial disposable income. Indeed, she rejected the notion that philanthropy could or should be part of business. If she had her way, the marginal income tax rate for the ultra-rich would be dramatically raised so that the government could receive the plaudits currently enjoyed by private philanthropy. Despite her ideals, Eileen was no utopian dreamer, and was realistic enough to appreciate that her socialist dream would not be realised in her lifetime. In the meantime, she was happy to play the role of Robin Hood.

Winston took an entirely different approach. Eileen's team, so he argued, at the minimum should be on the front line promoting the Lee Family Office's suite of services. Winston knew the importance of including philanthropic activities, particularly amongst the ranks of the inherited wealth.

'She makes our clients feel good about themselves,' Winston reasoned. 'If they're not sitting down for a few hours each quarter pontificating on the merits of some grants here or there, what would they do? God, they might start questioning their entire privileged role in life and throw their wealth away. And that wouldn't help our bottom line.'

In fairness to the bulk of the extended Lee family, Winston was primarily concerned about the mind-set of one family member; namely his eldest son. Winston was keen to ensure that his favourite child followed in the family footsteps. Further, many of the younger generation Lees had found gainful employment away from the family. They were not bemoaning the fact they did not have to get out of bed each morning. A mass revolt was unlikely.

Alfred provided a more measured response to the role of Eileen's team. Like his son, he rejected the contention that business and philanthropy should be separate. Instead, each should support the other. However, Alfred expressed the firm view that philanthropy was the glue that kept the family in sync and bound them in business together. Alfred did not believe that family members were likely to throw their wealth away, but without Eileen and her team's efforts, they could well take that wealth elsewhere.

When it came to the practical importance of Lee Family Office philanthropy, Alfred and Winston were more or less on the same page, but they differed on what they wanted from Eileen's team. Winston was adamant that the team should at least pay its way, if not turn a profit.

'You are not a charity,' I heard Winston once say to Eileen. 'You are no different to anybody else here. I expect you to properly budget, properly cost your services, and above all, properly invoice. It's not that hard.'

It would be fair to say that there was no love lost between Winston and Eileen. Indeed, I cannot recall a conversation between the two where Winston did not lose his cool, if not his temper. Not that Winston's lack of self-control bothered Eileen in the slightest. She seemed to relish Winston's animosity. I genuinely liked her.

Alfred's appreciation of Eileen and her team was obvious. Unsurprisingly, he whole-heartedly rejected her political and philosophical leanings, but at the same time, did not share his son's preoccupation with the profit motive.

'We should not measure the success of our philanthropy by Eileen's revenue or operating profit,' lectured Alfred. How much did those thirty-odd PPFs that she looks after give away last quarter? I don't know. Winston, you don't know. Our management accounts don't tell us that.'

When his father was on a roll, Winston at least knew to keep quiet.

'If you're going to continually question Eileen's profitability, then she should have a right of reply. Son, do you really want her at every board meeting? If not, let's drop the matter.'

Alfred's approach to Eileen's effectiveness was consistent with his views on Lee Family Office profitability as a whole. Alfred was a shrewd businessman who had personally transformed a sizeable, but not vast, inheritance into an extensive, diverse portfolio of listed and unlisted investments. The income alone from his privately owned rental properties dwarfed his regular Lee Family Office dividends.

Above all, Alfred was a man who knew how to prioritise. Whether Eileen and her team made or lost $50,000 a year for the Lee Family Office was immaterial. Again, whether, the bottom line of the Lee Family Office's financial services business was up or down several hundred thousand dollars or so was mostly irrelevant. The critical issue was that Lee Family Office philanthropy supported a host of charitable endeavours, while the financial services business protected and promoted the financial interests of the family, and external clients, as well as protect the investments held by the Lee Family Office in its own name.

Intuitively, I struggled with the idea that Eileen's team should continue indefinitely as a loss-making venture. I reasoned that no one else would be afforded that luxury.

'Your right, if you're referring to Winston,' said Martin Flynn, 'but you know he only tolerates Eileen because of his father. Greg, I think you're dead wrong about Alfred, though. He could cope with us all making losses for years.'

'Really?' I queried. 'Alfred didn't make a fortune by subsidising lost causes.'

'Sure, but that's not the issue. If we're all working hard, Alfred will back us one hundred per cent.'

Martin went on to explain that the Lee Family Office lacked the economies of scale that many other Australian family offices enjoyed and that, even in the best of circumstances, it was challenging to make a profit in the sector.

'Greg, he's all about individual effort and responsibility. Alfred's got to get someone to prepare his accounts and tax returns and manage his portfolio. He doesn't want an outsider doing that. He wants to control the process and that's why we're here.'

Martin was far too discreet to discuss Alfred's private affairs with me and would only reveal details of Alfred's financial circumstances on a need-to-know basis. Even so, I did once hear a rumour that Alfred had willingly spent $100,000 on legal fees, just to avoid a $50,000 tax liability. That story was probably exaggerated, but it succinctly reflected Alfred's attitude to money. He simply hated being told by others what to do or not do with his finances.

Winston could not be more different. According to Martin, Winston's hopes for the financial services business were naïve and unrealistic, although his actual choice of words were far more diplomatic.

'How can I put this nicely? Winston's no Warren Buffett. Sure, he's got the qualifications and can read a balance sheet, but his business acumen is questionable.'

For once, I found myself defending Winston.

'But his concerns about Eileen's team is all about profitability and cost savings.'

'That's what he says, but that's not why he berates her. The truth is that she simply doesn't respect him, and he knows it. He can't handle criticism.'

'Oh, come on, Martin,' I said. 'Are you suggesting we should all suck up to him?'

'No, that's not what I'm saying. We shouldn't have to grovel, but we can be more subservient. The sad fact is that Winston lacks confidence. If we take issue with him the whole time, it will only make matters worse, and I'm not just saying this to you. I've also tried with Eileen.'

I could tell Martin was giving me a warning, although I was struggling with the very idea that Winston wrestled with self-doubt. Martin put me straight: 'Winston is the Lee family patriarch in waiting. He's next in line. I bet you'd have a crisis of confidence if the weight of Lee family expectations rested on your shoulders. I know I would.'

I had never thought of Winston in that light, but Martin's critique made sense. After all, Alfred's contribution to the family had been an unqualified success. Winston had big shoes to fill. I thanked Martin for his candour, but our chief financial officer was not yet done. He felt I needed a more direct warning: 'Be careful, Greg, be very careful. Alfred appreciates us, but I'm not so sure about Winston. None of us are secure. Eileen, you, me. We're all vulnerable. You must be careful what you say to him and what you say about him. It's a small company.'

Martin had never spoken to me like that before. In fact, I do not recall him talking like that to anyone. The message was clear that, but for the grace of Alfred, I could be joining the dole queue to Centrelink. I felt a cold shiver run down my spine.

Chapter Fifteen
The Investigation

had been entrusted with my very own ASC investigation file. It was one of the few small, low-profile complaints that had slipped through the organisational cracks. It was, therefore, a novel experience and I vowed to make the most of the opportunity. Yet, classifying the file as small was an understatement. The brown manila folder contained a single letter of complaint and a meaningless one-page assessment from the ASC's Complaints Handling Unit.

I read the letter slowly. The complainant was a professor of psychology and early learning specialist from the University of New South Wales. He had founded KnowData Oz, which distributed educational computer games and toys in Australia under an exclusive licence from a USA based manufacturer, KnowData Inc.

KnowData Oz had been established in the early years of household computers and interactive technology. The professor's complaint concerned a series of compact disc games that had been developed to improve the arithmetical ability of young children—left brain stuff. By today's standards, the discs were basic with limited graphics and user capabilities. You simply would not want them now, even if they were being given away.

Still, in those days, they were state of the art. The professor had been overwhelmed by the responses. Boxes of discs were sold to schools and childcare centres. Even the Royal Children's Hospital in Sydney had purchased a few. Those successes led the professor to approach Borders bookstores and other retail outlets, including a small Chinese convenience store on Little Bourke Street, Melbourne. They, too, showed keen interest.

So far, so good, I thought. What has the good professor got to complain about? However, in the second paragraph of the letter, his problems started to become apparent. On a routine trip to Melbourne, he had visited a Borders bookstore and found some KnowData discs on the shelves. There were a dozen or so different compact discs each packaged in a separate box. The professor was surprised but initially unconcerned. He had had no direct dealings with that particular store. Presumably, Borders often moved stock between stores. Also, neatly stuck on each box was the obligatory KnowData Inc label with the words: *Distributed under licence from KnowData Inc, USA.*

For a micro-second, the professor was relieved, but as he moved to examine the box, the KnowData Inc label came into clear focus. It was a forgery and not a particularly sophisticated one. The size of the label was a bit small, and the background b ue was too navy. The font was different, and the overall appearance was somewhat blurred. You did not have to be a forensic investigator to conclude that the label was not genuine.

Over a few visits by the professor, the full story emerged. He had picked up all the boxes of discs and had demanded to see the store manager. Apparently, the manager was professional and extremely helpful. The manager was himself familiar with KnowData Inc products and had even bought a couple for his children. He also appeared to know that the compact discs were sold under a licence. The manager explained that a certain Marcus Stein had approached the store with KnowData Inc discs a few months before and had offered to sell them at an attractive discount. The manager had initially refused and mentioned to Stein that he could only purchase them from a licensed distributor.

The next part of the professor's story was fascinating. When questioned by the Borders manager, Stein claimed that he did hold a distribution licence and had merely forgotten to place a label on each box. Stein had returned to the store a week later. On each of the thirty boxes was a fake label.

According to the professor, the manager stated that he had not scrutinised the labels, and even if he had, he would have had no reason to doubt they were genuine. After listening to the professor, the boxes which had not been sold were removed from the shelves. Of course, the professor had no idea of how many other outlets held stock provided by Mr Stein.

Later, while interviewing the professor for his witness statement, I learnt that the professor had approached Mr Stein for an explanation. His letters had been ignored and his only telephone call had been met with a firm and concise: 'Get lost!'

I cannot now recall what it was about the complaint that attracted me. In part, there was the travel. The professor was based in Sydney and that meant I would need to fly there with a colleague, spend a couple of nights at Woolloomooloo Waters Hotel and prop up the bar at the Bourbon and Beefsteak in Kings Cross.

My interest in the professor's woes was also aroused by the way I had received the complaint. The boss had given me the chance to run an investigation of my own. That was scary, real scary. But the case did not seem that hard, or so I thought, and the boss clearly had faith in my capabilities. I did not want to let him down and I did not want to lose an opportunity.

Over the next few weeks, I squeezed an investigation into Marcus Stein between my usual tasks of bar-coding documents and running errands for the senior and principal investigators. I took formal statements from the professor and the Borders bookstore manager and took possession of the thirty-odd compact discs from Borders as well as a couple of discs from KnowData with the genuine label.

Of course, my primary concern was to establish the links between Marcus Stein and the suspect labels. Just because the bookstore manager could give evidence of his conversation with Mr Stein, that did not mean the latter had instigated the production of fake labels or was even aware of them. At best, the evidence from the manager was circumstantial. At worst, there was a gaping hole in my case. I knew that my first task was to plug the gap. I did not have the luxury of clinging to a file in the hope that evidence would somehow miraculously appear. The boss had taught me well.

'Deal with the hard shit first. If you can't, there will always be another case.'

With the help of the boss, I drafted a 'section 30 notice,' addressed to Marcus Stein's company. The founding legislation of the ASC provided ASC staff with compulsory powers to require specific company book and records. Section 30 of the ASC Law was one such provision. My notice was for: *All books, records, files, working papers, and notes from or concerning KnowData.*

I had drafted numerous ASC notices in the past, but that was the first notice issued under my name. As an Administrative

Service Officer Class 4, I was at the bottom rung of the delegation authority. Before, I took comfort that the boss's name was all over the relevant notice. But now it was my turn, and that was extra motivation to ensure the document was drafted correctly. I double-checked the address of Stein's company against the ASC national database and triple-checked the wording of section 232(2) of the Corporations Law, which I had identified as being the appropriate 'alleged or suspected' contravention. It was a criminal offence for an officer of a company to fail to act honestly in the exercise of his or her powers or the discharge of his or her duties. Sticking false labels on a product to beat licensing limitations seemed rather blatant to me. Despite my nerves, I had no reservations that I had identified the correct offence.

I served the section 30 notice on a bright and surprisingly warm winter morning. I was accompanied by a fellow assistant investigator whose own sunny disposition added to my sense of purpose. The ASC gods were shining on me. I was no longer nervous. I knew what I had to do and I was comfortable with the task ahead.

My positive demeanour was slightly shaken by a receptionist who informed us that Mr Stein was on the ski fields and uncontactable for at least a week. The disappointment was only momentary. We produced our ASC identification cards and the receptionist quickly identified herself as Maria De Marco. Ms De Marco was not just the receptionist but also Stein's long-suffering external accountant and company secretary. She had stepped in to mind the office during Mr Stein's absence and to attend to his filing. We got the distinct impression that Marcus Stein's attempts at filing were problematic, and that poor Maria was now questioning her whole involvement with him. For our purposes, we had got to her at an opportune time.

'What's he done now?' was her initial response to the notice. She had never seen an ASC notice before but was aware of our compulsory powers to demand books and records.

Before we could answer, Ms Marco muttered something about KnowData filing, walked straight to one of three grey metal filing cabinets and produced a manila folder from the top draw with the word 'KnowData' scribbled on the front. As we took hold of the file, we could see that the contents had been thrown together with little semblance of order. But the material was relevant and corroborated the c aim of the Borders' manager that Stein's company was tied to the KnowData compact discs.

'Filed it yesterday, or rather located all the contents yesterday. I was going to put it in order, but I've got a mountain of invoices to pay and tax returns are overdue. I wish he would get himself a bloody assistant. Sorry, I shouldn't swear, but he's really testing my patience. Oh, I think it's all there,' referring to the KnowData file, 'but with Marcus, you can never be sure.'

Ms De Marco was hardly painting a glowing picture of her fellow officer and client. It seemed an ideal chance to question her on her knowledge of KnowData. She said she had never heard of the entity before attempting the recent filing, and as Mr Stein was a one-person band, the only person who wou d have had relevant information was Marcus Stein himself. I queried whether that had always been the case noting that the oldest document in the 'KnowData file' was eighteen months old.

'Yes, there's no one else. I've been Marcus' accountant for three or four years now and company secretary for a couple.

I think I would know if there had anyone else working here. Look, there are only two desks, and both are covered with his stuff.'

I decided there and then to test the boundaries of Ms De Marco's cooperation.

'Will you give us a statement to that effect?' I asked, hoping but not expecting a positive response.

'Is he in trouble? Actually, am I in trouble? As I said, I had never even heard of KnowData until this week.'

The 'am I in trouble?' or the similar, 'am I a target?' response was a fairly typical reaction from the many persons ASC investigators had questioned over the years. We merely responded by stating that we believed that the person, in that case, Ms De Marco, had information relevant to our enquiries and that if we thought she was in trouble, we would not be asking for a voluntary witness statement. We also quietly mentioned our powers to conduct and record compulsory examinations. The latter often did the trick and Ms De Marco's case was no exception.

'Okay, let's get this over and done with. I haven't got time to mess around with, what did you call them, compulsory examinations? If you really need a statement that I know nothing about KnowData then so be it. I must say, this all seems a waste of time if you ask me.'

We spent the next hour drafting a handwritten statement along the lines that Ms De Marco knowledge of KnowData was limited. However, we also included the fact she was an officer of Stein's company and its accountant, and to the best of her knowledge, Mr Stein was the only person that could have dealt with KnowData. We also included a few paragraphs to the effect that the contents of Stein's KnowData file had been collated by Ms De Marco across Mr Stein's office desks. That was not a waste of time, even though she did not directly tie Stein to the fake labels. Ms De Marco signed the statement on the spot.

Later, when we returned to the office, we examined the contents of the KnowData file. I carefully reviewed each letter, invoice, statement, remittance notice, demand and yellow sticky note that comprised the file. It was not a big file and any seasoned investigator could have completed a review in a couple of hours. All up, I must have taken a couple of days. But it was worth it. My eureka moment occurred when I located an invoice from a small firm of printers. It was a relatively simple invoice for $300, but it was the narration on the document that interested me:

Item: One round blue label with 'Distributed under licence from KnowData Inc. USA.' Quantity 150.

I quickly searched the ASC's database and obtained the corporate details of the printing firm. Within a few minutes, I had contacted the friendly proprietor, Mr Inkerman, or 'Ink Man' to his customers. He was the father half of a father-and-son outfit, or at least that was in theory. In practice, Ink Man was running the show with a couple of middle-aged contemporaries who had been in the printing caper for years. His sole offspring, on the other hand, was more interested in property development, and according to his father, had bought up half the Gold Coast on the back of some highly geared transactions and personal guarantees from his supportive parents.

'He's a good worker, my boy,' laughed Ink Man, 'and I'm okay so long as the bank loans keep flowing.'

Ink Man's good humour did not, however, extend to Marcus Stein. After the usual pleasantries and a brief explanation of our investigation, I asked if he knew Mr Stein.

'Yeah, I know him,' he said. 'Know him too bloody well. Always up to something. What's it now?'

There was something in Ink Man's voice that suggested that he would be very willing to co-operate in proceedings to discredit Mr Stein. Ink Man readily accepted my invitation for an interview. Indeed, I got the distinct impression he would have been disappointed if he had not been asked. Not only was he thirty minutes early for the interview, but as promised, he had brought his file of his dealings with Stein.

I showed Ink Man the invoice and two compact disc boxes, one with an original KnowData Inc label and the other with the fake. The conversation was all too easy.

'Yeah, that's our work,' said Ink Man, pointing to the fake label. 'We did try our best to match with that one,' at the same time pointing to the original, 'but our machines are old and our colours are limited. Spent a lot more than three hundred bucks, but even then, the old bastard complained. In the end, I said take it or leave it. Guess what? He took it.'

There was clearly no love lost between Stein and Ink Man. Stein had used Ink Man's printing services for years and had been quick to haggle quotes, argue invoices and delay payments. Further, Ink Man had long suspected that Stein was up to no good, and he expressed no surprise that the labels had been used for improper purposes. What luck, I had found two key witnesses in Ms De Marco and Ink Man. The only difference was that Ink Man was exceptionally keen to help.

From his file, Ink Man produced a letter which purported to be signed by Marcus Stein. The letter was a request for one hundred and fifty identical labels to the enclosed original. Unsurprisingly, the supplied label was genuine, and I assumed

Marcus Stein had bought a KnowData Oz sourced compact disc box. Ink Man produced his copy of the invoice that he had sent to Stein. With one notable exception, the copy was identical to the invoice I had found in Stein's file. In the corner of Ink Man's copy was a 'Paid' stamp,' with the word 'NAB' and seven numbers handwritten next to it. I asked Ink Man to explain the notation.

'That's just his cheque number. Always like to keep a record of his bounced cheques,' sniggered Ink Man, 'but I can't recall this one bouncing back.'

Ink Man's file and his explanations were all good evidentiary stuff. I had documents and witnesses that tied Stein and his company's need for fake labels to the person who had printed them. I also had payment details that I would later corroborate by obtaining the NAB cheque from the bank itself. My confidence in our case was growing each minute. Yet, I felt something was missing.

'What did Mr Stein say when he first saw your reproduction label?' I asked quite innocently.

'Oh, he wasn't pleased, gave me mouthful over the phone telling me that a six-year-old kid could draw better than that. Wanted me to redo them.'

'Over the phone?' I queried. 'But you've met him, right. You know who he is?'

'No, no...never met him. All dealings have been by mail and phone calls. Wouldn't know what he looks like from a bar of soap, but do I know he's crook? Too right I do, over many years.'

Ink man's response did not feel right. It seemed to be a little extraordinary that he could display so much animosity to someone he had never actually met face to face. Of course, you did not have to be a Holocaust survivor to detest Hitler or a rabid Essendon Aussie Rules fan to hate Collingwood. As it turned out, the incident was just one of the numerous dealings between Ink Man and Stein.

However, it quickly dawned on me that Ink Man could be digging a hole for himself. I could see our ASC lawyers spending months pouring through the law on aiding and abetting or being knowingly concerned in the commission of an offence. Ink Man was unequivocally stating that Stein was a crook and here he was readily providing details of his involvement in the production of fake labels. I needed Ink Man as a witness, not as a co-defendant.

'But you didn't know that there was anything amiss with Stein's order at the time, now did you?' I said quite deliberately and in an intentionally leading manner. Somewhat unnecessarily, but at least to stress the point, I observed my offsider slowly shaking his head as a prompt for Ink Man's response.

Thankfully, Ink Man was quick on the uptake.

'No, no, course I didn't. Knew he was a bit of a scallywag, but nothing specific. I wouldn't get involved with such things. Never, been in any trouble you know? Not so much as a speeding ticket.'

It was time to wrap up the interview. We thanked Ink Man for his attendance and took possession of his file. A week later, Ink Man swore a statement with his firm's stamped invoice duly referenced as 'Exhibit A.'

The boss was pleased. Indeed, I heard a rumour that the 'pommy sook' had received a special mention at one of the boss's weekly meetings with the Director of Investigations. Two weeks later, I was called by the director to provide an update in person. There had not been too many Administrative Service Officers

Class 4 who had called up to brief the director. I was nervous but prepared.

'Not one of our usual matters,' the director remarked. 'Hear you have led this one from the front. That's what we like to see. What have you got for us, Greg?'

I provided a brief overview of the complaint and an outline of section 232 of the Corporations Law. I then got stuck into the evidence.

'The professor has stated that his company holds an exclusive licence from KnowData Inc to distribute educational compact discs across Australia. He will produce the licence agreement and a sample disc with a KnowData Inc licence label. The professor also states that he found boxes of discs with fake licence labels at a Borders bookstore in Melbourne.'

'Okay,' said the director, 'but let's cut to the chase. What have you got to support this?'

'A Borders manager,' I replied. 'He states that he was approached by Marcus Stein to buy the discs and only did so after the KnowData labels had been attached.' The director nodded.

'We have a statement from Stein's accountant and company secretary. She produced a file from Stein's office, which included an invoice from the local printer of the fake labels and also the relevant book of cheque butts, in Stein's handwriting, showing payment. She also states Stein was the only one who could have organised the transaction.'

I was on a roll, I summarised the evidence of Ink Man, emphasising that he knew Marcus Stein and that Stein had approached him to produce 150 labels that he had eventually paid for. I mentioned that we had also obtained a book of NAB cheque butts from Stein's company along with a statement from a bank manager who could produce the original cheque. I also told him that I had drafted an investigator's statement, referencing my notice on Stein's company to produce books and records and the results of my company searches.

'What do we know of Stein?' asked the director. I was so glad he asked, or rather I was glad I had previously requested full police and bankruptcy checks.

'He's no cleanskin,' I replied. 'He has a string of theft and fraud-related offences going back twenty-odd years. Oh, he's got form for escaping lawful custody and had to be extradited from Germany. Also, he was bankrupt not so long ago. I should say he's now a discharged bankrupt.'

'Is he now?' said the director somewhat rhetorically. 'I think you need to have a little chat with him. How about early tomorrow morning? Take your boss and one of our Federal Police officers. Pick him up. With his record, he isn't going to respond kindly to a simple interview invitation.'

That was the director's way of saying I had done a good job compiling the evidence and that we had enough to at least to put our allegations to Stein in a formal record of interview. Perhaps the decision to arrest Stein was a little dramatic, but he did have a long and colourful criminal history. Both the director and the boss reasoned that Marcus Stein would be more likely to provide a 'voluntary' statement if he was forcibly frog-marched into Australian Federal Police headquarters in the custody of a 130-kilogram cop.

Chapter Sixteen
The Children

Alfred Lee's whole demeanour was impressive. Standing barely five feet five inches in imperial measurements, he was striking. Imperial is the appropriate term. He was a modern-day Mandarin.

Before moving into his Toorak mansion, Alfred had spent much of his late twenties and thirties in Hong Kong where he had learnt the family freight and property trades. At that time, the southwestern sky was alight with American choppers. Colonial policemen on their regular duties would be interrupted by aggrieved Yankee pilots using the same short-wave frequency on their beat radios. Above all, Alfred remembered the refugee boats and faces of the boat children, whose only crime was to have been born in the wrong place at the wrong time. To say those memories weighed on him is an understatement. Those young faces were etched indelibly on his waking and unwaking mind. Alfred, that imposing figure, feared business adversary, would awake at nights in a pool of water. He just knew he had to do something.

'They have suffered so much,' was often all he could utter before tears welled in his eyes.

Refugees had started to arrive in Hong Kong shortly after the fall of Saigon. The influx reached a peak four years later with up to 1000 Vietnamese and other Indochinese arriving each day. During that period, Hong Kong did not turn back a single boat, but that policy would be short-lived as so-called 'refugee fatigue' swayed public and government opinion.

The original camps were open, and refugees were allowed to travel freely. Yet, the forces of inhumanity would soon wrestle control. Within a few years, outright hostility would replace humanitarianism. Refugees would languish in the dozen Hong Kong detention camps, sometimes for years and with no sense of hope. Riots, disturbances and conflicts between ethnic Chinese and ethnic Vietnamese were a daily occurrence. The most prevalent clinical problems were depression, PTSD, and anxiety disorders, all exacerbated by the cramped nature of life behind the razor wire. Conditions such as diarrhoea, scabies, tuberculosis, and asthma were also common.

However, you didn't need to be a doctor, psychologist, or camp guard to appreciate the consequences of life as an asylum seeker. It was a miserable existence, where women and girls feared being alone. Repression and poverty at home had been replaced by flimsy vessels, pirate-infested waters and later by violence, drugs, and forced isolation.

Alfred watched on with despair. He visited, or at least attempted to visit, many refugee camps, but spent most of his time at the inaugural camp just up the street from his Chatham Road hotel and at the infamous camp near Kai Tak Airport. He and members of his extended Hong Kong family initially brought food and clothing. Still, it was the absence of education that Alfred found most troubling. Adult illiteracy was rife and child literacy almost non-existent. While even he was powerless to influence Hong Kong government policy, he could do more than a bit to aid those lucky enough to find their way south.

Upon his return to Melbourne, Alfred established the Middle Kingdom early childhood learning services. Initially in Footscray, separate early learning centres were quickly opened in Richmond, Box Hill, and Doncaster; anywhere where there was a significant Chinese or Vietnamese community. Within a few years, twelve centres had been opened in the Melbourne metropolitan area.

The growth of the business and early learning facilities went hand in hand, but Alfred was less concerned with profitability than he was with the quality and reach of childhood education. The business was only a secondary consideration. Although he would dutifully pore over the quarterly management reports, he took no pride in the bottom line, even in those years where the business made a reasonable profit. Instead, Alfred focussed on the social improvements that Middle Kingdom's services provided. I will never forget Alfred's beaming face as he introduced a fresh-faced University of Melbourne graduate to the Lee Family Office staff. Originally from South Vietnam, and via numerous refugee camps in the Philippines and Hong Kong, the student and his mother had finally settled in Melbourne's western suburbs. He was one of the first children to attend the early learning centre in Footscray. His father never made it to Australia.

To survive, the Middle Kingdom business needed more than just a healthy number of individual success stories. Unfortunately, as interest rates and rental costs soared, margins were squeezed. Winston often moaned that he and his father spent too much time and money propping up the business. In truth, it was Alfred and the Lee Family Office that provided both the time and the money. Winston's personal contribution was non-existent.

Winston, it should be noted, was like his father, merely a director of Middle Kingdom. In theory, father and son were non-executive officers. There was a separate managing director with years of industry experience. However, Ms Ma was far more concerned with the practical running of the early learning centres than preparing board and committee papers. She openly admitted that she was more comfortable with the duties of a chief operating officer than those of a managing director. Therefore, she was quite relieved that Winston had taken on many of the governance requirements associated with running a company. To give Winston his due, he did make a point of attending all board and committee meetings, notwithstanding he was officially only a member of Middle Kingdom's remuneration committee.

There was another reason for Winston's involvement in executive decision-making. Put simply, it was almost impossible to separate the business operations of Middle Kingdom from those of the Lee Family Office. The Lee Family Office provided Middle Kingdom with a host of services. Nauru House was Middle Kingdom's registered office, and Ms Ma's office was literally in shouting distance of my own.

The Lee Family Office provided tax and accounting, IT maintenance, risk management, recruitment, human resources, and payroll services. I was responsible for overseeing all Middle Kingdom's leasing arrangements and other material contracts. In short, Middle Kingdom did not have the infrastructure to operate independently of the Lee Family Office. The only outsourced functions concerned corporate administration, including statutory record-keeping and reporting. The role of company secretary was contracted to one of Winston's many mates, although in practice Martin did much of the work.

In fact, as a wholly owned subsidiary of the Lee Family Office, the arrangements between Middle Kingdom and the Lee Family Office were perfectively standard. Tensions between the two entities would only emerge with the listing of Middle Kingdom on the Australian Securities Exchange (ASX). In truth, the decision to list was more Alfred's initiative than Winston's, but eldest son and family were one hundred per cent behind the decision. Even amongst us mere workers, there was a supportive buzz.

For Alfred, public listing was motivated by his desire to expand the scope of early learning to a new mix of refugees from the Horn of Africa. That new wave of asylum seekers had experienced many of the profound social and psychological problems that had affected the Vietnamese and Indochinese a generation before. ASX listing would be accompanied by twenty-two additional early learning centres in Melbourne and country Victoria.

Winston's desire to list was far less altruistic. At that time, Winston resented the success of ABC Learning, the world's largest provider of early childhood education services, and he envied the aggressive business tactics of its founder, Eddy Groves. An expanded early learning business would help propel Winston into the spotlight currently occupied by Mr Groves.

With the benefit of hindsight, the decision to publicly list Middle Kingdom was not commercially savvy. We all should have listened to our chief financial officer who expressed grave reservations from the outset. After all, Martin had always brought a different and often valuable insight into the business affairs of the Lee Family Office.

I recall reading some law school lecture notes that included a short article from the American sociologist, Professor C. Wright Mills. It was a bright light in an otherwise dull jurisprudential collection. Wright Mills had a fascinating thesis. The 'sociological imagination,' so he argued, required making links between personal challenges and broader social issues. He was not suggesting that when a Peruvian boy scout flaps his arms that the good people of Vienna end up choking on their schnitzels. Wright Mills was not professing a simplistic causal argument based on dubious connections. Rather, there existed a complex interdependency between the micro and the macro, and to have a sociological imagination, one must be able to step outside his or her personal world and think from an alternative viewpoint. Thankfully for the Lee Family Office, Martin literally practised that sociological imagination in his daily communications.

'I'm not sure that listing now is ideal,' said Martin. It was his polite way of saying that Alfred and Winston had got rocks in their heads. He continued: 'The talk in America is of a housing bubble. Didn't you see that recent article in *The Economist*? The status of all those CDOs is effectively junk.'

At the time, I had barely heard of a collateralised debt obligation and had no idea what it was other than some fancy financial product. More importantly, I had no understanding of what the status of a financial instrument could mean for the purchase of a dozen or so additional early learning centres in Victoria and the listing of Middle Kingdom.

Martin spoke more deliberately and slowly. He was not attempting to be patronising. He knew I was not the only one in his audience that was struggling with his argument.

'Let's put it like this, Winston. If there is a bubble and that bubble pops, then you can rest assured that there will be major flow-on effects to Australia, and it won't just be in the residential housing sector. Loans will dry up, business confidence will get hammered, unemployment will rise, and consumer spending will fall.' He finally got to the point. 'And in those economic circumstances, there won't be money for childcare.'

Time, of course, would prove Martin right. Yet, back then none of us, Martin included, would have thought that the acronym 'GFC' stood for anything other than the 'Geelong Football Club.' Martin's prophesy was quickly dismissed.

'God, you're such a worrier,' was Winston's immediate put-down. 'If we listened to you, we would still be a bloody tax compliance business with a total client base of eight.'

'Well, at least that's a lucky Chinese number,' laughed Martin. He had known Winston far too long to be upset by his ravings. He returned to his more measured communicative style.

'As I said,' Martin continued. 'There are some fundamental problems with the US economy right now, and if I'm right, there will be some huge implications for the Australian service industry. Unless you're publicly listing as an exit strategy, now would not be a good time to invest in more centres.'

Alfred, who had been listening intently to the interchange between Marin and his son, had heard enough.

'We control what we can control; nothing more, nothing less. There will always be ups and downs in the economy, but we are a family of triers. We are not going to sit back and wait because of the failings of some American banks. And let me make one thing clear. We are not buying twenty-odd new centres and investing

$20 million-plus of our own money for, what did you call it, an exit strategy?'

I could tell Alfred was unusually dismissive. Over the years, Martin and Alfred had developed a strong professional relationship. They were not friends outside of work, but they worked well together. It was rare that Alfred would voice his dissatisfaction about Martin's views, let alone while Winston and I were present.

In case Martin had not got the point, Alfred continued: 'We can make a real difference here. Early learning is currently a disaster. It's expensive; it's badly managed and has a poor reputation. Just look at ABC Learning. Mothers, who would rather be at work, stay at home because they can't afford professional help. It won't be the biggest, but I want Middle Kingdom to offer the best early learning experience in Australia. Martin, if you think this is just business, then you're wrong. We will provide a top-quality service and make money if we can. Now let's get back to work.'

My involvement in the listing of Middle Kingdom was limited to several peripheral matters. The bulk of the ASX listing application, including the public offer, underwriting arrangements and purchase agreements for the new early learning centres, was farmed out to teams of professional advisers, including a lead manager, stockbroker, and top-tier law and accounting firms. Without exception, the charge out rates were obscene.

To help satisfy ASX shareholder spread requirements, the Lee Family Offices' holding in Middle Kingdom was transferred to family members and clients of the Lee Family Office. I drafted and negotiated the terms of the share sale and purchase, although with considerable input from Martin and Alfred. My involvement in the necessary prospectus was restricted to reviewing the references to the Lee Family Office and the biographies of Alfred, Winston, Ms Ma, and the outsourced company secretary. They would all retain positions as company officers. I reviewed the escrow arrangements for Alfred's and Winston's shares, and at Alfred's request, the so-called roadshow material for meetings with institutional investors and his underwriting agreement. At some stage during the reviews, I must have mentioned my unease at providing legal services to Alfred and Winston directly, as I was probably in breach of my corporate practising certificate. Alfred's response was immediate and unequivocal.

'We need you on this now,' he said in no uncertain terms, 'and I'm sure Middle Kingdom is going to require your services in the future. If you believe you need a sole practising certificate, just go and get one.'

In all probability, Winston would have dismissed my concerns on the grounds of unnecessary cost and needless pedantry. Accordingly, I wasted no time with the application to the Legal Services Board. By the time Winston queried the expense, I was officially registered as a sole practitioner. I was no longer restricted to providing legal services to the Lee Family Office, and I was enticed by the possibility of providing legal services to a publicly listed entity.

Middle Kingdom, or 'MKL' as it would be known on the exchange, opened to great fanfare, or at least to a ten-second summary on the ABC news and a short paragraph in the *Australian Financial Review*. Under its prospectus, Middle Kingdom offered twenty million shares at $1.00 per share and would list with a market capitalisation of close to $40 million. The good news was that the offer was fully subscribed. The bad news was that by the close of the first trading day, Middle Kingdom was trading lower at $0.89 per share and over the next six months or so the share price would fall by a further ten per cent. For Winston, the falling share price was a constant irritation.

'This wouldn't be happening if we had Eddy Groves on the team,' I heard him remark.

Alfred was suitably unimpressed. 'Focus on the end goal, son. We have over 2,500 places mainly for disadvantaged toddlers and preschoolers, the most critical time of their lives. We don't measure this company's worth by just its share price, and we don't applaud a business that is notorious for paying poor wages, cost-cutting, and unsustainable debt. I don't want to hear talk of ABC Learning.'

However, while talk of Middle Kingdom's opposition ceased, questions began circulating about the role of Middle Kingdom's company secretary, particularly as his fees had substantially increased following listing. There was nothing to suggest that Winston's mate had acted illegally or unethically in the position. At the best of times, he was just a difficult person to contact. At the worst of times, it was impossible to find him. Simply, he was providing little more than the legally required basics. Ultimately, even Winston agreed that the role should be brought in-house. As company secretary of the Lee Family Office, Martin was the obvious choice. Yet, Alfred, in particular, was keen not to add to Martin's already extensive workload. I was the second choice.

My appointment as Middle Kingdom's company secretary was a promotion of sorts. While the change to my salary was minimal, the role would undoubtedly increase my public profile. I was certainly proud that the Lee family would entrust me with such a position.

'There you go, Tich Allen. I bet you didn't expect that,' was my initial response to Winston's invitation.

'And that wasn't the reaction I expected,' was the immediate reply from a slightly quizzical looking Winston. He had no idea what I was talking about, and I had no intention of explaining. I thanked him for the offer and muttered something sycophantically to the effect that I was honoured to serve in any way possible.

Chapter Seventeen
The Interview

I first met Marcus Stein one weekday morning, just as the sun was rising from the back of the Dandenong Ranges, fifty or so kilometres to Melbourne's east. It was a bright and glary morning with the wet on the roads and footpaths glittering in the first rays of daylight. The boss and the AFP Officer wore black designer sunglasses. But for the absence of headwear, they would have looked right at home at a Blues Brothers' fancy dress party. The boss must have read my mind.

'Practical, Greg, just being practical,' as he delicately wiped the lens of his expensive Ray-Ban glasses.

'Greg, you know the best time to execute a warrant?' said the boss, and before I could even shake my head, he continued. 'I'll tell you. It's four-thirty on a Tuesday morning. Best time as you get them when they're at their most vulnerable. In a deep sound sleep.'

I am not sure why Tuesdays were particularly special, but the 'deep sleep' logic made sense. Nevertheless, I was relieved that the boss had proposed a 7:30 am start. He later admitted that he was too old to be running around in the middle of the night. He had also suggested that the Australian Federal Police officer leave his handgun in the police armoury, but that request had fallen on deaf ears. Our AFP officers refused to go anywhere without their standard-issue Smith & Wesson revolver and handcuffs. The boss was somewhat bemused.

'For Christ's sake, he's used some phoney stickers to flog some goods,' was the way the boss described the ASC's allegations against Stein. 'This won't be a gunfight at the O.K. Corral.'

'It's the rules, mate. Just following procedures,' came the response.

I must admit the show of force was a little over the top, but our AFP officer was diligent and had gone out of his way to help. He had had even driven past Stein's house on a couple of occasions to establish whether the suspect was at home or not. The black Mercedes was the giveaway. Once our AFP officer had spotted the vehicle in Stein's driveway and conducted a simple licence check, we knew Stein was back in town.

I half expected our knock on Stein's front door to be accompanied by the cries of 'come on then, open up, it's the police.' Thankfully, clichéd commands were unnecessary, as a scantily dressed twenty-something female answered the doorbell almost immediately. Our AFP Officer produced his badge, introduced the boss, and asked for Marcus Stein, in that order.

For a moment, I thought we had disturbed Stein's daughter. However, her verbal reaction suggested a different relationship.

'Hey love, it's for you. The police are here for you, doll. Better get down here. They don't look happy.'

None of us were unhappy, but, given the circumstances, we did look as though we meant business. Yet, as a somewhat bedraggled fifty-something male made his way to the front door, it was hard not to laugh. His grey trackie pants required some industrial strength washing detergent while his ripped T-shirt was beyond repair. Clearly, he needed sleep, a shave, and a decent hairdresser. What luck, I thought, we've got him while he's down.

'Mr Stein? Mr Marcus Stein?' our AFP officer asked.

'What is it? How can I help?' came the terse response. 'Don't tell me; I've forgotten to renew the car rego or pay the dog licence?'

'No, nothing like that,' said our AFP Officer, who again flashed his badge, this time introducing both the boss and me. Without as much as a pause, our AFP Officer continued: 'Mr Stein, I'm here to arrest you in connection with an alleged breach of section 232 of the Corporations Law, insofar as you acted dishonestly as a director by making false representations concerning licensing arrangements with KnowData. I must inform you that you do not have to say or do anything, but anything you say or do may be given in evidence.'

Marcus Stein must have stood there for at least twenty seconds as the impact of the caution took effect. When it did hit home, the reaction was explosive.

'You what!' exclaimed Stein with a loud rising inflexion, 'What the hell are you talking about?'

I must admit, any advantage that had arisen from Stein's nocturnal activities was lost. We were dealing with one highly agitated and self-righteous bully. However, between his outbursts, the boss provided Stein with a bit more colour to the allegations, including the publishing of false labels.

'Oh dear,' said Stein somewhat sarcastically. 'Is that the best our corporate watchdog can do? Why the fuck are you arresting me? If you had a concern, why not just phone me up. This is bullshit. Alright, at least let me get dressed.'

Fifteen minutes later, Stein was in the back of the federal police car on his way to the AFP headquarters. In the meantime,

Miss twenty-something had telephoned Stein's lawyer who had, with the boss's support, successfully persuaded our AFP officer to put the handcuffs away.

'You think I'm going to leg it over some bullshit licensing disagreement?' Stein asked rhetorically. 'This is just plain bullshit.' Still, somewhat predicably, he went at least temporarily quiet when the boss calmly suggested that Stein's German escapades left us with little option.

'Oh yeah, I suppose you would know about that, wouldn't you? But I'm a changed man now. Let's sort this out.'

Back at the police station, Stein was efficiently fingerprinted, processed, and reacquainted with his longstanding defence lawyer. He knew the routine.

It was the first time that I had operated a 'Triple Deck,' which was the obvious name for a large tape recorder that recorded three audio cassette tapes simultaneously. There was one tape for the external transcription service, one tape for the defendant and one for us. I somewhat nervously removed three blank cassette tapes from their plastic wrapping, inserted them in the machine, and hit the red record button.

The Triple Deck was the only object of note in an otherwise uninspiring meeting room. It had pride of place on top of a standard government-issue table, while four matching chairs reflected the number of persons that could comfortably fit in the room at any one time. In the ceiling was a couple of sixty-watt downlights. It was a dour room, appropriate, I thought, for the likes of Stein's lawyer. He was a glum, quiet little man who displayed little concern for the plight of his client.

Unlike many modern television cop shows, there was no two-way mirror or radio contact with the interviewers. The boss could not scrutinise the facial expressions of the defendant or project manage the proceedings to implicate the defendant. Therefore, he departed to the canteen for a cup of tea and a cholesterol-enriched currant bun. In the meantime, the AFP officer and I commenced our formal record of interview with Stein. The fourth seat was reserved for his dispassionate lawyer.

Our AFP Officer laboriously repeated the allegations and the caution. Stein was still agitated, but his aggressive tone had mellowed, and his sentences were no longer punctuated with the 'F-word.' His lawyer sat in stone-cold silence.

It was over to me. I asked Stein about his dealings with Borders bookstores and the professor. His answers surprised me. Every step of the way, Stein agreed with the facts as I knew them. Yes, he had brought back a few box-loads of KnowData Inc compact discs from a trip to California.

'All the way, from Los Angeles, via Port Melbourne,' Stein added with a slight suggestion that he was somehow proud of his shipping arrangements.

Yes, he had been to various Borders bookstores and turned to Ink Man to print up some blue sticky labels. He agreed that he signed the cheque for $300 to Ink Man's printing firm and had physically stuck on the labels before delivering several boxes to Borders. He even agreed that his sole motivation for printing the labels was to ensure Borders purchased his discs. During the entire interchange, he only became emotional once. That was when I produced a copy of Ink Man's invoice and Stein's NAB cheque butts.

'Where did you get these?' He asked in a manner that suggested Ms De Marco had not briefed him on our visit a few weeks earlier.

'These are my documents. You can't have them.' He turned to his lawyer in what appeared to be a plea for reinforcements. Unfortunately, the plea went unanswered. His lawyer just continued to sit there and stare into space.

I explained that I had, in his absence, served a notice on Ms De Marco, who had been compelled to hand over the documents. That explanation appeared to satisfy Stein, although again he turned to his lawyer for re-assurance. Unsurprisingly, the lawyer continued with his impersonation of a statue. Indeed, the only time I saw the lawyer show the slightest bit of interest in the proceedings was when Stein claimed he was near broke and had only a couple of hundred dollars in his bank account. The lawyer was probably dealing with the ethical dilemma of whether he should continue to act for a client in circumstances where he was unlikely to get paid. His frequent glances at his watch only supported my hypothesis.

The factual evidence, or at least the central facts, were not in dispute. The chain of events that we had constructed through our interviews was not questioned. Stein even acknowledged that he had contacted Ink Man, written the cheque and narrated the invoice. Also, when I produced a box with the fake labels, he readily agreed that he placed Ink Man's label on that and every other box.

However, Stein did provide a different interpretation. He should, he contended, be applauded for his efforts, not victimised or criminalised for his actions. On the contrary, it was the professor who was the real villain in the affair. He was the one who was selling educational software at inflated prices. It was the professor who was exploiting children for the sake of a quick buck. According to Stein, KnowData Oz had an unfair monopoly. All he was doing was facilitating children's education at a reasonable price.

'If you genuinely believed you were lawfully entitled to distribute KnowData products in Australia, why did you organise the fake labels and ignore the professor's correspondence?' I asked. 'I suggest you deliberately embarked on a course of contact that was designed to deceive potential customers.'

'I'm not talking about lawful entitlements; I'm talking ethically and commercially. Also, look here—if I really were trying to be fraudulent, I would have arranged something better than this. Look,' he said, pointing at one of the fake labels. 'They're pathetic. They are not even the right size, right font or shape.'

'Why do you think I went to Ink Man? He's been totally hopeless over many years. Vowed I'd never use him again, but when this came up, I thought, well, all I need is something like the labels. I wasn't trying to be fraudulent. Look, I didn't respond to the professor. It was damn obvious that he would think that I was passing off his stuff. But that's all this is. I wanted a slice of his unfair market. So, it's a complaint about passing off. It's not criminal for Christ's sake.'

Soon after, we wrapped the interview up and released Stein into the care of his dispassionate solicitor. They left on the understanding that a brief of evidence would be prepared, and the Director of Public Prosecution may instigate criminal proceedings again Stein.

'You haven't listened to one bloody word, have you?' was Stein's departing comment. His solicitor merely smiled, skillfully escorting Stein through the glass doors and onto a La Trobe Street bathed in sunlight.

The weather reflected our cheery disposition. I almost ran the short distance back to the ASC offices. I was already mentally assembling the brief of evidence. Indeed, most of the work had been done. I arranged for the first cassette tape to be transcribed, and I prepared a neat one-page summary of the record of interview, in somewhat dry and matter-of-fact language. Within a few days, the brief of evidence was complete and with ASC lawyers.

Chapter Eighteen
The Misconduct

The Lee Family Office's most competent client adviser, James Powell, had not been seen for a couple of months. Although I missed his company, I was not overly concerned as I knew he had taken some leave. In any case, James was spending more and more working hours away from Nauru House. He never told me what he was doing, but it was quite usual for client advisers to spend a large amount of their time with clients away from the office, especially if they lived in or around Toorak. The Powells had bought a renovated property in nearby Malvern, so it made sense for James to base himself at home. Many of his clients were just around the corner.

However, early one morning, he walked into my office. He was visibly tired and shaken.

'What's up, mate?' I asked.

'It's just one thing after another. I don't want to bore you with my problems, but Lucy's struggling. School fees are due, and my Macquarie Bank shares have tanked. Have you seen their price recently?

'Sorry no, I haven't, but is there anything I can do? I'm here to help?'

James explained that the GFC had hit their finances badly. School tuition fees alone were close to $50,000 a year, and that was excluding uniforms, learning materials, excursions, sporting paraphernalia, and the latest BlackBerry that all private school children just had to have. Also, back home in Northamptonshire, Lucy's parents had recently been accepted into a nursing home. The expense of their aged care would be Lucy's responsibility. Three dependent children were bad enough without such costs and an appalling foreign exchange rate.

At that time, my own finances were not great. The mortgage on my Fitzroy home was already taking away a sizeable portion of my salary. It was a relief to find out that James wouldn't be touching me for a loan; my weekly slabs of Carlton Draught beer would remain a staple within my disposable income.

'I'll be straight, we have gone and got ourselves financial advice and we're just working through some of the recommendations.'

'What?' To say I was surprised would be an understatement. 'You're the best financial adviser out there. You of all people do not need financial counselling.'

'Well, sometimes you can't see your own wood for the trees. In any case, just getting an external opinion has helped. I love Lucy dearly, but she won't always listen to me. To be honest, Greg, things are not good between us. I'm trying my best because of the kids, but it's difficult to talk with Lucy, and I don't get home until late.'

It was not obvious to me why James would be getting home late. The Lee Family Office clients were hardly renowned for their work ethic beyond 5 pm. Stephen Powell would be a notable exception, but I could not believe even Stephen would regularly take up James's personal time. Stephen was far too organised and considerate to do that. I knew I must be missing something and tried broaching the subject. However, I quickly realised it was best to let James talk at will. It was obvious that he was deeply distressed. I had always known him as someone who liked to keep his problems to himself. Yet, there he was in my office, explaining his money problems and hinting of marital strife. He slowly got around to revealing his need to see me.

'We've changed banks, but we need access to extra credit. We're applying for new visa cards, so could you please witness our signatures? Oh, by the way, Lucy gave me a power of attorney that also needs witnessing.'

It had taken James a full twenty minutes to get to the point. It would not be the first time I had been asked to witness a signature for a bank card application or for granting a power of attorney. I assumed that James wanted a friend to talk to just as much as the Powells needed a witness. I also assumed that Lucy would be in the building or nearby. After all, her workplace was just across the road at Macquarie Bank.

'Of course. I'm only too happy to be a witness. Sure, there's nothing else I can do? Can I see the documents?'

My review did not take long. The visa card application forms were typical bank documents, and the enduring power of attorney (financial) was just over one page. Again, it was a standard document with a broad authorisation. James was authorised immediately to do anything for Lucy that an attorney could lawfully do. There were no conditions, limitations, or instructions. However, there was a problem with the documents.

'Mate. Lucy has already signed. I cannot witness something that she's already done. She has to sign in front of me and

I have to be sure she knows the effect of giving a power of attorney.'

James's reaction was immediate. 'Oh, come on, mate. How long have you known us? If you think Lucy doesn't know what a power of attorney is then you don't know us at all. Come on. You know Lucy, you know her signature, and we need this now.'

By then, an unusual desperation had crept into James's voice. Of course, I should have stuck to my guns, but James was a friend, and he was clearly distressed. I did not want to add to his woes. Also, I took some comfort from the fact that Lucy's power of attorney needed two witnesses and the first had already signed. Unfortunately, I did not recognise the signature and forgot to ask James who that witness was.

'Mate. At the very least I've got to talk to Lucy, and I'm sorry, but actually, I don't know her signature.'

'If you must,' came the quick response, 'but we have to do this now. I've got to get to the bank this morning.'

My resulting telephone conversation with Lucy was far from pleasant. I got an abrupt 'Lucy speaking.' As I started to talk about the credit card application, she cut me off. 'Greg, I don't want to be rude, but we're in the middle of a flipping credit crisis, the markets are stuffed and probably so is my job.'

I started to interject, but Lucy had not finished her tirade.

'Our heads are just above the water, but only just. I have not got time for this.'

Over the years, I had attended many Lee family social functions where spouses and partners had been readily welcomed. James and Lucy were regular invitees, and I had thoroughly enjoyed their company. I had even visited their Malvern home. It was a memorable dinner party for one reason. Lucy had set me up with a blind date. I knew she meant well, and there was absolutely nothing wrong with my date. Still, it was an uncomfortable experience and the following day James had phoned to apologise. He knew I was still besotted with Lena.

He simply said, 'When you're ready to move on, be sure to let us know. We care about you and Lucy has lots of single girlfriends.'

Of course, I never did move on, but I had no doubts that Lucy would have made a fine matchmaker. She was just as determined and focussed in her private life as she was with her work. I knew she could be a formidable opponent, especially when angry. I quickly realised that my telephone call was heading into dangerous territory. I let her speak.

'I signed last night. We need that credit. Can you please just do us a favour and sign your name. That's all we ask.' By then, her voice sounded more desperate than impatient.

'Yes, of course,' was my weak reply. I put the phone back on its hook and duly stamped and signed the documents.

'Thanks, Greg. We won't forget this.' As he spoke, James quickly slipped the signed application form and power of attorney into his briefcase and turned to the door to leave.

Perhaps I should have been more uneasy about 'witnessing' Lucy's signature. However, I was more concerned about James. He was definitely not telling me the whole truth. Something did not ring true and all I could think that, whatever it was, it somehow concerned working late. James's brief comments made no sense to me. Years ago, James had worked incredibly long hours to understand his clients' financial affairs and to build healthy client relationships. The hard work had been done, and his clients literally loved him, so what could have changed? Perhaps Winston had dramatically increased his workload. I had to say something. I was concerned for his welfare.

'James, if you would like me to talk to Winston about your workload, I can...' I stopped mid-sentence. The look on James's face was enough to tell me that the conversation was at an end.

'It's nothing, don't worry. I'll see you later.' They would be my last words on the subject of James Powell's wellbeing until everything went wrong.

Chapter Nineteen
The Prosecution

Six weeks after I had completed and submitted the Marcus Stein brief of evidence, I was called into the boss's office.

'You had better read this,' he said, handing me a four-page memorandum from the ASC legal team headed: *Brief of Evidence – Marcus Stein: Legal Review*

It took me barely a paragraph to appreciate that the document was hardly an objective, constructive review. Instead, it was a scathing attack on both the evidence and my understanding of directors' duties. While the language was formal and overly wordy, the criticism from my beloved ASC lawyers fell into two underlying concerns. First, the evidence relied too heavily on Stein's record of interview.

In particular, I read that the evidence to prove Stein penned the request for printed labels, that he signed the cheque and completed particulars of the payment on relevant cheque butt was limited. Further, as Ink Man and Stein had never met, their telephone conversation was only of marginal relevance. My anger rose as I read the relevant part of the advice: *The lack of expert evidence from a handwriting expert to link Stein to the transaction is problematic. Indeed, there is nothing to suggest the investigator has ever turned his mind to the need for such evidence.*

Thanks for nothing, I thought as I muttered something along the lines that we were all supposed to be on the same side.

But the second criticism packed the biggest punch and was presented under the heading: *No ASC involvement warranted.*

The legal team essentially agreed with Stein's interpretation of events. If there was any illegality, it was of a civil nature, such as the tort of passing off. The professor could have and should have pursued civil action against Stein. Yet, there was more. The memorandum provided a lengthy treatise on how section 232 of the Corporations Law was limited to conduct that harmed the company itself; in this case, Stein's company. Indeed, far from acting improperly, Stein, having bought the compact discs from company funds, was only doing his best to maximise a return for the company. The fact that Stein owned and controlled the relevant company appeared to be irrelevant. The memorandum concluded by advising that Stein was acting in the best interests of his company, and accordingly, could not be found to be acting dishonestly.

The reaction on my face must have sent a clear message to the boss.

'Don't look so glum, Greg. Our lawyers hardly have a reputation for being helpful. Really, what did you expect?'

For a split second I thought of Lena.

'Yeah, I know. Don't cross your bridges before they're hatched,' was all I could say.

'You what?' said the boss. 'Gee, sometimes you're a real comedian. But what I want to hear is what you are going to do about Dear Mr Stein?'

I started to address the issue of the handwriting and suggested, as the timing was not crucial, that we could still arrange for expert evidence. The boss cut me off.

'Yes, it's bullshit; a waste of time and energy. If the DPP thinks that a handwriting expert is necessary, we'll do that later. For now, forget the handwriting. The lawyers are just being their usual defensive selves. I want to hear about 'acting dishonestly' and what the courts have said that means.'

I must have looked at the boss quite blankly.

'Get up to the library, do your research, and if there is even a half-decent legal justification, then we'll send the brief across to the DPP and tell upstairs where to stick their advice. But you have to prove to me first that there's a legal basis for the charge.'

By the time I reached the ASC library, my head was spinning. I was angry with the uncollegiate nature of the memorandum, but I had an increasingly nagging suspicion that the ASC legal team had a point. Given my legal research skills had been limited to reading a couple of tax office rulings for a tax law essay at RMIT, I entrusted the aid of the kindly ASC librarian. Together, we identified a couple of corporate law textbooks, isolated a few relevant cases, and importantly, re-read section 232 of the Corporations Law. The provision essentially held that company officers must, in the exercise of their duties, act honestly. If the contravention is accompanied by fraud or deception, the officer may face a fine of up to $20,000 or five years in jail, or both.

Much of the legal team's response to my brief of evidence focussed on fraud or rather, in their view, the absence of fraud. There was a brief acknowledgement that the manager of the Borders bookstore may have been 'taken in' by the false labels but that in itself would be insufficient to prove fraud beyond a reasonable doubt. On the contrary, the poor quality of the labels themselves was itself evidence that Stein's motivations were hardly calculated to deceive.

'That's it,' I quietly said to myself out loud. 'No fraud, no dishonesty, so no offence.'

'But look,' responded the kindly librarian. 'Stein may not get a jail term, but the section provides for different penalties. Surely, we don't have to prove fraud in all cases of dishonesty, otherwise what is the point of subsection b?'

The librarian was right. Section 232(3)(b) provided for a fine of up to $5,000 where fraud or deception could not be proved. This revelation was sufficient to warrant further investigation, but our initial enthusiasm was short-lived. Indeed, the legal team had referred to a Victorian Supreme Court case where dishonesty had been considered in the absence of fraud. Dishonesty, so the court held, was only established if the defendant knew what he did was not in the interests of the company. Further, it must also be established that the defendant engaged in deliberate conduct in disregard of that knowledge.

'Oh dear,' I again muttered. 'How is this going to help?' I asked rhetorically. 'Stein's not ripping off his own company. Indeed, he's making money for his company and his conduct is consistent with that motivation.'

Just as I was about to admit defeat, the librarian picked up one of the textbooks. After a brief review, she pointed to a paragraph and remarked, 'Look, that Victorian case is twenty years old, and a different view has been taken recently by the Chief Justice of the South Australian Supreme Court.' As she spoke, she pointed to a reference to *Australian Growth Resources v Van Reesema* in the Australian Corporate Law Reports.

Thankfully, the ASC library held copies of the reports. It did not take us long to locate the South Australian case or to rekindle my enthusiasm for the prosecution of Marcus Stein. I read the judgement with interest. His Honour had expressly referred to the differential penalties that were by the 1990s set out in subsection 232(3) of the Corporations Law. He had no doubt that an officer could fail to act honestly if he or she acted improperly, albeit with a subjectively honest purpose.

I was excited. Here we had current authority that an officer could be held to act dishonestly even if he or she believed they were acting honestly. Stein may well have thought he was working for the best interests of the company, but even by his admission, he had engaged in passing off, a purpose judged by the law to be improper.

I reasoned that ASC lawyers were stuck in the past. They obviously did not appreciate the increasing desire of the courts to judge the conduct of officers criminally by reference to social standards and without the burden of proving criminal intent. The collapses of the State Bank of Victoria, Estate Mortgage, Pyramid Building Society, and the Interwest group were still sharp in the public mind. The misconduct of those connected with those collapses would undoubtedly influence parliamentarians and courts alike. Put simply, we expected more from our captains of industry. Whatever their individual beliefs or motivations, it was clear that criminal misconduct on the part of corporate citizens was increasingly being judged by reference to society's notions of reasonableness or, as the lawyers would say, objective standards.

Of course, just as one swallow does not make a summer, one precedent does not fashion a compelling brief of evidence. But the more we dug, the more the librarian and I felt vindicated. We turned our attention to the Victorian Supreme Court's approach to the offence of dishonestly obtaining property by deception. Dishonesty, the court held, was an awareness that the deception would detrimentally affect the interests of the victim in a significant practical way. While the court was not advocating an objective standard of dishonesty, its reasoning presented a good back-up argument. Stein had readily agreed that his conduct was designed to undermine the professor's distribution monopoly and thus cause considerable economic harm. Even though we could not prove fraud or deception, we had enough to prove 'dishonesty.'

I wrote up our research in the form of a memorandum and anxiously awaited the boss's reply. I did not have to wait long for a favourable reaction. However, I suspect his appreciative response was due more to his personal dislike of the ASC legal team than the compelling nature of the legal research. Yet, his enthusiasm was real and was actioned in two ways. First, the Stein brief of evidence, together with the legal team's memorandum and my response, was delivered to the Commonwealth Director of Public Prosecutions. There was no argument about the quality of my legal reasoning. There was no good reason to delay the prosecution of Marcus Stein.

Secondly, and just as importantly, from that day on, the words 'pommy sock' were banished from the boss's vocabulary. I had been officially reinstated as the 'pommy bastard.' But it was a hollow development. That evening, as I trudged back to a dark, uninviting home, I was acutely aware of my loneliness. I had no one to share my pride in investigating Marcus Stein or preparing the brief of evidence. There was no one on the home front to call me a pommy bastard or to reflect on the warmth and support of the boss. I returned to a sterile, heartless abode with nothing but a six-pack of Carlton Draught and the bedside photo of Lena to keep me company. It would be the happiest day of my career, but I would spend that night in a flood of tears.

Looking back, I suspect I must have waited anxiously for the DPP's response. I figured the 'legal boys club' would stick together and write the case off. At the very least, I expected the DPP to require evidence from a handwriting expert and probably statements from a bunch of potential witnesses that I failed to identify. I said as much to the boss, who just laughed.

'There's no love lost between the DPP and our legal team. Have faith in yourself; the matter's not going to be written off,' he said convincingly.

The boss was right. A few weeks later we received correspondence that the DPP would summon Marcus Stein to appear in the Melbourne Magistrates' Court to answer one count of failing to act honestly in contravention of section 232 of the Corporations Law. Contrary to my expectations, the correspondence was concise, and the list of required requisitions was mercifully short. The DPP did not need a handwriting expert or other evidence to support the admissions provided by Stein in his record of interview. All the DPP required was a current extract of Stein's criminal history and an up-to-date list of witness addresses. My faith in the legal fraternity had been restored. The requisitions stood in stark contrast to the demands of ASC lawyers. It was not even clear that the DPP had read the legal team's memorandum. Indeed, at no stage did they object to my assessment of section 232 of the Corporations Law.

With the aid of an AFP officer and the police database, I quickly dealt with the DPP's requirements, although it would take a few more weeks before Stein was 'brought to justice,' or rather, 'brought to mention.' On the court mention date, either Stein would plead guilty, or the matter would be adjourned for a contested hearing at a later date.

Appropriately, at least for Stein, he fronted the Melbourne Magistrate's court on a dark and dank Melbourne morning. The stroll from the ASC offices to the corner of Lonsdale and Williams streets was just a few minutes, but it was a cold and miserable walk for any individual who forgot their overcoat. I was therefore pleased to find a crowd of persons milling around the foyer. Their combined body heat was a welcome relief.

I looked around the crowd of individuals. It was hard to tell who was who, apart from a few that wore the distinctive attire of the Victoria Police uniform branch. I assumed that the rest of the throng comprised of defendants, their families, witnesses, lawyers, and reporters. But it was not obvious who was who. There were no wigs and gowns to distinguish the lawyers and no handcuffs or hooped T-shirts to identify the crooks. Further, the collective noise and bustle only added to my sense of confusion. Of course, it was just another ordinary day in the life of the Melbourne Magistrates' Court. Thankfully, the notice board listed the relevant court. Otherwise, I could have been lost for hours.

Eventually, I found the court and DPP prosecutor who had been assigned to the case. He was a quiet, thoughtful lawyer who seemed impervious to the commotion that was around us. I reasoned that he was well versed in court proceedings. In one hand, he held a copy of my brief of evidence. In the other, he gripped the handle of the obligatory legal briefcase. I later discovered it only contained a sandwich and can of Coco-Cola. Still, he looked impressive, and given the number of yellow Post-It notes that protruded from the brief of evidence, it was clear that he had done his homework.

'No, I think we've got everything,' he said confidently, 'but can you see him? I don't know what Stein looks like.'

By then, Marcus Stein, or rather his dispassionate lawyer, had spotted me and was heading in our direction.

'Leave this to me,' said the DPP lawyer and headed off with Stein's lawyer for pre-hearing negotiations, or rather what appeared to me, less than twenty seconds of casual pleasantries. They could well have talked about their favourite coffee shop or the football results for all I knew. However, upon the DPP lawyer's return, I realised that they had discussed the case.

'You were right, Greg,' said the DPP Lawyer, 'Stein's as angry as ever. He won't plead, so be prepared for a hearing in a few weeks. If you want to head back to the office, by all means, do. Leave it to me.'

Just as I was about to re-embrace the chilly Melbourne air, there was a flurry of activity outside of the relevant court. The list of proceedings had been amended. We walked over and saw that Stein's case was now listed for another court, albeit just around the corner. (I am reluctant, Dear Reader, to disclose the number of the new court for fear of identifying the new magistrate. In the circumstances, I trust you will understand my hesitancy.)

Almost as soon as we had glanced at the amended list, Stein's dispassionate lawyer headed in our general direction. Surprisingly, he looked anything but disinterested. His hair was ruffled, his necktie hung to one side, and he was clearly out of breath.

'I have taken fresh instructions from my client,' blurted Stein's lawyer, which of course was lawyer-speak along the lines that he had just had a heated discussion with his client and had managed to drill some sense into him.

'Go on,' said the DPP lawyer. 'We're listening.'

'In the circumstances,' Stein's lawyer continued. 'While we feel a sense of injustice, my client does wish to move on. He does not want to be a burden on the system; therefore, he will plead guilty.'

As soon as Stein's lawyer had walked back to his client, I saw the look on the DPP lawyer's face. There was more than a hint of a smile. The look of bemusement on my face only added to his sense of hilarity.

'You've got to laugh, Greg, you've gotta laugh. He'll only plead because the new magistrate has a strong reputation for being defence-friendly. In fact, I couldn't think of anyone more defence-friendly. Come on, Greg, when it's over I'll buy you a coffee.'

Momentarily I felt deflated. Resolution of the prosecution would hinge on the perception of the arbiter, not on the merits of my case. Nonetheless, those thoughts were fleeting. Less than a couple of hours later, Marcus Stein left the Melbourne Magistrates' Court. He walked away with a $2,000 fine and a criminal conviction. In the circumstances, it was probably the best result I could have hoped for. The sanction was no token punishment, given the maximum penalty was $5,000. I would like to think the strength of my case influenced the presiding magistrate's penalty. More likely, the magistrate was swayed by the eloquence of the DPP lawyer. More likely still, the magistrate was influenced by the volume of Stein's prior convictions.

By the time the DPP lawyer and I had finished our coffees, the chilly morning had given way to a bright and sunny afternoon.

As I walked down Little Lonsdale Street to the rear of the ASC offices, I felt rejuvenated. I had almost single-handedly prepared a brief of evidence that had resulted in a conviction. There were not too many Administrative Services Officers Class 4 who could say that. The boss had supported me throughout, and the DPP had treated me as a professional. While my domestic life was a disaster, I could at least claim that my work life was on the ascendency.

Unfortunately, my elation was short-lived. On the steps to the ASC offices, I passed the head of the ASC legal team.

'Heard you got a conviction today,' she remarked.

'Thanks. Yes, I did,' was my immediate reply.

'You were lucky,' was the terse response, and with that, she turned her back on me and walked away in the opposite direction.

Chapter Twenty
The Studies

'You were lucky.' The dismissive words of the most senior ASC lawyer repeated inside my head.

'Christ, you know the legal team is filled with morons,' was the boss's take on my reaction. 'The matter would not have gone through the DPP and magistrate if there wasn't a case.'

Despite the boss's attempts at reassurance, the ASC's lawyer's belittling reference to 'luck' continued to haunt me. I reasoned that the ASC lawyers were either jealous or embarrassed. They had been undermined by a very junior investigator with nothing but a straightforward business degree. Nonetheless, I recognised that if the Stein prosecution were just about luck, then no amount of legal logic would convince them otherwise.

Of course, I would be surprised if any of the lawyers would have given the matter a second thought. Apart from those three cutting words, nothing else was said. It was as though the prosecution had never happened. In the months that followed, I must have bumped into ASC lawyers on numerous occasions. The conversations were polite and generally in good humour; however, there was no mention of Marcus Stein or my victory in the Magistrates' Court.

Nonetheless, the passing comment of having luck on my side, ate away at me. In fairness, I was more agitated by the lawyer's dismissive attitude as there was nothing I could say or do to persuade her otherwise. In her eyes, I was not qualified to have an opinion. Put simply, she had no reason to listen to me. Of course, if I had been a practising lawyer, then the situation would have been entirely different. I must have muttered something along those lines to the boss.

'Cut the whinging,' he said. 'If you can't beat them, join them. You've done a business degree by correspondence, why not a Bachelor of Laws?'

A few days later, the boss pointed to a small article in *The Age* that addressed the burgeoning establishment of Australian law schools. In Victoria, La Trobe and Deakin universities had joined the list of tertiary institutions that offered law degrees. But the article also gave special attention to Macquarie University, in Sydney's north-west, for being instrumental in designing a part-time course for mature students in full-time employment.

The article intrigued me. Memories of Perry Mason and John Mortimer re-emerged. I thought of Tich Allen's put-downs and my fantasies of Farrah Fawcett-Majors. Suppressed memories from two decades back rose to the surface. Could I really be a lawyer? I must have procrastinated for an hour or so before I realised that I had been smiling throughout my deliberations and had not for one moment stopped to think of Lena. Perhaps that was an omen. A law degree would not only legitimise my standing amongst those ill-informed ASIC lawyers but may offer me broader salvation. It was a chance to move on with my life and seek new opportunities, unclouded by past fears and failures.

One telephone call and one application form later I had enrolled in a Macquarie University Bachelor of Legal Studies Course. It was not a Bachelor of Laws or Juris Doctor, but it was a law degree recognised by the various State legal services boards.

I didn't know whether to laugh or cry. The application process appeared all too easy. I had expected a series of formal interviews and some proof that my secondary school education was on a par with Scotch College, Melbourne or Geelong Grammar School or equivalent institution. Yet, a simple application form, proof of employment and a certified copy of my RMIT degree were all that was required.

In reality, the next few years felt like a repeat performance of my RMIT days, or at least my RMIT days following Lena's departure. I would attend the ASC during the day and hit the law books at night. The only difference was that attendance at Macquarie University was limited to a couple of weekend visits per year. There would be no mid-week seminars or late-night drinking sessions at The Oxford Scholar Hotel. In hindsight, I now believe the process exacerbated my loneliness. Far from offering redemption, I generally became more introverted and insular. I would leave work, often early, with the sole intention of reading course materials or locating some obscure journal article designated by the law school as 'extra reading.' Needless to say, I was a regular patron of Dan Murphy's.

The Macquarie degree offered the usual suite of courses. Torts, contracts, constitutional law, property law, criminal law and procedure were all part of the mix. Along with a foundation course entitled 'History and Philosophy of Law,' there were also compulsory units covering judicial remedies in tort and contract, business organisations and litigation. I was attracted to the fact that Macquarie University prided itself on offering a socially aware law curriculum. Legislation was not merely presented as a reflection of the will of parliament. The doctrine of precedent was but one force that shaped the form and content of case law. Instead, the law was presented as a dynamic phenomenon, which in the western legal tradition had generally facilitated the rise of capitalism.

In part, the sociological and historical approach to the study of law kept me sane. I would reflect on whether the Australian Constitution reflected popular sovereignty or a vision for a shared good through a compact between the various states. I was never asked to merely recite the thirty-nine legislative powers of the Federal Government listed in section 51 of the Constitution. I submitted a torts assignment on whether or not the common law had developed workable criteria for negligent acts and statements. There was no mention of snails in ginger beer bottles. Indeed, I only cited *Donoghue v. Stevenson* as an illustration of how far the judiciary had recognised changing economic circumstances. I was fascinated to learn how far the rise of administrative rationalism had challenged the notion of private will as a basic concept of contemporary law. I was not required to consider the powers of the NCAT (NSW Civil & Administrative Tribunal) or role play my way through a Local Court's mention hearing.

To the 'black-letter' purists at the universities of Melbourne and Sydney, Macquarie University's approach to the study of law undoubtedly lacked intellectual rigour. In retrospect, it would have been to my long-term advantage to have taken a more conservative approach to my studies. If I had spent more time on the letter of the law, or if I actually learnt the basic principles of statutory interpretation, I might not have ended up in the mess I did. However, blame could not be levied at Macquarie University. I had been taught that law must be understood in a social, political, and economic context. The problem was that I was just too focussed on the context.

I did not, of course, forget another context. Each day at the office, I would be reminded of my reasons for enrolling in a Bachelor of Legal Studies. An internal ASC newsletter referred to the fact that I was studying for a law degree. Now and then, a colleague would ask how my studies were faring, but there would be no response, good or bad, from the legal team. If I really wanted to be taken seriously, it would take a lot more than a few years of legal studies.

The legal team's deafening silence stood in contrast to the continuing support from the boss. He took a keen interest in the subject matter of my various courses and was more than generous with the regulator's time. On numerous occasions, I was granted study leave, and it would be fair to say that my devotion during work hours to the Macquarie University curriculum extended well beyond the one-hour lunch break.

I also received support from an unlikely source. A few months into my studies, I was thrilled to receive a letter from the professor thanking me for my role in bringing Marcus Stein to justice. It was the start of a long-term, albeit long-distance, friendship. Like myself, the professor was a single man whose wife had traded him in for a more home-bound model. His passion was researching and developing educational software; he had spent most of his thirties at the University of New South Wales undertaking a doctorate while lecturing in computer studies and establishing a software distribution business. By the time he was forty, he had his doctorate and a successful business. At some stage during the journey though, his wife had pressed the escape key.

The professor's initial correspondence developed into a series of regular catch-ups. Thankfully, he also enjoyed a beer and would seek me out for a drinking session when business brought him to Melbourne. The watering holes along King Street were our favoured destinations, but over the years I think we discovered every pub in Melbourne's CBD. We also caught up when my studies took me to Macquarie University. Just to the south of the campus and close to my motel accommodation was The Ranch Hotel or El Rancho as the pub was more commonly known. The professor would join me after class and provide me with his wisdom of thirty plus years in academia.

Over time, the professor became my mentor. He took pleasure in discussing the lessons I had learnt from my course materials and on-campus lectures. He challenged my arguments but did so respectfully and refreshingly. Learning had never been so much fun, mainly as the professor was not one for a dry argument. As long as the schooners of beer were lined up, he would talk for hours. Away from the pub, he proofread my various essays and even hand-delivered a few of them to the law faculty to ensure they arrived on time. Those were the pre-internet days when Australia Post was the preferred means of submitting assignments. Without a doubt, the professor's friendship and encouragement ameliorated my feelings of being a legal interloper and offered a welcome respite from loneliness.

Thirty-odd assignments and a dozen trips to the university later, I was the proud holder of a Bachelor of Legal Studies. Pride, though, is a relative concept. In truth, the qualification itself did not mean much, and I didn't even attend the graduation ceremony. It was not as though I had passed the eleven-plus or achieved anything as equally important. There was still a long way to go before I could call myself a lawyer. When I received my results, I briefly thought of Tich Allen. However, that was wasted energy. He would have passed away years before, and even if he were still alive, he wouldn't remember one eleven-plus failure from another. I also thought of Lena. She would have said all the right things and smothered me with kisses and smiles, but that would have just been for show. I knew that, deep down, she could not have cared less about my newly developed legal skills. Academic prowess was no substitute for a devoted husband; she had craved that attention during our marriage, and on that front I had clearly failed.

I may have still been a recovering divorcee, but at least the boss was happy. Even the new head of the legal team offered me his congratulations. In those days, the ASC undertook organisational restructures on an all-too-regular basis. Staff morale was low and both turnover and redundancies were high. Accordingly, the composition of the legal team had changed significantly since the Marcus Stein prosecution. Indeed, it had changed for the better. The new head was eager to 'break down the barrier,' as he called it, between lawyers and investigators. I was a welcome beneficiary as he offered me articles of clerkship.

In reality, the nature of my employment duties hardly changed. For a year, I would spend two afternoons a week with the legal team. On occasions, I was required to review and advise on minor statutory offences, including failing to provide a liquidator with a 'Report as to Affairs' and failing to display a company's name at its principal place of business. I recall reviewing a brief of evidence that was used internally to ban a high-flying financial adviser. Further, I relished the opportunity to personally attend the Supreme Court to file a writ in a significant class action.

Nonetheless, the lows outweighed the highs. Most of my tasks for the legal team were numbingly mundane. As an assistant investigator, many of my chores involved photocopying and sticking barcodes on documents to identify them as exhibits. The bulk of my time with the legal team followed the same pattern. The only difference was the photocopying machine. The legal team had a larger and more expensive variety. On one occasion, I was summoned to a senior lawyer as a matter of urgency. I was surprised but pleased. At last, I thought, I would be asked to participate in a significant legal case. Unfortunately, my enthusiasm was quickly dampened. The legal team's photocopier had jammed, and I was the number one lackey.

I am sure that the Council of Legal Education was not aware of the quality of my articles of clerkship. If they had, then the comprehensive changes to practical legal training that occurred years later would have been introduced considerably sooner. As it was, the year came and went, and in early autumn of the following year I was admitted to practice as a barrister and solicitor in the Supreme Court of Victoria. Technically, my apprenticeship with the ASC's legal team had concluded, but now and then I was called back to help out on a piece of minor advice or to draft an affidavit. Thankfully, my time as the chief photocopying officer had come to an end.

While I toyed with the idea of seeking employment elsewhere, I was contented in my role as an assistant investigator, particularly as the boss had been considering me for promotion. I was also reasonably comfortable with my informal arrangement with the legal team. In fact, they genuinely seemed to accept me as one of their own. Half a decade of study and a year of articles had paid off.

Still, I felt something was missing. I was only a lawyer of sorts. I was not employed in a law firm or even engaged in legal practice on an ongoing basis. Even if it were possible, I could not have looked Tich Allen in the face and claimed to be a practising lawyer. Further, I was fast approaching forty years of age. If I had sought a legal career elsewhere, then my competition would have been at least fifteen years younger than me. Thus, I put my feelings to one side. I was resigned to the fact that I would be going nowhere.

However, not even a few months later, my world would change dramatically. The professor was in town and, as usual, after-work beers had been arranged. As I was no longer travelling to Sydney to study, it had been a long time between drinks and there was much to discuss. Since graduating, our conversations focussed more on politics than anything else. We did not discuss party politics or matters of ideology or philosophy. Instead, the professor was obsessed with the office politics of the University of NSW, and I was usually preoccupied with consequences of the ASC's latest organisational restructure.

It became clear though that the professor was keen to move our conversation in a different direction.

'Remember that convenience store in Little Bourke Street? It was the one that stocked my KnowData compact discs.'

I immediately twigged the professor was referring to the Marcus Stein prosecution.

'Vaguely,' I replied. 'I do recall you mentioning it, but I don't think we ever took a statement. Not sure I even visited the place. Why do you ask?'

'Well, I happen to know the owner. Actually, I have known Alfred for a long time. He's a truly nice man. I assume you've heard of Alfred Lee?'

'No, I haven't,' was my honest response. 'Is he in trouble or something?'

The professor laughed and clarified that Alfred was too much of a gentleman to get into trouble himself. I was intrigued as the professor went on to explain in detail.

'Alfred is a very astute investor and successful businessman. That little shop in Chinatown is just a fraction of what he owns. He has properties all over the place, but also runs a family office with his son. They've got accountants and advisers and the like all taking care of their family's private wealth.'

Just as I was about to ask what this talk of Alfred Lee had to do with the professor, let alone myself, the professor got to the point.

'Well, I see Alfred quite often. In fact, I saw him last week in Sydney. He's looking for a lawyer as there is some legal issue developing with their cash management trust. He didn't tell me what the problem was, but he said they were looking for a lawyer with ASC experience. I hope you didn't mind, but I told him about the sterling work you did prosecuting Stein, and the fact that you led the charge. Alfred's very keen to meet you. Here, take his business card.'

'I don't mind at all. But I am shocked. As you well know, I might be nearing forty, but I don't have much legal experience.'

'Look. I know you have only been a practising lawyer for a short time,' replied the professor. 'But don't tell me you lack experience. You have plenty of experience. In any case, I explained your situation to Alfred. He was even more interested. They have a bevy of law firms that do work for them. All they need is someone on the inside, and preferably someone who knows the regulator. They're not going to pay you partner or even senior associate rates. But the role sounds right up your alley. At least speak to them. What have you got to lose?'

Little did I know then that I would have a lot to lose, but, at that time, I was excited, and over the coming few days, my elation grew. I confided in the boss who, in no uncertain words, suggested I would be a fool not to apply.

'You'll make decent investigator someday, but you'd have a screw loose if you do not go for this opportunity.'

A couple of weeks later, I sat nervously in a Lee Family Office meeting room, awaiting an interview with Mr Winston Lee. I had anticipated an interrogation and desperately tried to re-read the notes I had scribbled in preparation. Before the meeting, I researched cash management trusts and discovered that new laws were being considered that would affect the regulation of collective investment vehicles. Such vehicles included trusts that looked a bit like saving accounts that you would open with a bank. Research is probably too strong a word. My research was limited to accompanying the boss and a colleague from ASC's licensing section to the Golden Age Hotel. There is, of course, a limit to what one can learn in the middle of downing a dozen pots with Drambuie chasers. However, at the very least, I staggered away knowing the basics of the regulatory environment.

As it turned out, cash management trusts and the regulatory environment were plainly not on Mr Lee's mind. The interview itself was a mercifully brief affair with no technical questions. Winston Lee spent most of the time fidgeting in his chair and looking at his rather expensive Rolex watch. His plump physique and protruding belly were strong indications that he enjoyed the finer things in life. I noticed that Mr Lee had an unhealthy number of red and pink spots on his face, and he appeared to sweat easily. I reasoned that he needed a wholesome diet and some serious exercise.

It was apparent from his manner that Mr Lee had more pressing matters to attend to. He asked a few general questions concerning my background and work experience, which suggested he had not read my curriculum vitae. Otherwise, all he wanted to know was how much the ASC was paying me and how much resignation notice I was required to provide.

I had barely responded when Mr Lee enquired, 'How would you like to make twenty per cent more than you earn now?'

'Of course,' I replied. 'I'd be delighted.'

Winston Lee immediately rose out of his chair to shake my hand. As he did so, he merely said, 'In that case, we look forward to seeing you next month. Our HR Manager will sort out the details with you.' With that, he promptly ushered me out of the meeting room. Within half an hour, I was back at the Golden Age Hotel enjoying a celebratory beer or three with the man I would forever regard as the greatest boss I'd ever had.

At the time, I was not sure what to make of Winston Lee. I cannot claim I warmed to him, but I was not with him long enough to develop any negative feelings. In fact, given I had walked out of his door with the offer of a fantastic job, I had every reason to like him. As I staggered back that night to my Brunswick pad, I was in a jovial mood. Just weeks before I could never have dreamed of a legal career. Yet, there I was in my late thirties being offered the position of legal counsel to a remarkable family. There would be no missing Lena that night.

I reflected on Tich Allen and the old head of the ASC legal team. If they could only see me now, I thought to myself. Despite their respective put-downs, I had made it. I had realised my childhood dreams. An eleven-plus failure had joined the ranks of the profession. To claim I was joyful would be an understatement. I was absolutely euphoric.

Of course, I could not have realised my ambitions without the help and encouragement of others. In particular, I was indebted to both the boss and the professor. There were also two other individuals I had to thank. One was a gentleman I had never met. The other was the gentleman's son whom I had barely known for a few hours. I fell asleep that night thinking only good things of Alfred and Winston Lee.

Chapter Twenty-One
The Dreams

was fascinated by the ease in which someone could withdraw amounts from the Lee Family Office's cash management trust. In part, my interest in the Lee Fund was a professional concern as my functions covered operational compliance. It also seemed an easy way to get rich quick. Eileen, perhaps ironically given her position as head of the firm's philanthropy team, and I spent many a drunken lunchtime 'theoretically' working out how we could relieve the Lee Fund of a few million dollars while dreaming of what life would be like in South America.

'If you're gonna do a crime, then make it worthwhile,' she argued. 'Sticking a dodgy label on a box of compact discs isn't worth the effort. Poor bugger. Bet he didn't reckon Chief Inspector Mason would be on his case.'

Eileen was a laugh. Her language was coarse, but her passion and zeal were infectious. She would refer to Alfred as the 'old bastard' to his face, but her favourite phrase was 'How's it going, me old China?'

Said by anyone else, they would have been hauled up to HR, read the riot act about racial discrimination and been summarily dismissed, and not necessarily in that order. I once asked her how she got away with talking to Alfred like that.

'Thanks for fucking nothing,' she replied. 'You should hear what I say to that rotten, selfish son of his. Anyway, you're pretty much a Cockney boy. Have you never heard of "me old China," as in china plate meaning mate? It's rhyming slang, Greg. Are you sure you've got those business and law degrees? Sometimes you aren't half slow.'

Before I could respond with a witty retort, Eileen had reverted to our favourite topic.

'Come on, Greg, just a couple of million each. We'll paint Rio Janeiro red. I'll make you forget about that Greek tart you keep crapping on about. Just me and you on Ipanema Beach.'

It was an unlikely scenario for many reasons. No matter how hard I tried, I could never think of Lena as a tart. Also, I had the sneaking suspicion that Eileen's husband would not appreciate his wife of thirty years destroying their marriage and her public reputation by heading off to some extradition-free beach resort with a toy-boy. Bonnie and Clyde, we were not. Obviously, it was just merry banter, and neither of us would ever have hopped on a Rio-bound 747 together or seriously engaged in fraud.

Of course, one could not extract monies from the Lee Fund at will. Checks and balances had been built into the withdrawal process. A payment request form was required from a client or one of his or her nominated signatories. In most cases, the form would be accompanied by an invoice, statement or the like. The form and attachments were then forwarded to the accounts team for processing. In reality, that team consisted of two administrative assistants who reported directly to Martin.

In my early years at the Lee Family Office, payments were made by cheque from the Lee Fund's bank account with the accounts team laboriously writing out each cheque. In turn, each cheque, together with supporting attachments, would be reviewed and signed by two client advisers from different teams.

Later, when the bank provided us with online software, electronic funds transfer became the preferred method of remittance. However, the process remained mostly the same. Two independent client advisers were required to access the software platform to review and authorise all payments. Finally, a daily reconciliation of Lee Fund records with the fund's bank statements would be conducted by a junior accountant. Any discrepancies would be promptly referred to Martin, who had been instrumental in establishing the withdrawal procedures.

For Winston, the checks and balances built into the payments process were unnecessary diversions from income-generating activities. Over the years, he had grown to respect Martin, and would rarely criticise an initiative that had Martin's support. However, there was one notable exception. I once tried to introduce a 'call-back' policy where all payment requests above a specified sum would require confirmation through a telephone call to the client. I suggested $20,000, knowing full well that the daily number of payments exceeding that amount was less than half a dozen. Despite Martin's backing, my suggestion caused widespread consternation and was dismissed by Winston as just another uncommercial contribution from the business prevention unit. The policy was never implemented.

To claim the Lee Fund compliance processes were robust would be an overstatement. Martin was acutely aware of the limitations. Even though the online software had reduced the number of mistakes attributable to human error, blunders continued regularly. They were often left for Martin to fix up. Most of the problems stemmed from the inaccurate completion or reading of the payments forms. Incorrect account numbers, wrong amounts, payee typos were all part of the bungle mix. Most errors were easily identifiable and, in theory, should have been spotted by the two client advisers before authorisation. Nonetheless, with Winston's blessing, most advisers conducted little more than a few cursory checks.

Martin, though, was concerned about possible collusion, particularly as many client advisers had been nominated as authorised signatories on client accounts and didn't personally complete payment request forms. That task fell to their personal assistants.

'What if one of the accounts team conspires with an assistant and processes a fake form or more likely a fake invoice?' he said. 'We can't rely on the checking by client advisers. I don't know how we can mitigate that possibility.'

Martin was right. The whole efficacy of the payments process relied on the dedication of our client advisers. Before signing off on a payments request, the client adviser needed to know the payment was genuine. The lack of adequate checks within the payments platform was only one challenge. The more serious problem concerned the front-end of the process. A slack client adviser and a couple of criminal assistants could wreak havoc.

'Yes, I know,' I replied. 'Really, anything can be done with collusion. We just have to keep on stressing the importance of proper checks.'

Secretly, though, I was less concerned about criminal assistants than I was about fraudulent client advisers. Collusion might well occur, but I was never convinced it was a necessary pre-requisite for ripping off the Lee Fund. I was concerned that the Lee Fund could be easily manipulated by a client adviser acting alone.

The scenario was simple. A client adviser, as an authorised signature on a client account, could simply authorise payments from the Lee Fund to other bank accounts. As long as the client adviser's signature appeared on the payment request form, then the withdrawal would be processed. Provided the relevant client's books and records were falsified and the amounts kept small, the adviser could make regular payments for years. The client would not know unless he or she were extremely diligent. After all, the very same client adviser was maintaining the client's books and records, preparing the client's accounts, and lodging their tax returns.

I hoped our checking processes would be sufficient to identify payments to bank accounts held in the name of client advisers. However, if you are committed to engaging in serious fraud, it would not be difficult to open a bank account in a different name. You may need to elicit the services of a crooked friend or relative, but you would not need to collude with another staff member.

To be honest, I never seriously thought that a Lee Family Office client adviser would ever engage in such overt criminal activity. Except for James Powell, I was not particularly friendly with the fifteen or so client advisers. That was the nature of the professional relationship and, to be fair, where there was bad feeling between us, Winston had usually instigated the problems. Indeed, one of the most significant risk issues concerning the Lee Fund was identified by a client adviser.

For years, Winston, with the aid of a junior accountant, had managed the investments of the Lee Fund. 'Managed,' though, is a very generous interpretation of Winston's involvement in the investment process. The assets of the Lee Fund were, in the main, a series of short-term bank products with various maturity dates. Unfortunately, without exception, they were all with one bank. Winston had never got around to spreading counterparty risk across multiple financial institutions.

I found out later that the junior accountant assisting Winston had expressed dismay about the lack of spread and had raised the matter in a team meeting that included a senior client adviser. To give that adviser his due, he directly approached Martin and Winston. I am sure Martin was aware of the issue, but it would not have ranked highly on his list of priorities. Also, I am sure Martin would have handled the conversation with Winston more diplomatically.

It was later that I heard that Winston did not take kindly to being lectured on 'risk management 101' from a subordinate. Nevertheless, what he said must have worked. Within just a few weeks, the Lee Fund had accounts with all four major banks, and Winston had signed off guidelines to ensure Lee Fund assets were evenly spread. The client advisers were not a bad lot.

Chapter Twenty-Two
The Loss

The Middle Kingdom company secretary role was hardly glamorous, and, unfortunately, I significantly underestimated the dull administrative nature of the position.

'It's not as though you have to prepare the financials and management reports. Martin's our man for that,' was one of Winston's many ongoing remarks.

Winston did have a point. The financial well-being of Middle Kingdom was invariably the main topic of board discussion, and Martin would spend countless hours preparing accounts, statements, reports, and analysis in preparation for the inevitable interrogations he would receive at the hands of directors. Martin's contributions dominated the board papers.

Nevertheless, Winston consistently ignored the many, almost invisible compliance tasks that make up a company secretary's role. Statutory recording-keeping and reporting, attending to ASIC and ASX lodgements, as well as minute taking and board correspondence were all part of the mix. However, it was the organisation and management of board and committee meetings that necessitated an unhealthy amount of time and effort.

Six board meetings a year plus an annual general meeting was how Winston initially presented the challenge. And it was a challenge. Just arranging a simple calendar of events for directors was hard enough, let alone the packs of board and committee papers and e-mail communications that preceded and succeeded each meeting of directors. Getting ten directors to agree on suitable meeting dates was a constant battle.

'Greg, I know you're new to this, but why don't you give us a choice of two or three alternatives,' was the response from one of the more condescending directors.

Unfortunately, that gem of a suggestion resulted in the creation of a further eighteen unsuitable proposed dates. I learnt quite quickly that by 'locking in' Alfred, Winston and Ms Ma, in that order, to the proposed dates, the others would fall quickly into line.

In addition to the board, there was an audit and risk committee, a remuneration committee, a separate nominations committee and an advisory committee. Each committee had a different chair. And the advisory committee did not just comprise of directors, it also included industry experts. Along with three directors, there was a former Victorian State Minister of Health, an academic, and a respected member of the Chinese community. Their availability was as limited as that of the directors.

Juggling the calendar and ensuring that papers were available at least one week before the meeting and draft minutes within one week after each meeting were the most arduous part of my role. Unfortunately, it was rare that I would meet that timetable. Martin, for all his attributes, could never provide management accounts more than seven days before board or audit and risk committee meetings. He was just too busy. Winston, who would insist on reviewing all draft board and committee minutes before they were more broadly circulated, would take at least a week to review. His feedback was usually terse and often incomprehensible.

Administration and compliance were just one facet of the company secretary role, and, in fairness, most of the administrative hack work was ably handled by my secretary. Still, the role demanded more. I needed to behave as a manager or supervisor with responsibilities that were difficult to delegate.

It was not enough to merely convene board and committee meetings or to ensure the circulation of agendas, minutes, discussion papers, and reports. I was required to action board and committee recommendations, oversee and update the board and committee charters, arrange board performance reviews, organise and draft large slabs of each annual report, as well as facilitate board induction and professional development. Most importantly, I was expected to oversee and report on compliance with the ASX Corporate Council's Corporate Governance Principles and Recommendations.

With my legal hat on, I was Middle Kingdom's moral conscience. If I wore my company secretary hat, then I was the company's chief governance officer. Yet, it seemed obvious that there was an interplay between the two roles. Whether I wore my legal hat or my secretarial hat, it was vital that I behaved ethically.

Much of the material and information required for board and committee meetings was internally generated by Lee Family Office staff. Such meetings would invariably require the attendance of Lee Family Office staff, notably Martin and the Lee Family Office's HR manager. As employees of the Lee Family Office, such personnel, myself included, were answerable to Winston. I do not doubt that the reliance on the Lee Family Office and Winston's practical involvement in the operations of

Middle Kingdom undermined the ASX governance principles, in particular the concern for independent oversight.

Legally speaking, Winston was the directing mind and will of the Middle Kingdom. He was too far ingrained in the significant business and financial affairs of the company. In other words, from a legal perspective, whatever Winston knew about matters concerning Middle Kingdom would be attributed to the company itself.

Each year, I would struggle drafting Middle Kingdom's annual report, given the ASX requirement to disclose the extent of compliance with the ASX governance principles. However, I figured that as long as the interests of the Lee Family Office and Middle Kingdom were aligned, Winston's hands-on approach would not cause any practical governance problems.

I was also comforted by the presence of Ms Ma. I cannot recall one incident where Winston ever sought to challenge her authority or decision-making. Indeed, Winston was not alone. The entire board had nothing but praise for her industry knowledge, professionalism, and dedication. My own dealings with Ms Ma were mainly limited to collecting reports and data from her for board and committee papers. She was never once late, and her contributions were invariably relevant and insightful. Under her watch, management of the various early learning centres had become more coordinated and efficient. She had overseen a review of occupational health and safety that had led to improvements across the centres. Indeed, the acronyms 'LTI' (lost time injury), 'LTIFR' (lost-time injury frequency rate) and 'LTISR' (lost time incidents severity rate) became part of the corporate vernacular. Inadequate safety standards and poor governance would not be tolerated.

Unfortunately, the reign of Ms Ma as Middle Kingdom's managing director was far too short. At the time of her departure, her list of outstanding tasks remained long and detailed. When Winston announced her resignation, I was with Martin. The look of disappointment on Martin's face said it all, but I could tell by his reaction that he was not surprised. He knew something that I did not.

'What's going on, Martin? What have we done to upset her?'

'You've got it all wrong, Greg. She's not upset. Winston will probably kill me for telling you, but she's off to Hong Kong to head up his nursing home.'

'This is getting more absurd by the minute,' was all I could think and say. 'Hong Kong? Winston's nursing home? What are you telling me?'

'Winston's nursing home in Chai Wan. She agreed to be the head registrar. She was always going to return to Hong Kong at some stage to be with her family, but Winston just accelerated the process.'

Martin was talking to me in a manner that assumed I knew what he was talking about. Yet, I had never heard of a Chai Wan nursing home, let alone one run by Winston. I needed more answers.

'Martin, I vaguely remember Chai Wan being mentioned, something about being next to a big cemetery. Oh, and I assume you mean Alfred's nursing home?'

Martin laughed.

'You're right, at least about the cemetery. Chai Wan is at the arse end of Hong Kong Island, surrounded by a mountain of headstones, far away from the tourists. But you're wrong about

Alfred. The nursing home is all Winston. His idea, his money, his time.'

The look on my face must have mirrored my thoughts. Martin continued.

'Come on, Greg, how long have you known Winston? He's not just golf and the Sandringham Yacht Club. Alfred has always demanded more of his children?'

'But I've never heard of the Chai Wan nursing home. It's not a client. It hasn't got an account with the Lee Fund.' I was on a roll. 'Winston's never mentioned the facility, and how come you know so much?'

'Okay, okay,' he responded. 'Well, I've been honorary secretary for a few years now, and the reason why Winston hasn't said anything is because he wants to keep his philanthropy quiet. He's a real Lee. Like his father, like his uncles. He's no different.'

However, Martin revealed one crucial qualification.

'Whenever there's any talk about Chai Wan then it's all from Alfred. He never discusses his own charities but won't shut up about his children's. I bet you Winston will behave exactly the same once his kids join the office.'

Almost as an afterthought, Martin mentioned that he had visited the nursing facility on a couple of occasions to meet its bookkeepers.

'I suppose you do the accounts as well? Do you do all that for nothing, out of the goodness of your heart?'

I immediately regretted those sarcastic comments. They were rude, unnecessary, and undeserving. Martin was not only a friend, but he was loyal to the Lee family, and his compassion was never in question. Given the circumstances, he responded with a somewhat restrained put-down.

'If that's a serious question, then you don't know the meaning of "honorary." There's a dictionary on my desk, go and look the word up.' I deserved that response, but I could tell from Martin's tone that he was only fleetingly disgruntled. Almost immediately, he returned to his usual professional demeanour.

'Yes, I do oversee the accounts, but I only have a basic knowledge of Hong Kong accounting standards, so Deloitte signs off,' Martin modestly explained. I immediately took his explanation as code for, *'I know a hell of a lot about Hong Kong tax and accounting, but they need to be signed off by a local accountant.'*

The source of my agitation most likely stemmed from the fact that I simply did not want to believe Winston could be so silently committed to a worthy social cause. I later found out that the facility housed a hundred-odd beds and a seven-days-a-week clinic staffed by two doctors and half a dozen full-time nurses. The nursing facility provided valuable support to some of Hong Kong Island's most frail and impoverished. It was a well-run, efficient operation that had required considerable capital and operational expenditure.

Had I really read Winston so wrong? I had always thought I was a pretty good judge of character, but there was a lot more to Winston than I had appreciated. Perhaps Winston was just involved to please his father or merely to save face? In any case, my assessment was demonstrably challenged when I broached the subject of Chai Wan with Winston. He was decidedly agitated by the conversation.

Martin was right. Once 'Chai Wan' was planted firmly in my memory bank, I noticed that it was always Alfred that raised the name in conversation. He was openly proud of his son's philanthropic achievements. Winston was far more discreet.

Yet, my discussions with Martin highlighted a more profound, troubling concern. There I was talking to a fellow colleague who was supporting Lee family philanthropy. Martin did not just supply his expertise. The corporate secretarial function, his oversight of the local bookkeepers, and correspondence with the Hong Kong accountants, were all done out of office hours and at home. What had I ever done to foster the charitable endeavours of my employer? What sacrifices had I made as a reasonably paid corporate lawyer to help the socially and economically deprived? Well, Dear Reader, the answer to those questions should be of no surprise. Not only had I not done anything, I had not even thought about doing anything charitable.

However, I digress from the main issue. We all knew Ms Ma's departure to Hong Kong would be trouble, or at least Martin did.

'She will be a big loss. Who's going to deal with the government?' he once asked rhetorically. Martin answered his own question with another. 'Winston, right?' before adding, 'Winston, dead wrong. Greg, you're ex-ASIC, now company secretary, you'd better take charge. I want you on the executive leadership team. You're going to have to babysit the new managing director, whoever that will be. I'll sort it out with Winston.'

I said nothing. There was nothing to say. Winston would do what Winston wanted to do, but I felt honoured that Martin thought highly enough of me to nominate me as a member of Middle Kingdom's executive leadership team.

Martin's main concern was the childcare regulator. Initially, Middle Kingdom's thirty-four early learning centres had been licensed and overseen by the Department of Human Services. Following a government restructure, those tasks then fell onto the Department of Education and Early Childhood Development or DEECD. Even with the introduction of the so-called 'National Quality Framework,' the relevant legislation and regulatory framework essentially remained the same. Even the names and faces of authorised officers were unchanged. These were the bureaucrats that responded to new approved provider applications, provided a daily monitoring or supervision function, investigated serious incidents, and prosecuted owners for various offences.

Following my brief conversation with Martin, I obtained a copy of the newly enacted Education and Care Services National Law Act and its regulations. These legislative instruments provided for the responsibilities and obligations of Victorian early learning centres. They also detailed the rights and duties of DEECD and its authorised officers.

I was not at all surprised to learn that the expected standards of governance and behaviour by early learning operators were onerous. The clear intent of the legislation, supported by a National Quality Standard and Approved Learning Frameworks, was to provide for a positive and safe environment. Mums and dads should be able to relinquish control over their young children for a few hours a day and do so in the knowledge that their children would be nurtured in their absence and returned in one piece. The required standards of care were hardly controversial. Public interest demanded that early learning centres be professionally operated and managed. There were strict rules governing opening hours, child quotas, records of registers, health and safety, equipment and facilities, and, importantly, approval of nominated supervisors.

Effectively, each early learning centre was separately approved by DEECD. Each centre was required to employ a 'nominated supervisor,' being a person of sufficient experience and education to be entrusted with a range of responsibilities. Amongst other things, each nominated supervisor was required to deliver appropriate educational programs, protect the safety of children and provide for their sleep and rest, supervise the provision of food and beverages, administer medication, and ensure adequate staff levels were maintained.

Although not a legal requirement, it was common for Middle Kingdom to appoint each centre's nominated supervisor as the centre manager. That, of course, was just a cost-saving device which did not sit well with the managers, particularly after Ms Ma's departure.

'I spend more time talking to Collins Street than I do with the kids,' admitted one disgruntled manager. 'When Ms Ma was here, she would deal with all the reporting and money problems. Now I spend my days responding to Martin's offsiders and putting out bushfires for the new boss.' It was a common complaint.

In practice, each of Middle Kingdom's nominated supervisors had worked for several years in childcare services and had obtained an Early Childhood Certificate from a TAFE college. I later learnt that such workers would themselves fill the ranks of DEECD's authorised officers. Mainly women, these were committed workers that sought to protect and promote the best interests of Victoria's young. However, there were other comparisons between nominated supervisors and authorised officers. Both groups were overworked, under-resourced, and underpaid. If money was to be made in early learning, it would flow through to the likes of ABC Learning's Eddy Groves. Workers and bureaucrats were motivated by intrinsic rather than financial returns.

Dealing with passionate people can be difficult, particularly if they have an arsenal of rights and powers at their disposal. I knew that from my ASC days. In that previous life, I had issued notices for books and records and compulsory examinations almost at will. Authorised officers under the Children's Services Act had similar powers. They could compel answers to questions.

I knew enough to know that dealing with DEECD on a day-to-day basis would require tact and diplomacy. Ms Ma had it. Indeed, her involvement had been mandated in the policies and procedures for each of Middle Kingdom's early learning centres. She was the first point of contact for each manager. If she did not herself communicate with the department, then she would at least have known what the issue was and provide the wisdom of her twenty years' experience. Yet, more often than not, she was on the phone to DEECD, explaining, negotiating, helping and protecting not just the 2500 odd children in our collective care, but the name and reputation of Middle Kingdom.

Even if I had the time, I was never inclined to follow in Ms Ma's footsteps. Indeed, that was not the expectation. Instead, my role on Middle Kingdom's executive leadership team was to lend support and provide direction to the various centre managers when requested. Most of the time, my services were sought in response to complaints from parents. However, each early learning centre underwent an annual inspection by DEECD authorised officers. Their focus was mainly on staffing levels, security arrangements and general cleanliness. For the most part, the feedback was constructive, but I do recall one incident where an authorised officer insisted on the removal of a 'dead' tree from a children's play area. That requirement was only withdrawn when I politely explained, in formal correspondence to the department, the meaning of the word 'deciduous.'

Even after the appointment of Middle Kingdom's new managing director, Dr Danny Chan, I made it a point to attend each DEECD visit, and I was authorised by the board to act as a negotiator. Site inspections often resulted in demands for costly operational improvements, and, thankfully, I had the delegated authority to approve operational expenditure up to $50,000.

In truth, I could count on one hand the number of times I actually approved expenditure. In reality, most finance decisions were worked out in consultation with Winston, Martin and the new managing director. As a matter of practice, I was no substitute for the old managing director. I felt I was tinkering at the edges of executive decision-making. More importantly, it was pretty evident that we had collectively failed to mitigate the loss of Ms Ma.

Two months after Ms Ma's departure, the full force of the credit crunch took effect. As Martin predicted, the Middle Kingdom share price dramatically fell as enrolments tumbled. Parents who had lost jobs could no longer afford or simply no longer required early learning services. Cutbacks on overtime meant that household priorities were reassessed. Grandparents had replaced outside service providers as primary day time carers. Families were doing everything possible to save a dollar or two. The demise of Middle Kingdom Ltd and its early learning centres had begun.

Chapter Twenty-Three
The Project

The jaggedly picturesque Strathbogie Ranges are just a couple of hours north of Melbourne. I cannot now recall when Winston agreed to plunge significant funds into a large olive plantation business in the area. Regardless, like many of Winston's pet projects, it was a rushed decision that we would live to regret.

The ownership structure of the Strathbogie olive business was complicated. Investors would neither own the land nor directly hold shares in the syndicate, but financial returns were solely dependent on the success or failure of cultivating olive trees. Further, the business was a closed investment with a committed sum payable over three capital calls. Such industry jargon was just a fancy way of saying that the venture was a one-off deal and that its trustee would hit us for three equal payments covering the total investment sum. The trustees, so I was told, had agreed to Winston's request to allow our clients to contribute under the Lee Family Office subscription.

The Lee Family Office's financial services licence authorised us to operate 'investor directed portfolio services,' commonly referred to within the industry by its acronym, 'IDPS.' An IDPS is a generic term that covers platform operators, wrap accounts, and master funds. Broadly speaking, the arrangement allows investors to manage and retain control of their portfolio and access a range of different investments. At the same time, the IDPS operator commonly provides investors with custodial, transactional, and reporting services.

Over the years, the Lee Family Office provided numerous investment opportunities that were structured as an IDPS, and the clients loved them. By pooling client monies together, the Lee Family Office was able to access financial products that would usually be restricted to institutional funds. Clients could grab a piece of the investment action and rely on our accountants and custody staff to handle the large and often complex administrative requirements that accompanied such transactions.

As far as the regulator was concerned, operators could either register each IDPS as a registered managed investment scheme or rely on ASIC 're ief.' The problem with those two options was that both invoked significant disclosure and audit obligations, and, in the case of the former, specific registration with the ASIC. Oh, how Mr Gladstone would have loved an IDPS. Still, if you bothered to read the managed investments provisions of the Corporations Act carefully, there was a third alternative. Provided an IPDS was limited to wholesale investor monies, or no more than a total of $2 million from twenty retail investors, then the arrangement was excluded from IDPS regulation. Like so much of the Lee Family Office's financial service offerings, the wholesale client test was our regulatory escape.

Our stake in the Strathbogie olive business was structured as an IDPS. Formally known as the Olive Bend Syndicate, or casually referred to as Project Olive Oil, the IDPS attracted reasonable client interest. Following consultations with Lee Family Office client advisers, three Lee family members invested in their own names, two through corporate trustees of family trusts. Stephen Powell and several non-family clients invested through their respective companies, including a couple of non-family clients who subscribed through their self-managed superannuation funds. All up, the aggregate subscription was nearly $9 million. It was a substantial investment, but our other IDPSs had attracted more investment funds. As each client had either contributed more than $500,000 or was covered by a wealthy investor certificate, all nine clients were, so I believed, wholesale investors. Therefore, I was confident that Project Olive Oil was unlikely to attract the attention of the regulator.

The first two capital calls came very quickly. One was for the leasing of the land and project set-up costs, and the second for the purchase of plant and equipment. I do not believe I ever fully appreciated what makes a plantation grow. Still, I reasoned it could not involve much more than top-quality seeds, fit for purpose yellow equipment, suitably trained horticulturalists, a fair array of Orica insecticides, and good old Aussie sunlight. The third capital call came about a year into the project. Initially, the call had been scheduled to facilitate the first harvest of fruit, but that was some three to five years away.

Olives flourish where there is good drainage, coupled with hot, dry summers and cool winters. In theory, the Mediterranean-like climate of the Strathbogie Ranges provided an ideal environment for setting up an olive crop. However, you have to maintain the shape and health of each olive tree through fertilising, watering, and pruning. It was clear that there were several related problems with the project. First, young olive trees require extensive watering but the drought that had swept through most of southern

Australia had restricted supply. Secondly, the irrigation channels were inadequate through dubious design and poor quality soil. Finally, the experience and skills of the management company that had been engaged to cultivate acres of supposedly 'prime' land were questionable. It was all a recipe for disaster.

Martin was the first to realise that all was not well. As an unlisted investment, the Lee Family Office was reliant on the valuations of the business provided by the trustee of the operation. It was believed that the carrying value of the investment would be at cost, at least until the first harvest. Unfortunately, shortly after the third capital call, the trustees' quarterly updates dried up and their management accounts raised more questions, particularly around expenses. The notes to one set of management accounts indicated, albeit somewhat vaguely, that the carrying cost was 'optimistic.' Martin's telephone calls and e-mails to the trustees went unanswered, while Winston heard through the grapevine that the management company had abandoned ship due to unpaid management fees.

'Yes, it was the grapevine,' I heard Winston say. 'Because there's no fucking olive vines to talk about.'

The extent of the Olive Bend Syndicate's problems was confirmed one hot, sticky February afternoon. Winston, who would rather have been swinging his three iron around the Huntingdale Golf Course, found himself in country Victoria thumping on the locked front door of the recently vacated offices of the trustee. His subsequent site visit confirmed our worst fears. The land had never been properly or fully cultivated. The earth was parched and dry and littered with old, rusted farm machinery and pieces of plastic irrigation pipes. Few of the olive trees were more than the size of a pot plant. Scores of plants were dead, broken or otherwise unloved. Many had not even been planted. Yet, the adjacent fields of flourishing grapes, wheat, triticale, and oats told a different story. Quite simply, the geological and climatic problems could not in themselves account for the demise of the project.

'How did this happen?' I asked Martin. 'What do we know of those trustees? Didn't we do any commercial due diligence?'

Martin gave me a sheepish look before replying, 'Don't go there, Greg, and you're asking the wrong question. The question is, how are we going to square this with our clients. Their $9 million won't even produce one bottle of extra virgin olive oil.'

Later, I overheard an interchange between Winston and his father. Alfred, in no uncertain terms, suggested that former Scotch College classmates do not necessarily make the best of business partners. I also heard, in his disparaging tone, something about business plans being drafted on the back of coasters at the nineteenth hole. The fact that Winston's response was solely in Cantonese indicated that father and son were in a heated debate.

To be fair, the due diligence process was not as limited as Alfred suggested. True, the commercial and operational focus had been found wanting, and that would likely return to bite us. However, I had been asked to review the constituent legal documents of the project before our client advisers approached clients. The trust deed was a standard unit trust document drafted by a reputable mid-tier law firm. The information memorandum that set out the benefits and risks of the investment, along with pricing and the application had been carefully drafted and included the required general advice warnings. The trustees appeared to have the correct authorisation under their financial services licence, and our credit, bankruptcy and personal property securities register checks produced no adverse findings. The information memorandum stated that a related party of the trustees owned the property. My title searches confirmed that claim. Nothing in my legal due diligence process raised any red flags. The problem with the project was not its legal set-up or structure, and, from the Lee Family Office viewpoint, the project's failings were squarely within Winston's domain.

At Alfred's initiative, Winston and Martin held meetings with each of the nine client investors. Those were not easy meetings and serious questions of the Lee Family Office's due diligence process were raised. Indeed, Alfred was called in on at least two occasions to gently persuade clients that, notwithstanding the Olive Bend Syndicate hiccup, their long-term financial interests were best served by the Lee Family Office.

Alas, the collective efforts of Alfred, Winston and Martin fell short. Several clients sought, in somewhat colourful language, compensation for their loss. Winston's eventual total offer of $3 million was not sufficient for at least a couple of the clients who closed all their accounts and dealings with the Lee Family Office. Indeed, all clients expressed displeasure, except Stephen Powell, who took personal responsibility for his own decision-making and loss.

Over the coming months, we waited with bated breath as to what the former clients would do next. At the very least, we expected a writ of summons and statement of claim from one or more of them. We notified our insurance broker and literally sat back and contemplated the inevitable. However, what we got were formal notices from ASIC. Rather than waste their own money, one of the former clients had lodged a formal complaint with ASIC. I gathered from Winston it was one of the self-managed superannuation fund trustees, although that did not elicit any immediate alarm bells.

Looking back, I was surprised that the regulator had commenced an investigation into the Olive Bend Syndicate. ASIC had never shown a propensity to protect wealthy investors and could easily have written the matter off. After all, Winston had been running the project and, by any reasonable standard, his lack of proper due diligence could readily be held to be negligent. The complainant could, therefore, take civil recovery action themselves.

The regulator's notices to produce books, which were served on the company and Winston personally, supported my conclusion that the focus of concern was squarely limited to issues of Winston's competence. Indeed, at the time, I mentioned to Martin that I was worried that Winston had compromised our ability to hold a financial services licence. Ever the diplomat, Martin advised me to keep my views quiet.

Of course, we responded to the regulator's notices to produce every item of correspondence, every board minute and every Lee Fund and bank statement that in any way, shape or form referred to the Olive Bend Syndicate. My IDPS compliance spreadsheets were handed over, together with the management accounts supplied by the trustees of the project.

In truth, we probably provided documents that were not strictly covered by the notice. Martin and I agreed that a limited response to the notice might draw attention to the gaping due diligence hole. Our idea, therefore, was to swamp the regulator with our books and records. Given the nature of the investigation, its low priority, and the limited resources that ASIC would have assigned to the case, the approach seemed sensible. With a bit of luck, the sheer volume of material would overwhelm ASIC's junior investigators, who would seek to close the file at the earliest opportunity.

I had mixed emotions when we heard that Winston had been called to attend a compulsory examination at ASIC's new Collins Street offices. On the one hand, it was clear ASIC was not readily prepared to close its investigation file. On the other hand, I took pleasure from the fact that the culprit for our woes had been singled out and called to account. I quietly smirked the day Winston and his old Scotch College classmate, then an eminent QC, left for their date with the regulator.

A few hours later, Winston returned looking somewhat shaken and tired. He had plainly received a grilling. Martin asked how the examination had gone. Winston slowly raised his head, took one look at Martin and then at me.

'Can't say anything,' he said. 'Confidentiality orders and all that. Mason here knows all about that, don't you?'

Winston spoke in an unusually subdued and reserved tone. Yet, he was correct, and I agreed with him. However, I was a little surprised that he was so willing to comply with a regulatory direction, particularly given his usual selective approach to law and order. Perhaps the ASIC examination had taught Winston a valuable lesson in professionalism. Unfortunately, the next chapter in the Project Olive Oil saga would prove me wrong.

Chapter Twenty-Four
The Escape

They were extraordinary times, and something had to give. For months I had assumed that the financial impact of the global financial crisis would be Middle Kingdom's Achilles' Heel. To my surprise, that was not the case. What did give way was a wonky service door at the White Horse Early Learning Centre in the eastern Melbourne suburb of Box Hill. In hindsight, the repercussions would have been minimal but for a basic design fault in the entrance area of the centre, unseasonal weather, and the absence of a full complement of staff.

It was towards the end of a working week when the manager of the centre received a telephone call from a highly agitated parent. The parent advised that her child, together with her four-year-old friend, were playing happily at home in the back garden with her daughter's new tricycle. Those facts were hardly alarming and would not in themselves cause agitation to a reasonable parent. However, as the manager immediately realised, both children had attended the centre that day, and according to the timetable, should have been participating in a painting activity in the classroom next door at that very moment.

The parent's distress was both obvious and warranted. Having escaped from the centre, the two children negotiated a busy arterial road, traversed a nearby park and creek, and most likely skipped along a deserted back alley en route to the family home. Thankfully, both children were in good health and spirit and had no appreciation of the dangers they might have faced. For the then highly stressed manager, that was good news. The bad or rather disturbing news was that the children had, according to the parent, merely pushed open a door to effect their escape. Given the two-kilometre distance between the school and home, the two escape artists must have been gone for a good hour or two. No one noticed the inviting open door, let alone the two missing children.

There was immediate work to be done. A headcount was hastily conducted, and the problem service door was promptly identified. Thankfully, all other children were accounted for, and the manner of the escape was readily explained.

The service door itself opened outwards to a small laneway to the side of the centre where the rubbish and recycling bins were usually positioned. The lane led to a small gate that was mainly for show rather than security. Therefore, the door needed to be firmly closed when not in use. The door itself was of a self-closing variety, with the top of the door attached to the doorframe with a robust hydraulic closing mechanism. The doorknob was deliberately positioned and structured so that a small child could not ordinarily reach or turn the knob. Unfortunately, either the spring had weakened, or the fluid in the closer had leaked. Whatever the reason, the closing mechanism did not function properly. Further, the cedar door itself had expanded due to unusual high temperatures. The result was that the door did not close properly. It rested on the edge of its frame. In that position, the door was no barrier to even the small hands of a couple of four-year-olds.

Of course, the question remained as to why the malfunctioning door had not been noticed. In part, the answer lay with the staff member who last used the door. Cleaning usually required two full-time employees, but due to sickness and the absence of back-up staff, only one staff member had been assigned to cleaning duties. The cleaner was so busy she could not remember accessing the rubbish bins, let alone checking to see if the door had closed properly. Moreover, the door itself was effectively invisible from the main entrance due to a small partition wall and cupboard. It appeared that the original architect had deliberately obscured the rather unappealing exit. What the centre made up for in aesthetics and storage capacity it lost on surveillance capabilities.

To comply with the Education and Care Services National Law, a notification was sent to DEECD (a.k.a the department), and within a couple of days, two female authorised officers descended on the centre. They interviewed staff, checked the obligatory roster book to determine who was on duty, took photographs and statements, and in Winston's words, generally made a nuisance of themselves.

We knew DEECD would prosecute Middle Kingdom, or at least we all did except Winston. The situation was not unique. It would not be the first or last time a child would make a unilateral decision to leave a childcare or early learning facility. It was, nevertheless, completely understandable that the legislation and department took a zero-tolerance to such matters, and, as a matter of course, prosecuted the approved provider, in this case, Middle Kingdom. The department expected operators of early learning centres to adequately supervise children and take reasonable precautions to protect them from harm. By any usual standards, those expectations were uncontroversial. Yet, predictably, news of the prosecution infuriated Winston, and he made his feelings known at a hastily convened board meeting.

'We've done all we could reasonably be expected to do. We've provided facilities that have made escape difficult. If there is a failure, then it squarely rests with the manager and the staff involved. What's your take on this, Greg?'

Given the circumstances, I would have been surprised if Middle Kingdom could escape vicarious liability. Usually, an employer is responsible for the conduct of employees who have acted within the scope of their employment. There was no suggestion that White Horse Early Learning Centre staff had acted outside their authority. Still, vicarious liability was not a topic I could provide off-the-cuff advice on, and I was about to admit as much. Nevertheless, before I could even open my mouth, Alfred had cut in.

'Winston, do you genuinely believe we've done everything we could? I don't think so. We know from Dr Chan that keeping up with maintenance across all centres is difficult, and the more we cut costs the more safety problems we will have. That is our problem.'

As Winston attempted to argue that there was a difference between doing everything reasonable and doing everything possible, Alfred quickly changed track.

'In any case, we stand behind our people. That's how the Lee family got its good name. There will be a fallout from this, and I refuse to make it worse by blaming our hard-working emp oyees.'

Alfred's response signalled the end of Winston's outburst and, of course, Alfred was right. There would be fallout. While the fine itself was only $200, the potential reputational damage was significant. Middle Kingdom's finances were precarious enough, without any adverse publicity. Martin, ever the astute observer, tried broaching the subject with Winston. I later asked Martin about Winston's reaction.

'He's got his bloody head in the sand,' was all Martin said.

Martin rarely swore, but when he did, it was usually for a good reason. *The Age* referred to the incident as the 'Great Escape,' and the *Herald Sun* would publish a three-column article under the heading: *Kids in danger at Chinese Kindies*.

Within days, Middle Kingdom's telephone lines were clogged with calls from concerned parents. For Middle Kingdom, the fear was that the media coverage would further decimate enrolments. Due to the global financial crisis, child numbers had already suffered significantly. In an attempt to limit the adverse repercussions, Winston, who by that time had obviously extracted his head from the sand, had drafted a media release and announcement to the Australian Stock Exchange.

'Any issues?' were the limits of his instructions as he dumped the draft documents into my in-tray. 'Oh, and we need board sign-off. Get a meeting arranged for this afternoon. I want this out by this evening.'

Of course, the contents and the truthfulness of the announcement were crucial. There were severe penalties under the Corporations Act for providing false or misleading statements to the market. I read both the media release and announcement very carefully and noted a predictably dry response with a good deal of corporate spin. There were comments about how concerned the officers of Middle Kingdom were by the incident and how Middle Kingdom's number one priority was the safety of children and staff. There were other statements about the robust quality of Middle Kingdom procedures and that incidents of that nature were extremely rare.

Amidst Winston's attempt to smooth over the unfortunate incident, there was one paragraph in both the media release and announcement that captured my attention. It read as follows:

Middle Kingdom officers take security breaches very seriously. Accordingly, we have commissioned forensic investigators to conduct a full controls review of our safety procedures and arrangements. All recommendations concerning the White Horse Early Learning Centre have been addressed and recommendations that concern Middle Kingdom's early learning centres as a whole will be implemented as a matter of urgency.

An external review was undoubtedly a good idea, even though Winston's motives would have had more to do with protecting Middle Kingdom's share price than a real concern for child safety.

Despite being company secretary, a forensic investigator's review was news to me. Of course, I was hardly surprised by the lack of consultation. My elevation to company secretary had not opened up my lines of communication with Winston. Yet, Winston was asking me to review public statements. It was not a time to keep quiet. Before I could sign-off, I had to be sure the statements were true.

Thankfully, I found Martin close by. He confirmed that Winston and Danny Chan had approached one of Winston's University of Melbourne buddies, who was by then a partner at KPMG. A review had, in fact, been commissioned and an interim report had been received, although neither Martin nor Danny had seen the document. So, there was no way I could avoid seeing Winston. I needed to know that the references to the KPMG report were complete and accurate.

I found Winston at his desk, staring at the ASX website. He was probably fixated on Middle Kingdom's declining share price. There was a definite air of uneasiness in the room.

'I hear KPMG has reported on the security problems at Box Hill and that they've been resolved. I take it you've got their interim report?'

'Yes, Greg,' he started with a deep but impatient sigh. 'I've got the KPMG report. I'm onto it. I'll table it at the board meeting.'

'Can I at least make a copy so that I can match it up to the public statements?'

'No. Not until I'm finished. I'm still going through it. You'll get a copy at the meeting. If you're worried about getting your precious board papers out, I'll deal with the board. We haven't got the luxury of time. They'll understand.'

'Winston. No. I'm not worried about the board paper timetable,' I replied almost apologetically. 'Of course, the matter is urgent. I just need to check the report itself, because the ASX and media releases explicitly reference a forensic investigation.'

'I know there's a reference. I wrote the damn things. Gee, what is it? What do you need to check?'

By then, the air of uneasiness had given way to outright hostility, but I had to know what KPMG had recommended, as well and what Middle Kingdom would be doing in response.

'Well,' I began. 'First off, I need to know if the Box Hill foyer has been fixed up. I am assuming that was a recommendation. Also, I need to know the status of the other safety recommendations. What's happening there?'

'Listen, Mason. I haven't got time for this.'

Winston's tone of voice was both aggressive and dismissive. I had overstepped his precious mark. However, he did at least stop looking at the ASX website and respond to my questions.

'Yes, KMPG recommended we fix up the foyer and the side gate. Of course, they looked at all the safety procedures. Child supervision, lifting and moving kids, staffing levels, quality of the kids' furniture, how often the floors are cleaned, even where the bloody fire extinguishers are located. You know, all the common hazards. There's a list of them here.' Winston pointed to the interim report. 'There'll be more details in the final report.'

'So I take it we have repaired the foyer and the gate? Are there any other recommendations that have been followed through?'

'Yes, yes and yes,' was the terse reply. Winston took a deep breath and continued. 'Yes, the door problems have been fixed. Yes, KPMG suggested changes to the incident reporting register, and yes, the changes have been made.'

Before I could even reply, Winston pointed to his door.

'Now shut it on your way out,' was all Winston said as he turned his gaze back to the ASX website.

If anybody else had spoken to me in the way Winston had, I would have been angry and upset. Yet, when I look back on that conversation, his behaviour was pretty typical of our many interactions. Indeed, I took comfort from the fact that I was not the only victim of Winston's wrath. On occasions, even Martin wasn't spared. Putting aside Winston's terse manner, my concerns about the public statement had been allayed by Winston's brief response. The White Horse Early Learning Centre had undergone physical repairs and implemented a safety recommendation.

I recall feeling assured as I closed Winston's office door that both statements were factually correct. I, therefore, fixed up a couple of spelling errors and circulated the documents to the board. A few hours later, both papers were approved by all directors with minor changes. There was little chance of serious opposition to any document drafted by Winston. By the close of business that evening, the announcement and media release had been faxed to the ASX and Australian Financial Review respectively.

In one respect, Winston was true to his word. He did circulate the KPMG interim report at the hastily convened board meeting. It appeared that a thorough review had been conducted at Box Hill. But the problem was that the interim report was limited to the White Horse Early Learning Centre. I, therefore, assumed the final report, with its recommendations for the entire cohort of early learning centres, would be imminent.

In hindsight, I should have picked up on what Winston didn't say, as much as what he did. At that time, I had understood Winston's comments to mean all problems with the foyer and side gate at Box Hill had been repaired. Indeed, KMPG's interim report mentioned the wonky service door in the context of the problem layout, but as later events would reveal, only the door itself had been repaired and not the side gate or the flaws in the design of the foyer. Of course, I now wish I had done more than just listen to Winston. At a minimum, I should have contacted the centre manager. I could have even taken a half-hour taxi ride to Box Hill and checked myself. My lack of due diligence would come back to haunt me.

Chapter Twenty-Five
The Fraud

Winston had received a complaint. $65,000 had gone missing from Stephen Powell's account with the Lee Fund. The funds had been paid to the Powell Family Foundation. As it turned out, the matter ended up being referred to me, since the complainant was not from Winston's immediate family or close friends.

My first port of call was James Powell, Stephen Powell's client adviser. James looked decidedly embarrassed and agitated when he advised it was just an oversight and that he would fix the problem.

'Yes, it's my mistake, Greg. A simple error. I'll get the money back to Stephen's personal account and discuss what he wants to do next.'

I listened to James in extreme discomfort. The brief explanation just made no sense. Why, I thought to myself, would Stephen Powell be so upset about donations being made to the wrong foundation? Since the Powell Pride Foundation, Stephen had established at least three further foundations. They were all controlled by him. It would be a simple job to transfer funds to the right entity, and our accountants were masters at fixing up errors with a few journal entries and reversals here and there.

Further, it was not like Stephen to complain. From what I could see, he enjoyed a very healthy working relationship with James. Nonetheless, I reasoned I should just record the matter as a complaint and have James confirm that the monies had been paid to the appropriate Stephen Powell account.

To this day, I do not know why I did not let go. Maybe it was the regulator in me. Perhaps I never really trusted James or was jealous of his domestic bliss. Whatever the reason, I ordered a full ASIC company extract on the 'Powell Family Foundation' from ASIC's national database. Less than five minutes later, I had the extract in front of me. It was a bombshell. My stomach rose to my throat, and I felt my heart pumping outside of my chest.

The Powell Family Foundation was not a Stephen Powell company at all. Of course, Stephen was upset; the Powell Family Foundation had nothing to do with him. The Powell Family Foundation was James Powell's company. James had set up a public company limited by guarantee with his wife and his eldest son as directors. All he had needed was to complete and lodge with ASIC an application form together with a constitution. He probably even copied the Powell Pride Foundation constitution.

To say the ASIC extract made my blood boil would be an understatement. At best, James Powell had lied or misused his position. At worst, he had attempted to steal $65,000 from Stephen Powell. That was my worst nightmare. No collusion was required. All James had needed to do was supply his foundation's bank account details to our accounts team and complete and sign a payment request form. After all, James was an authorised signatory on all Lee Fund accounts associated with Stephen Powell. In the absence of a 'call back' policy, James could move Stephen Powell's monies at will. Thankfully, Stephen had checked his statements. If it had been any other client, James would have got away with it.

I sat at my desk for maybe thirty minutes or so as the enormity of James's conduct sunk in. During that time, I went from disbelief to anger, and from disappointment to finally resolution. James Powell had to go. I should have handed the matter over to Winston or the HR Director, but by then I was on a mission. James would repay the money and leave, and, with that on my mind, I stormed into his office and slammed his door so hard the hinges shook.

'What's wrong, Greg? Not happy? If this is about the Powell Pride Foundation, I've handled it. The money has been repaid.'

'No, not that foundation. The Powell Family Foundation. Your bloody company!' And with that, I threw the ASIC extract on his desk.

James never even took a second glance at the document, although his grin promptly turned into a stern frown.

Finally, he raised his head and in a slow, deliberate voice said, 'I see.'

'Well, what are you going to do? Resign, I trust, because my next conversation's with Winston.'

'No, it's not,' came the even more deliberate and this time menacing response.

'Are you threatening me or what?'

'I don't have to, mate, because you're not saying a thing.'

For a few moments, I could not work out whether James was bullying or attempting to blackmail me. I quickly realised it was the latter.

'You're not saying a thing,' James repeated. 'Not what you've done.' I was confused and practically speechless. I had no idea what I had done that could compel my silence. James needed to explain, and he needed to do so fast.

'What the hell are you talking about?'

'You won't be saying anything. So that you know, I used a power of attorney to set up a bank account for my foundation. You know the one. The power of attorney with Lucy's signature that you witnessed when she wasn't here. Well, surprise, surprise she knows nothing about the bank account or of the foundation. In fact, she knows sod all about the power of attorney.'

By then, I was in a daze as James appeared to leave the best bombshell to last.

'I also used that power of attorney to mortgage the house. Christ, there's no way else I could have repaid sixty-five grand.'

'And Lucy? What does she say?'

'Aren't you listening? She knows nothing, mate, and you're not telling her.'

That miserable excuse for a human being smugly finished with, 'If you take this further, then it's you and me both. I won't be going alone.'

He was right. I would lose as much as him, maybe more. My job and practising certificate were on the line. I tried to recall what Lucy had said when I had phoned her all those months ago. I couldn't remember her exact words, although it was only a short call. I remembered that she was agitated and in no mood to chat. There was talk of the credit card applications, but that was it. I had no recollection of us mentioning the power of attorney.

I left James Powell's office wholly stunned. My God, I thought, if I dobbed him in he would immediately retaliate with evidence of my professional misconduct. So, instead of standing up and taking the high moral ground, I compounded my misconduct by saying nothing and shredding the ASIC company extract. After all, Stephen Powell had his money back and the complaint had been withdrawn.

I never spoke directly to James again, or at least not until near the end. Weeks later, fate intervened. One morning, an e-mail to all staff was circulated.

Good morning,

Yesterday James Powell tendered his resignation and has decided to rethink his career options. James joined us as an accountant ten years ago working with a focus on high net worth and philanthropic clients.

There will be no formal presentation. However, his team will arrange an appropriate farewell.

We thank James for his years of service and wish him well in his future endeavours.

Winston Lee

So that was that. In fact, James left that very same day on 'gardening leave,' which was ironic given he had never mown a lawn or weeded a garden bed in his life. Gardening leave was granted when the employee was taking up a position with a competitor. The leave minimised the risks of outgoing staff taking confidential information with them that may be used by the new employer.

Months later, I found out that James was working for a suburban accountant, primarily doing tax and compliance work for self-managed superannuation funds. It was strange that his new firm would rank as a Lee family competitor, but that was that. James had left the building and good riddance. Nonetheless, I continued to reflect on why James had attempted what, in retrospect, appeared to be a rather crude deception.

I had heard that James and Lucy had been struck hard by the global financial crisis, but that was only part of the problem. Lucy did lose her job at Macquarie Bank, but she was soon snatched up by Deutsche Bank. The problem could not be blamed on either Lucy or the state of the economy. James's real problem, as I heard on the rumour mill, was gambling.

So, I was told, James was frequently seen at Crown Casino, be it on the pokie machines or at the roulette table. I thought back to that meeting with James in my office and his tale of financial woe. It was not hard to do so. I should have insisted Lucy sign her credit card application and the power of attorney in my presence. My conduct that day had hardly been a beacon of professionalism. What I remembered most was James's comment that he was arriving home late, and his reticence or inability to explain why. Of course, there was me believing that his problems arose from a heavy workload or unreasonable client demands. There was no suggestion that the Powell family's financial difficulties had been self-induced.

What a fool I had been, or rather James had played me for a fool. He may well have had evening engagements, but evidently, those appointments were with croupiers rather than clients. I hoped his brush with criminality had taught him a valuable lesson, although, by the sound of things, he was a hopeless addict. Poor Lucy and the kids, I thought to myself.

Chapter Twenty-Six
The Risks

As the globa financial crisis deepened, Middle Kingdom's revenue declined, as did its cash flow and ability to pay creditors. Cost savings were identified and the first to suffer were casual and part-time staff. Statistically, the number of person-hours across the centres were decreased by ten per cent in the space of a single month. Staffing levels barely met the legally prescribed ratios. Thankfully, the Lee Office Family was a steadfast ally. Middle Kingdom was regularly provided with financial accommodation through short-term loans approved by Winston and Martin.

By that time, Ms Ma had bid farewell for her new life in Horg Kong, but our collective memory of her remained vivid. Her knowledge of the industry and Middle Kingdom operations had been second to none. Her dynamism and professionalism had been addictive. She was a great loss across all levels of the organisation. She had been a trusted adviser to the directors and an astute manager of her workforce. Sure, Danny Chan was suitably qualified, but he lacked Ms Ma's experience. The loss of Ms Ma posed a significant risk to the ongoing operations of Middle Kingdom.

The implications of Ms Ma's exit were not lost on the directors, or rather, the directors were keen to understand the repercussions.

Over the following months, the audit and risk committee became increasingly worried about the efficiency of the early learning centres and quality of care. Danny Chan's quarterly reports were progressively littered with examples of client complaints, under-performing staff, maintenance concerns, and his futile attempts to improve enrolments.

The adverse publicity stemming from the two Box Hill escapees merely compounded the directors' concerns, but there appeared to be no plan B. Did the board really think that somehow, magically, the company would turn the corner and restore profits to the levels witnessed in the glory days of Ms Ma? Of course not, but I expect much of the continuing inertia was due to the presence of Alfred. Directors were fully aware of his passion and zeal and the circumstances that gave rise to his involvement in early childhood education. How can you recommend the closure of Middle Kingdom early learning centres when so many of the children were the descendants of boat people? Alfred had been one of the few to look after the children from the refugee camps. He would not desert the grandchildren.

Slowly, though, the need for change was overwhelming. While Alfred's passion for early learning was remarkable, so was his ability to read a set of management accounts. Even he began referring to potential 'cutbacks' and 'closures,' although he always qualified his comments with the words 'I deeply regret.'

It was in that environment that the audit and risk committee charged management with the responsibility of conducting a comprehensive risk review across Middle Kingdom, with a report to be lodged within three months. Initially, the committee had been keen to outsource the review, but Winston, who was in attendance at the meeting, readily offered up the services of Lee Family Office senior management.

I was chosen to establish and oversee the risk review. I was to lead a small team that included Martin, the HR manager, and the chief operating officer of the Lee Family Office. To be honest, I was quietly pleased just to be involved, let alone in charge. The review was of practical importance for Middle Kingdom, although I understood it could be used to justify closures of underperforming centres. Nonetheless, the risk review was no self-serving exercise. Cutbacks and closures were not the sole options, and the committee welcomed concrete commercial alternatives.

The nature and extent of my participation in the risk review involved more than just providing the board with information and advice. Risk identification and assessment are by their nature subjective. My formulations, characterisations and judgements of Middle Kingdom's risks would have a lasting impact on business operations.

'Mr Mason, you're heading up a project that will have a substantial bearing on how Middle Kingdom and its centres will conduct their operations,' noted the committee chairman at the time. 'We're relying on your wisdom.'

I left the committee meeting on a high. As a member of the executive leadership team, I had instigated and approved several operational improvements. However, the risk review was, as Lena would have said, a different kettle of worms. I had been approached to participate in significant commercial decision-making. Whether or not Winston would now recognise me as a business facilitator rather than business preventer was another issue. Regardless, I should give Winston his due. After all, he volunteered me for the role.

Together, the review team established broad categories of risk to cover legal, operations, people, financial, and shareholders.

Martin headed up the review of financial risk, particularly those surrounding tax, creditors, cash flow, and financial delegations. The HR Manager focussed on the people category, including payroll, unfair dismissal claims, and rates of sick leave. She even instigated an employee satisfaction survey. Together with the Lee Family Office's chief operating officer, I handled the other categories.

Our collective enquiries included interviewing all thirty-four early learning centre managers, managing director Danny Chan, and the company auditor. We reviewed the numerous registers and record-keeping requirements under the Education and Care Services National Law, conducted physical inspections, and reviewed samples of client agreements. Back at the office, I reviewed all leasing arrangements and material contracts, ASX listing rules, and spoke with the share registry.

Our approach to risk assessment was hardly novel. It deliberately followed the professional standard on risk management. At the heart of the risk assessment process was a matrix by which we could characterise each identified risk as either negligible, low, medium, high, or extreme based on an assessment of the likelihood of occurrence and its potential impact on the organisation. Of course, such assessments themselves were highly subjective, and the team's determinations would necessarily shape the audit and risk committee's response.

A couple of months and several hundred identified risks later, our findings were presented in a spreadsheet. Most identified risks were either negligible or low risk. The risk of not paying Middle Kingdom staff was negligible, given the Lee Family Office's involvement in the payroll process and the fact it provided financial accommodation. The individual early learning centres doggedly complied with the policies and procedures established by Ms Ma. Child enrolment and attendance records, child assessment evaluations, registers of teaching staff (or family day educators as they were formally known), were, by and large, complete and accurate. Without exception, the manager of each centre had continued to demand compliance with record-keeping and process requirements. In short, we uncovered a robust corporate culture. In turn, the strength of that culture diminished the legal risk of potential corporate liability.

However, more worrying risks were identified. Privacy and data security were a moderate risk given Middle Kingdom's antiquated IT systems and an increasingly onerous regulatory environment. Nonetheless, the more serious risks mainly arose from ongoing problems with cash flow and the demands of creditors. The fact that invoices would eventually be paid was not the only issue. The failure to meet payment deadlines caused potential reputational damage. Several suppliers had demanded cash on delivery terms, and the primary cleaning service had declined an extension of their contract on the grounds of late payments. Indeed, a few centre managers and deputies had been forced to use their own credit cards to purchase necessary supplies.

The centre managers were particularly concerned about the physical condition of their premises and provided numerous examples of where basic maintenance programs had been delayed or shelved. Our spreadsheet noted a litany of faults from a leaking roof at Sunshine, and a broken window at Gee ong, to a lifeless air-conditioner at Bendigo. In themselves, we believed that none of those faults constituted more than a low risk, but collectively the likelihood of harm to children or staff was more significant. Accordingly, the risk of inadequate maintenance was assessed as a medium people risk.

Unsurprisingly, one could not disassociate maintenance problems from the events at the White Horse Early Learning Centre. During the review, Danny Chan confirmed that a final report into the safety controls would not be forthcoming. I was told that Winston had balked at the cost of KPMG's services and unilaterally cancelled any further forensic investigation work. That worried me, not just from a broad safety angle, but from the public statements we had made, particularly to the ASX. It was also clear from our inspection of the White Horse Early Learning Centre that the problem foyer had not been revamped and that the side gate remained unsecured. Accordingly, we identified the contents of the company announcement to the ASX as a medium legal risk. Thankfully, at least the wonky service door had been fixed.

But the most severe identifiable risks focussed on the quality of staff morale. Reductions in staff numbers was merely one issue. Cost savings had diminished the funds available for staff training and development. The centre managers and other senior workers expressed concerns about the lack of leadership following Ms Ma's departure. In short, staff were overworked, undersupervised, and under stress. Staff confidence had hit an all-time low. Put another way, the risk of poor staff morale was high.

Of course, risk identification and assessment were just part of the review process. The next task was to summarise the findings and to present recommendations in the form of a report. In particular, the audit and risk committee expected a detailed timetable of proposals designed to manage the impact of all but the negligible and low risks. That would not be an easy task. I was particularly concerned, given Danny Chan was consistently in my office asking for feedback on the review. I suspect Danny had a good appreciation of how far staff morale had collapsed under his watch.

It turned out that my anxiety was misplaced. As the deadline for presenting the draft review to the audit and risk committee approached, the matter was partially taken out of my hands. Early one morning, I was summoned into Winston's office, who instructed me to close the door. That directive, combined with the fact that Martin was already in the room, were ominous.

'Good morning, Greg,' began Winston in an unusually pensive tone.

'Yeah, good morning, Winston, Martin. What's up?'

'Your risk review. Martin tells me that all the hard work has been done and you're working on the conclusions?'

'Yes,' I replied while thinking that Winston's almost apologetic tone of voice was bizarre. 'Yes, I am working on it, but I'll be sitting down with Martin and the other two on the team before it's finalised.'

'Don't,' came the prompt response. I was immediately perplexed and looked at Martin for direction, yet the chief financial officer deliberately avoided my gaze and said nothing.

'What's going on? I'm obviously missing something.'

'Look, Greg,' Winston continued in the same tenor. 'I understand you've identified insolvency as a minor risk, and you'll be recommending amendments to the funding process and financial delegations of the centre managers.'

'Again, you're right, these matters are being considered, but I wouldn't be presenting anything without Martin's input.'

It was at that juncture that Martin suddenly entered into the conversation.

'Insolvency—we have it as a moderate risk, right?' asked Martin.

I nodded.

'Actually,' he continued. 'It's a major, sorry, extreme risk.'

'Come on, Martin,' I replied dismissively. 'You know full well that insolvency isn't proved by temporary liquidity problems or just by looking at a balance sheet and comparing assets and liabilities. It's a real practical test. Can the company pay its debts when they become due and payable? Sure, there have been complaints and extensions of deadlines, but the Lee Family Office is always there for financial support.'

'Well, that's been the situation so far,' interrupted Winston, 'but there are limits on our appetite to bankroll Middle Kingdom's operations.'

I paused to reflect on this unseen development. It did not take me long to appreciate the seriousness of the situation. I took a deep breath as Winston continued.

'The Lee Family Office directors met yesterday and agreed that Middle Kingdom is an unacceptable drain on resources. We're getting some external advice. The main aim is to avoid voluntary administration, and, of course, the reputational damage that would flow.'

So, the main goal is to save face and stuff the hundred-plus workers who are stressed enough as it is. My God, I thought to myself, if Winston is talking like this, he must have his father's approval. I had read the recent management reports, but the situation was more dire than I had appreciated. I said nothing and dutifully continued listening.

'In the circumstances, there cannot be any references to funding. No references at all to insolvency or funding; pull them all. Also, pull out Martin's financial section in its entirety, well, all but the insurance risks. The committee is smart. There'll be looking to see an insolvency risk under financials, but if the section's not there, they won't be concerned.'

The Middle Kingdom audit and risk committee might not be concerned, but by that stage of the conversation, I most certainly was.

'Winston,' I interrupted. 'You have to tell the Middle Kingdom board. We've had this conversation before. I've told you that you'll be seen as an executive officer. You're the directing mind and will of the company. If you know Lee Family Office funds are drying up then you have a duty to inform Middle Kingdom fully, and...' I said almost as an afterthought, 'a duty of disclosure to the market.'

'No, I haven't,' replied Winston in a much louder voice. 'The Lee Family Office board has demanded this matter be kept strictly confidential. We're only letting you know to avoid any embarrassment with the risk review.'

'Great, thanks for letting me know,' I said sarcastically. 'Not only do you have directly competing duties, but you've placed me in a catch-22 situation. I'm inside the tent now. How can I give legal advice to both entities? How can I continue to satisfy my professional conduct obligations?' These were rhetorical questions. I did not expect a reply but received one anyway.

'Gee, I hadn't thought of that. It's ironic.'

'Really?' I replied sarcastically. 'What, perhaps, is ironic,' I continued to venture, 'is the fact that the whole need for the review is because of Middle Kingdom's precarious financial state. So we're now excluding the very matters that were crucial in the first place. What do you want me to say to the committee? How am I going to explain this?'

'Point taken, Greg,' replied Winston in a much calmer tone. 'Leave the committee to me. I'll deal with them.'

By that time, Martin had heard enough, particularly as my conversation with Winston had been heading off on a tangent.

'Greg. I was at yesterday's board meeting. I haven't done the minutes as yet. I'll check my notes, but I believe the funding decision is not quite as definite as you probably think it is.'

It was one of the few occasions that I suspected that Martin was economical with the truth. Martin continued in the same vein as if to reinforce his assertions.

'Sure, there are underlying concerns and we're exploring options, but nothing's fully decided. Nothing. The tap hasn't been closed,' he said, looking to Winston for reassurance. Winston did not disappoint.

'The Lee Family Office governance practices are tip-top. I know my director's duties. We might only be an unlisted company, but we follow the ASX principles just like Middle Kingdom. I would immediately declare my interest and leave the room if we were going to stop funding.'

I was not convinced by either Martin's summary of the directors' discussion or Winston's claim that he took his duties seriously. Although, I did draw comfort from the fact that Martin had not yet drafted the minutes of the board meeting. I suggested to Martin that the minutes simply state that the Lee Family Office directors discussed the affairs of Middle Kingdom and its early learning centres. Nothing else should be reduced to writing. Winston and Martin merely nodded and thanked me for my input.

As I left the room, Winston and Martin appeared to commence an intense conversation. I could not hear their words, but I concluded that they had a lot of back-pedalling to go. I had no doubt that a decision to curtail, if not cease funding, had already been made. The implications for the business were all too obvious and I quickly upgraded the risk of employees not being paid. If my conversation with Winston had taught him anything, it was that the journey of winding up Middle Kingdom and his role in the process would need to be managed carefully. ASIC was increasingly prepared to prosecute directors for trading whilst insolvent. I was glad I was not Winston's personal lawyer.

It was only later that I seriously reflected on my dual position as Middle Kingdom company secretary and in-house lawyer. Did I truly have a problem? To be honest, Dear Reader, I was not sure.

On the one hand, as company secretary, I had fiduciary duties as an officer of Middle Kingdom. While the majority of functions were administrative, such as filing reports, did the role of the secretary, as the gatekeeper of good governance, compel disclosure? Surely, the efficacy of good governance, for which I was responsible, was in part dependent on its officers providing full and honest disclosure of matters relevant to the company. Even though Winston and Martin had provided few but confusing particulars, there was no doubt in my mind that the days of Middle Kingdom's reliance on the Lee Family Office were numbered. Did I, as company secretary, have a positive obligation to inform the Middle Kingdom board, or was it just hypocrisy to refrain from doing so? To be honest, the more I contemplated my secretarial duties the more I became confused.

On the other hand, I was fully aware that I had fiduciary duties as a lawyer to both the Lee Family Office and Middle Kingdom, including acting in good faith and with absolute fairness and openness towards each client. I also had an ethical obligation to comply with the professional conduct rules that bind solicitors generally. In particular, I had a positive duty to avoid conflicts of interest between clients. That much was clear, but applying those duties to the situation at hand troubled me.

If I did describe my conversation with Winston and Martin to, say Middle Kingdom's Chairman, the disclosure would be to the benefit of Middle Kingdom and not the Lee Family Office. My conduct would be a clear breach of my lawyer's duty of confidentiality to the Lee Family Office. But, even if funding to Middle Kingdom had ceased, I would only have a conflict if I had been asked to provide legal advice on insolvency. In those circumstances, the dutiful response would be to refuse to act for both entities. As it turned out though, I was not called on to provide advice on such a topic.

I wondered if recent developments on legal or client professional privilege were relevant. In truth, I had never taken more than a passing interest in the topic given the Lee Family Office's reluctance to litigate. However, I understood that legal professional privilege was designed to protect free and frank confidential communications between a client and lawyer (provided those communications were made for the dominant purpose of providing legal advice, or for use in existing or likely legal proceedings). If the dominant purpose was satisfied then such communications would remain strictly confidential.

Over the years, I had attended numerous continuing professional development seminars. Invariably, there was always advice on protecting legal professional privilege. There was no silver bullet as such, but 'independence' was the key word. The lawyer, in providing advice, had to be seen and act independently of any non-legal roles they may occupy.

I dutifully maintained a current practising certificate, kept separate files for legal and non-legal work functions and maintained a confidential drive on the IT network for purely legal matters. Each legal advice commenced with the following disclaimer:

This document is confidential and subject to legal professional privilege. It has been prepared for the purpose of providing legal advice. The document is for internal privileged use only and not to be forwarded or circulated without the approval of Legal Counsel.

Finally, I signed each legal advice in my capacity as legal counsel. All these measures sought to evidence an independent lawyer-client relationship. But did I really have such a relationship with the Lee Family Office? How could an employee be genuinely independent of his or her employer?

A seminar on the Federal Court case of *Archer Capital v Sage* was more than opportune; it was encouraging. The court had acknowledged that 'independence' was already built into the professional relationship between an in-house lawyer and employer. Provided a person was recruited as a lawyer and consulted in a professional capacity to provide legal advice, that advice would be privileged.

That little phrase 'consulted in a professional capacity' made all the difference. So long as I was consulted in my professional capacity as a lawyer, privilege would attach to my communications. Put another way, if I was consulted in a different role, say as company secretary or risk manager, privilege would not attach. In other words, the courts had recognised that an in-house lawyer could have multiple roles within their employment. For each separate task, the trick was to identify the particular role one was performing. Great, I thought to myself, I was not asked to conduct the risk review in the role of either lawyer or company secretary. I was only asked to take charge when Winston mentioned to the audit and risk committee that I had relevant experience through my involvement in financial services licencing.

On yet other hands, I was an employee of the Lee Family Office and with a duty of confidentiality and a member of the Middle Kingdom executive leadership team. Gee, I thought to myself, how many hands I have got here? But, by the time I had counted my appendages, I had dismissed my fears of any conflict of interest.

In the end, I took comfort from the absence of any definitive decision to stop Middle Kingdom funding. More importantly, I was assured by the fact I had not been asked to provide legal advice and had conducted the risk review solely with my risk manager's hat on. Perhaps too conveniently, I concluded that I had no obligation to inform the Middle Kingdom board that they may soon be staring insolvency in the face. I came to this conclusion knowing full well that Middle Kingdom would be requiring legal services well into the future. Accordingly, I made a mental note to take care.

Chapter Twenty-Seven
The Inquisition

We didn't have long to wait for ASIC's next instalment on Project Olive Oil. A second compulsory notice arrived, hand-delivered, and addressed to me. I was to front a mandatory examination the following week.

'The glove's on the other foot now,' I muttered as the ASIC delivery boy disappeared from the foyer. Our receptionist just gave me a quizzical look.

Despite knowing the ASIC process intimately, I was a little apprehensive. It would be the first time I would be on the receiving end of an ASIC examination. My belief that the regulator would only be interested in establishing the scope of due diligence provided me with some comfort. The fact that I had undertaken a review of the constituent documents of the project, assessed the trustees' financial services licence, and conducted various probity checks was clearly relevant. Yes, I was nervous but, in my calmer moments, I rationalised that I was just being called as a witness. I had not compromised the Lee Family Office's financial services licence and, accordingly, I could not possibly justify the appointment of a solicitor to represent me.

The examination room in ASIC's new Collins Street premises was similar to one I remembered back at the regulator's previous office. There was a long, curved bench for the examinee and an assortment of legal representatives, if required. A couple of metres in front was a slightly raised bench that could readily accommodate four ASIC investigators (or inspectors as they were called for compulsory examination purposes). To one side was a large recording device operated by Spark & Cannon or some other professional transcription service. What I remembered most was the polished wood. The panelling on the walls, the glow of the floorboard, and sheen of the benchtops were beautifully harmonised. The design had more in common with a parliament or courtroom than a Swedish sauna. Exotic hardwood had been lavishly installed throughout. No plantation pine or cheap veneer was in sight.

Overall, the examination room projected an aura of quality and craftsmanship. It was a place for formality and seriousness. As I entered and took my seat in front of three inspectors, I glanced at the Hodder & Stoughton pocket Holy Bible and a copy of Corporations Act on the bench in front of me. I experienced an overwhelming sense of foreboding. Thankfully, I was provided with a large glass of water.

The examination commenced with a standard address from the lead inspector. He stated the time and date, referred to the notice requiring my attendance, and mentioned the delegation that authorised him to conduct the examination. Upon request, I formally stated my full name and residential address. With the basic formalities out of the way, the inspector addressed several standard requirements that covered all examinations. So far, so good, I thought to myself. I was on familiar territory, and I started to relax.

First, the lead inspector directed the representative of the transcription service to be present and record the examination. At the same time, I was informed that I would be required to read and sign the transcript. Second, I was given a confidentiality direction. I could not directly or indirectly disclose to any person any examination questions, any of my answers, or mention any documents provided to me during the proceedings for one year.

Third, I was told of my obligation to answer all questions, even those that might tend to incriminate me. There was no equivalent to the 'Fifth Amendment' under the Australian Securities and Investments Act. However, if I prefaced each of my answers with the word 'privilege,' any answer, unless it was a lie, could not be used against me.

This limited privilege against self-incrimination often appeared quite ridiculous, as a blanket claim for privilege could not be made covering all questions. It was therefore common practice to preface all answers with the word 'privilege,' even for those mundane or innocuous questions. Where a lawyer for an examinee was present, his or her role was often limited to reminding the examinee to use the word 'privilege.' On one occasion, back in my ASC days, I recall one high-profile examinee carrying into the examination a free-standing A4 certificate frame, which he placed on the benchtop in front of him. There was no certificate in the frame; just one sheet of paper with the word 'privilege' in large typeface.

Fourth, I was required to take an oath or give an affirmation that the answers that I would give would be truthful. Since my mother's passing thirty years before, my attendance at church had been limited to the occasional wedding and funeral. In any case, even if I could believe there was a God, he or she had better things to do than accompany me through a procedure that I was very familiar with. Accordingly, I affirmed.

Finally, before the lead inspector commenced with questions concerning the Lee Family Office and the Project Olive Oil disaster, he asked me if I had any questions concerning how the examination would be conducted. Like many examinees before me, I responded by clarifying my position regarding self-incrimination. A knowing smirk appeared on the inspector's face as I opened my mouth.

'Should I inadvertently forget to preface an answer with the word "privilege," that failure should not be taken as an indication that I have waived any right to the protection of against self-incrimination. I intend to claim the benefit of the protection to all answers to questions that might incriminate me.'

'Your comments are noted,' was the immediate response from the lead inspector, which was his code for, *'we know you know the process, smartass, but let's get on with it.'*

The next quarter of an hour or so was devoted to the Lee Family Office, its status as a holder of a financial services licence, and my roles as in-house counsel and compliance officer. Importantly, I was asked to comment on the validity of various ASIC documents that were produced during the course of the examination.

'Privilege. Yes, the Lee Family Office Limited is a public company that holds an Australian Financial Service Licence.'

'Privilege. The ASIC historical extract is correct. Winston Lee is the chief executive officer and I report directly to him.'

'I have numerous roles. Sorry, privilege. I have numerous roles in the Lee Family Office, including its compliance with all matters other than human resources and tax. The HR Manager deals with all staffing issues, and the tax and accounting sides are handled by the chief financial officer, Martin Flynn.'

'Privilege. Yes, I do oversee an approved product list for Lee Family Office clients. Before a financial product is placed on the list, it requires due diligence covering investment, tax, portfolio administration, and legal. Winston Lee covers the investment due diligence, Martin Flynn does the tax, the Custody Manager deals with portfolio administration issues, and I do the legal due diligence or instruct a panel law firm to do so.'

Of course, this line of questioning was designed to show that I was in a senior enough position within the Lee Family Office to have direct knowledge of client investments generally, and the Olive Bend Syndicate investment, specifically. The questioning also sought to identify the various internal processes for determining what financial products would be offered to clients. The examination was proceeding down a predictable path.

'I wish to ask you some questions concerning the Olive Bend Syndicate,' the lead inspector began, 'and I produce to you an ASIC notice for books and records addressed to the Lee Family Office. Have you heard of the Olive Bend Syndicate and seen this notice, albeit not this copy, before?'

'Privilege. Yes, to both questions,' was my initial comment. Unfortunately, my response led to more questions concerning the Lee Family Office's response to the ASIC notice. I agreed that Martin Flynn and I had worked together to respond to the notice. I also admitted that I had reviewed all the documents that were handed up to the regulator.

None of these lines of inquiry were particularly concerning. I was providing factual information and, given Martin Flynn's involvement, I was pretty confident we had fully complied with the regulator's notice to produce books and records. What was more worrying was the fact that the inspector's questions were moving away from concerns about the quality of due diligence.

'Mr Mason, are you familiar with relevant Corporations Act provisions concerning retail and wholesale clients?' the inspector asked.

'Privilege. Yes,' although in the circumstances that seemed a curious question, as we had been careful to include only wholesale clients.

'There is a copy of the Corporations Act in front of you,' continued the inspector. 'Please turn to the marked section.' I picked up the legislation and saw that section 761G(7) had been tagged.

'Privilege,' I said. 'Yes, I know this section and the associated regulations. The section allowed us to offer Olive Bend Syndicate as a wholesale investment. The first paragraph is the $500,000 threshold and the third paragraph provides for the wealthy investor certificate of $2.5 million assets or $250,000 of net income. All the syndicate clients are covered by at least one of these paragraphs.'

'I see,' said the inspector, but the way he muttered those words suggested that he did not see, or worse, he did not believe I understood the provision. I felt a chill as I realised that we were beginning to head into unknown territory. The inspector continued.

'I now produce to you a document headed 'Olive Bend Syndicate' with a list of nine names and dollar amounts next to those names. Have you seen this document before and, if so, what does it purport to represent?'

'Privilege. Yes,' I replied. 'I prepared the list. It's a summary of the nine investors that had invested in the Olive Bend Syndicate with their commitment sums.'

'Do you know these investors?' asked the inspector.

'Privilege. Not personally, but I know they are all clients or companies or trustees of our clients.' Although the questions were routine, by then I feared the inspector was just setting the scene for the inevitable hard-hitting questions that would follow.

'Are there any self-managed superannuation funds on the list?' This was a strange question, but I guessed that was because the complainant's superannuation fund was included on the list. But, as the next few minutes unfolded, it suddenly dawned on me that I had totally misread the direction of ASIC's investigation.

'Privilege. Two,' I replied, and I read out the names of the two superannuation funds and their commitment amounts of $400,000 each.

'How did these entities come to invest in the Olive Bend Syndicate?' continued the inspector.

I cannot now recall the exact words of my reply. Still, I believe I would have repeated my description of our diligence process and the fact that the investment opportunity was limited to wholesale clients. I also recall mentioning the input of Lee Family Office client advisers. Whether a particular wholesale client wished to invest or not would be a decision worked out in consultation with that client's nominated adviser.

Whatever I said did not seem to trouble the inspector. By that time, he appeared to be concentrating on producing documents. I started to relax a little.

'I now produce two coda files marked Lee Family Office client advice files.' Thankfully, the inspector had selected two files that were reasonably complete. I still wondered why he had chosen those particular investors and not others.

'Have you seen these files before?' queried the inspector. 'If so, what do they relate to and who was responsible for creating and maintaining them?'

'Privilege,' I answered. 'These are the client adviser files that cover the two superannuation funds. The relevant client adviser was responsible for the contents. The files cover client information, risk assessments, proposed asset allocations, and adviser recommendations.' At least in relation to those particular files, I was very confident my comments were accurate and, more importantly, truthful.

'Mr Mason, are the files complete?'

'Privilege. Yes, inspector, to the best of my knowledge they are.'

'How do you know?' was the instant reply.

I muttered something about collecting the files myself in response to the ASIC notice and checking with each client adviser. But the next question came straight from left field. The anxiety that had slowly dissipated over the last few minutes returned in full fury.

'Mr Mason, in each file, please identify the statement of advice.' The look on my face must have said it all. 'You look confused, Mr Mason?' That was an understatement.

'Well, yes, ah, privilege,' I replied. 'There are no statements of advice.'

'Why not, Mr Mason? Why not?'

'Privilege. As I said before, these clients are wealthy investors. They are not retail clients. They are each subject to an accountant's certificate. We needed to be sure we were not breaching the managed investment provisions.'

'I see,' said the inspector. 'I see' seemed to be his favourite expression. 'I'm not talking about managed investments. I'm talking about advice, financial product advice, Mr Mason; what part of section 761G don't you understand?' It was a rhetorical question. He proceeded to refer me to the legislation again.

'Mr Mason, let me summarise the legislation. If a client is given a financial product or service that relates to a superannuation product, then the client is only wholesale if the super fund has assets of $10 million or more? Do you agree, Mr Mason?'

It is difficult to read the Corporations Act at the best of times, but almost impossible when one is a bundle of nerves. I tried to reassure myself as I had read those provisions countless times before. I had even referenced and explained them in the Lee Family Office Compliance Manual. Despite my emotional state, I understood the inspector's question and, with a qualification, readily agreed with his summary.

'Privilege. Yes, I agree with your summary, but the Olive Bend Syndicate does not relate to a superannuation product. Our client advisers' advice just concerned an underlying investment. Recommending someone to become a member of a super fund is radically different to advising the trustees of that same fund what they should invest in. Any relationship is tenuous to say the least. It's indirect at best.'

The inspector cut me off to produce a further document.

'I will stop you there and produce to you an ASIC document titled "QFS 150." The document, on ASIC letterhead, was a one-page response to a frequently asked question concerning financial services regulation.

'Have you seen this document before?' asked the inspector. I shook my head, saying nothing. By then, I was too busy reading the one-pager and my throat was far too dry to say anything.

'Who is responsible for overseeing financial services compliance within the Lee Family Office?' asked the inspector, although he knew the answer. He was having fun at my expense.

'I am,' I managed to mutter, while spilling the glass of water that was shaking in my hands.

'And you haven't seen this ASIC release before?' Again, this was a rhetorical question. 'If you're capable, I suggest you read the document in full.' The line of questioning was patronising, but I had no grounds to refuse. I slowly read the ASIC release, which clearly set out ASIC's policy in respect to underlying investments of superannuation funds. For ASIC, the word 'relates' had a broad meaning. What the trustees of a super fund chose to invest in did, in fact, relate to membership of the fund itself.

I was literally shaken by ASIC's stance, but I didn't have to finish reading to understand the implications. The Lee Family Office had treated those two superannuation funds as wholesale clients on the back of wealthy investor certificates. Unfortunately, when it came to providing financial advice, ASIC only regarded a superannuation fund as a retail client if the fund had assets of at least $10 million.

You may think, Dear Reader, that this is technical stuff. If Lena had been there she would have said something like: 'Section 76 G what? Pull yourself together, you sook. Don't be so upset. It's not as though you've killed anyone.' Yet, for once in my adult life, Lena was not close to my mind.

I could guess the inspector's next question.

'And do these two superannuation funds have net assets of $10 million?'

Again, I shook my head. Both funds had considerable assets, but the Lee Family Office only managed one self-managed superannuation fund valued at over $10 million. That was Alfred's fund, and it was not on the Olive Bend Syndicate list.

'I see,' said the inspector in a tone that was bordering on confrontational.

The ramifications of the inspector's line of questioning were obvious. We had correctly structured the Olive Bend Syndicate to exclude the retail IDPS provisions. Still, I had ignored, or had never appreciated, the fact that we had provided retail advisory services to two superannuation funds. According to ASIC, we should have given those funds a Financial Services Guide and, more importantly, provided statements of advice that complied with the highly stylised content provisions of the Corporations Act.

The inspector was on a roll.

'You told me that you are responsible for ASIC compliance. You've told me that you understand the wealthy investor requirements, but you don't seem to have read section 761G or relevant ASIC policy. You're even a former ASIC investigator, so I understand.'

I recall thinking that I was never so vitriolic towards an examinee when I had been in the inspector's chair. Perhaps I had just caught him on a bad day, but his demeanour was disconcerting and bordering on unprofessional. Even his colleagues looked embarrassed. Not that they were any comfort to me. I said nothing; the inspector's acridity was not worthy of a response. All I could think of at that moment was that I needed a lawyer. My mind was spinning. I should have insisted on legal representation. Why did I affirm? I should have entrusted God's help.

The inspector continued.

'For the record, Mr Mason, here is what we are going to do. We are going to serve you with another notice. This time it's going to be for all your self-managed super fund client advice files for the past two years.' I said nothing and let the inspector finish his bitter spiel.

In contrast to the lengthy formalities that characterised the first part of the examination, the inspector's closing remarks were mercifully brief. He asked if I wished to address him on any matters raised during the examination, to which I just shook my head. I was reminded of the confidentiality requirement and informed that the ASIC reserved its right to recall me if necessary. The inspectors then hastily excused themselves. I figured they knew I would be happy to find my own way to the exit.

I left the examination in a state of bewilderment. I was stunned, breathless, and felt physically sick. I feared I would be the scapegoat for the Olive Bend Syndicate debacle. The shortcomings of Winston's due diligence would be forgotten or glossed over. All that would be remembered would be my failure to identify a technical compliance requirement based around a dubious one-page contribution from the regulator.

Back at the office, Martin Flynn and I prepared for the inevitable notice requiring production of all advisory files for client superannuation funds over the previous two years. Thankfully, the vast majority of those files were still on-site, with only a handful moved to storage. To our dismay, we discovered that the records were organised into client or family groups rather than by references to legal entities or specific investment vehicles, such as self-managed superannuation funds. Accordingly, Martin and I had to painstakingly review every single item of client advice that had been prepared during the last two years. That was a no-five-minute task.

The reaction of the board of directors was predictable. As a group, they had displayed little interest in our financial services licence for a decade or more. Overnight, and with the likelihood of ASIC taking enforcement action, their attitude changed. In the end, Martin was left with the primary task of reviewing client files while I prepared numerous reports to the board and fielded countless queries from individual directors.

Of course, there was one burning question. How many statements of advice had the Lee Family Office failed to prepare? The short answer, as Martin established a few days later, was thirty-two. Given the way I felt about ASIC's conduct and the pressure I felt from the board, the answer could have been one thousand and two. In particular, I feared Winston's reaction. He certainly did not disappoint.

At first, Winston had difficulty believing client advisers had breached their statutory obligations. He phoned one of his former Scotch College friends who was a leading corporate barrister. The answer was ambiguous. Winston was told that ASIC's legal interpretation was controversial, but did the Lee Family Office really want the expense and publicity of taking the regulator on? The advice was to respond in full, keep our mouths shut, and take whatever punishment was going to be dished out on the chin.

We did respond in full. Winston did, at least for the most part, keep his trap shut, and we did accept the enforceable undertaking that came our way. Thankfully, the Lee Family Office avoided prosecution, but the undertaking was hardly a desirable outcome. The ten-plus-page document set out in detail our failure to comply with the retail client protections under the Corporations Act and required us to remediate the identified breaches. The undertaking also directed us to engage an independent expert to review all client files and to develop compliance procedures to prevent future contraventions.

At first, Winston and the board were pleased to avoid prosecution, but were less happy when I informed them that the enforceable undertaking was a public document and would be accessible, free of charge, forever and a day through the ASIC website. For an organisation that shunned publicity, this was an unwelcome development. Fortunately, the whole sorry saga was only picked up by the *Australian Financial Review* and presented in a short non-descript article buried towards the back of the paper. Public attention was mostly noticeable by its absence. Nonetheless, internal scrutiny of Project Olive Oil would only cease with the occurrence of far more severe allegations of misconduct.

'Regulation has gone mad, Mr Mason. Regulation has gone mad,' said Alfred. He continued: 'Our clients are wealthy. Of course, their super funds haven't got $10 million, but that's only because of tax office restrictions. They have a lot more than $10 million across their entities, otherwise they wouldn't be our clients. Why should we have to treat one part of their group's affairs as retail and all their other parts as wholesale? It's absurd.'

I had no answer to what seemed a very reasonable assessment. As he shuffled out of my office, Alfred quietly concluded by saying:

'Sorry, Mr Mason. Sorry, you're the one that has had to fix it up.'

Winston's response was ultimately less measured and supportive.

'This is your doing, Mason. It's your job to be on top of this and you'll pay. How dare you jeopardise our financial services licence. If it wasn't for the tight labour market...'

He broke off, most likely realising that even in a normal labour market, he would have difficulty recruiting even a first-year lawyer on my salary. But Winston was right; I did pay. Other than consumer price index adjustments, I would never receive a salary increase, let alone a bonus, for the rest of my Lee Family Office career. Thankfully, at that time, I had no appreciation of how short the rest of that career would be.

✦

Chapter Twenty-Eight
The Advice

The Middle Kingdom audit and risk committee comprised of three independent directors, although with Winston in attendance, independent decision-making was largely a myth. The committee chairman not only deferred to Winston, he continuously kowtowed. Unsurprisingly, when the Middle Kingdom risk review report was presented, the committee showed no concerns about the absence of financial risks. Whatever Winston had said worked.

However, the absence of financial risks only served to highlight the importance of the other risk categories and, to give the independent directors credit, they had analysed the review in-depth, which was more than Winston could claim. The committee grumbled about the characterisation of certain risks, but thankfully did so in a productive manner.

The committee, for example, was dismayed at the high levels of staff sick leave and the results of the staff engagement survey. Poor morale, they argued, questioned the ongoing viability of the business and should, therefore, have been classified as an operational rather than a people risk. I begged to differ and looked at Martin for reassurance. There was no backup coming from his direction, as he just shrugged his shoulders. It was clear he didn't care one way or the other. Martin was right. The critical point was that the directors had recognised the risk and were sufficiently concerred to appreciate its consequences.

The discussion began to deteriorate when committee members suggested that the severity of certain risks had been overstated. The litany of general maintenance snags across the early learning centres was raised as an example.

'Of course, they're safety risks, but you're right just to call them snags. They are easy fixes,' proffered the chairman. They're a low, not a medium, risk. Martin, I want you to cost the necessary rectification work and request working capital from the Lee Family Office. I'm sure we all want these snags fixed, particularly that foyer at Box Hill.'

I saw Martin turn to Winston for encouragement, but the latter averted Martin's gaze and said nothing. It provided me with more convincing evidence that the Lee Family Office pipeline of funds had been switched off. The conversation quickly changed direction. Perhaps the chairman, who had witnessed Winston's response to Martin's stare, also concluded that future funding would be a problem. Maybe, it was just a coincidence. Either way, the directors become solely preoccupied with one issue: their own personal welfare.

Each officer of Middle Kingdom, myself included, had executed a deed of indemnity. In that document, Middle Kingdom agreed to indemnify officers for liabilities incurred by them as officers of the company, other than those prohibited by law. The deed also provided us with access to company documents for up to seven years after ceasing office, and the benefit of Directors and Officers (D&O) liability insurance. The committee members turned their attention to Middle Kingdom's D&O policy.

A copy of the D&O policy was, as a matter of routine, included in the committee papers. The policy itself was a risk mitigant, as it was designed to protect officers for alleged wrongful acts, including claims of mismanagement or wrongdoings that are typically brought by shareholders, employees, regulators, creditors, competitors, and liquidators and the like. As with many such policies, ours was divided into three parts or, if you are familiar with insurance lingo, three sides: A, B and C.

There were several concerns with the policy, some of which Martin and I had identified in the risk review. We were particularly troubled about the extent of cover for company reimbursement under Side B and, given poor morale, an absence of an extension for employment practices. We were further troubled by the level of compensation Middle Kingdom itself could claim for actions instigated by aggrieved shareholders under Side C. The number of class actions had increased dramatically since the GFC.

The committee, however, was squarely focussed on the benefits that flowed directly to officers, the so-called Side A cover. Such cover provided direct protection to officers for liabilities and legal costs of defending claims for wrongful acts. The policy extended to liabilities that Middle Kingdom itself could not cover legally, including circumstances where directors had failed to act in good faith.

The committee was uneasy about the insurer's obligations to advance defence costs, the protection for retired officers as well as the level of excess. The chairman queried his protection against any ASIC regulatory action, given the regulatory risk arising from the announcement to the ASX following the girls' escape from the White Horse Early Learning Centre. I confirmed that officers were protected against civil penalty orders under the Corporations Act. I was about to comment that I had been concerned for some years about the level of cover for such orders. A sub-limit of $250,000 would hardly go far. I stopped short, though, when Winston interjected.

'There was nothing wrong with our public statements. What was said at the time was one hundred per cent correct. The door was fixed, and safety matters considered. If Greg now has a problem with the wording, it's insignificant at best. We can't be expected to fix up every little issue. In any case, just think of the damage a further release would do to the share price.'

Winston had, as Lena would have said, 'taken the air out of my sails.' I would need to broach the subject of our ASX submissions at a more opportune time. In any case, I thought to myself, it would be sweet justice if Winston received such an order, preferably one above $250,000. Further, I hated the whole idea of indemnities; if directors did their job properly, there should be no need for them. I merely closed the copy of the D&O policy in front of me and refrained from further comment.

Meanwhile, I could tell the chairman was becoming increasingly uncomfortable. He was fidgeting in his chair and scribbling like mad on his committee papers. I suspect Winston's comments did not convince him, but in true sycophantic fashion, he was not going to argue with Winston.

'As usual, Winston, you make a very important point,' said the chairman. 'Let's not get carried away. But clearly, some legal risks may affect us as directors. I think Martin should organise a review of our insurance arrangements with our broker. Also, I think it would be a great idea if Greg here were to provide us with a summary of the legal risks we face as officers of Middle Kingdom.'

My immediate facial reaction to this request came as no surprise to Winston. He could tell I was uneasy.

'Greg, you're so predictable,' he began. 'Look. We all know you're not our private lawyer. You've repeatedly made that point. But, gee, we've just been discussing D&O cover. Don't you think the company would want to know where we all stand, even if it's just for insurance purposes?'

On one level, Winston had a point. There had been numerous occasions over the years where I had sought to gently remind directors, notably Winston, that the company was my client and not the directors personally. On another level, I was troubled by my boss's response. I had no doubt that the primary motivation for the advice was self-protection and little to do with the company. I politely began objecting but was cut off.

'Greg! We're not going to debate this,' continued Winston. 'All we want is a high-level summary of the key areas of liability. If any of us need to take it further, we'll do so with our own advisers. If you must, include one of your pesky sentences about how the advice is only for the company's use.'

In retrospect, I should have pushed back more. While I did not anticipate the harm the resulting advice would ultimately bring, I was unsettled by Winston's logic. He was suggesting that the directors could construct a Chinese wall inside their heads to separate advice received for the company from advice received for their own use. I decided to refrain from further comment. The last thing I needed was an accusation of racism.

Matters of motivation were but one concern. I was grappling with another problem but could say nothing. I knew that a request for a high-level summary was really a demand for comprehensive advice covering all areas of potential liability. One such area of liability was a real doozy. A director has a clear personal duty to prevent his or her company from trading whilst insolvent. There are severe civil and criminal penalties for failing to do so and, from my conversation with Winston and Martin, it was pretty evident that personal liability for trading whilst insolvent was the Middle Kingdom directors' most significant threat. Yet, the risk review had deliberately excluded insolvency risk and, for fear of breaching my own fiduciary duties, I had no desire to raise the topic.

I was in a bind. While I believed that I was not in a position to raise the topic of insolvency, I also believed that I would be negligent not to at least flag the dangers of poor cash flow. Thankfully, none of the risks identified by the HR Manager or myself were off-limits. Personal liability under the Fair Work Act was a good start, and I deliberately mentioned that turning a blind eye to employee underpayments was itself an offence.

I further pointed out that Australian Consumer Law governed early learning services. Any drop in the quality of such services could render directors personally liable for misleading or deceptive conduct, particularly as the standard agreement with parents made representations as to the care and skill of Middle Kingdom's services. I referred to the tax office's willingness to pursue directors for a company's unpaid PAYG withholding tax and superannuation guarantee liabilities.

It would not take a genius to link cash flow problems to concerns about service quality and underpayments or withholdings. Further, it wouldn't take rocket science to connect poor service quality to the Middle Kingdom's share price and the interests of investors. Shareholder class action against Middle Kingdom itself was a possibility. Shareholder action against directors brought in the name of the company was another.

There are hundreds of national, state and territory laws that impose personal liability on directors. Thankfully, the vast majority were irrelevant but, even so, I was necessarily selective. I reasoned the directors needed a sharp reality check, rather than a comprehensive treatise on, for example, the array of fiduciary duties owed by directors at common law. Therefore, most of my advice was limited to breaches of directors' duties under the Corporations Act and personal liability under occupational health and safety legislation.

Safety was of particular concern, as maintenance issues had figured highly in the risk review. Under the then new legislation, Middle Kingdom had a duty of care to ensure the ongoing health and safety of all persons, not just staff. That duty included providing and maintaining safe structures and an environment without risks to health and safety.

As far as the OH&S legislation was concerned, the design and workings of the White Horse Early Learning Centre, particularly the foyer and side gate, were a problem, and, to escape personal liability, directors had to exercise due diligence. Personal liability was limited to circumstances where directors were reckless as to the risks of death or serious injury. Thankfully, the robust processes, reporting lines, and training introduced by Ms Ma offered the directors considerable protection.

However, the ongoing failure to rectify the foyer and side gate and decreasing staffing levels compromised any claim that due diligence had been reasonably exercised. I could have added that reasonable due diligence required an inquiring mind, a willingness to actively question management, and not persistently defer to the Lee Family Office chief executive officer. I refrained from further opening my mouth out of fear of unnecessarily provoking Winston. He would be agitated enough.

The media release and, more importantly, the company announcement to the ASX following the 'Great Escape' became the main focus of my attention. I simply could not accept Winston's argument that the matter was an insignificant risk.

Continuous disclosure is based on the principle that all investors should have equal and timely access to information about a company. Therefore, my concern was not with the girls' escape from the White Horse Early Learning Centre, as the media had extensively covered the incident. The adverse publicity may have significantly affected Middle Kingdom's share price but, by its very nature, that information had generally been available. In any case, we had already made public statements to the media and ASX.

The problem was that the claims made in those statements were misleading. I re-read the relevant sentence:

All recommendations concerning the White Horse Early Learning Centre have been addressed and recommendations that concern Middle Kingdom's early learning centres as a whole will be implemented as a matter of urgency.

The facts were that only the wonky service door had been repaired. No re-design work had commenced on the layout of the foyer, and the side gate was as problematic as ever. I was also concerned that Winston had terminated KPMG's services. No broader recommendations for early learning centres had been received, let alone implemented as a matter of urgency. Of course, the public knew nothing of these failings. So, would a reasonable Middle Kingdom shareholder, I asked myself, be dismayed if a serious safety concern had not been adequately rectified or if the company had turned a deaf ear to any broader safety concerns. I knew what Winston's answers to those questions would be, but he was hardly a reasonable person.

I concluded that a failure to clarify the communique might itself constitute a breach of the continuous disclosure requirements, or at least amount to misleading or deceptive conduct. I quoted the relevant provisions of the Corporations Act, including the offence of supplying false information to the ASX by either act or omission. Further, I mentioned that directors could be personally liable if they aided or abetted or were knowingly concerned in a contravention by Middle Kingdom. The longer the ASX announcement remained unclarified, the more likely directors could be accessorily liable.

Finally, I provided a brief explanation of the civil penalty regime that had been introduced in the mid-1990s. Importantly, were Middle Kingdom itself held culpable, directors themselves could be personally punished for contravening the continuous disclosure provisions or their duty of care and diligence as officers.

It had been years since I had last reviewed the statutory duty of directors. Yet, I was aware that amendments at the turn of the millennium had introduced a 'business judgement rule.' The rule protected decisions made by directors who acted on an informed basis, in good faith and in the honest belief that their choices were in the best interests of the company. Those requirements limited the application of the rule. Indeed, it would be hard to argue that a failure to clarify a misleading statement to the ASX could be regarded as a decision made in good faith.

I skipped over the 'business judgement rule' and concluded that the directors had failed to act with due care and diligence. Of course, I did not present my conclusion in such a forthright manner. My advice was more along the lines that directors may struggle to defend an allegation of failing to act with due care and diligence. Nonetheless, I did not doubt that the message was clear.

I also knew that Winston would not take kindly to my advice. True to form, the subsequent audit and risk committee meeting was dominated by my take on the announcement to the ASX. Winston was his usual indignant self.

'I've told you before, Greg, there was nothing wrong with what we said. The door was fixed and we did consider the lay-out of the foyer. I'm not sure what planet you're on, Greg, or what dictionary you read but, in my book, the word "addressed" doesn't have to mean "fixed up." It also means "consider," and that we did.'

Winston abruptly stopped mid-monologue, but he had only paused for breath.

'And, yes I did cut off KPMG. The cost was prohibitive. But there is nothing dishonest about saying that their recommendations would be implemented as a matter of urgency. They would have been if we had got any.'

I could tell by the look on committee members' faces that they did not share the logic of Winston's argument. Despite this, the best I could hope for was a weak reaction.

'Let's not get into semantics,' responded the chairman, 'but it's evident there's a difference of opinion here. Ultimately, I think the sooner the Box Hill centre is repaired, the better. Let's get onto that, shall we?'

'Good idea,' responded Winston, 'and while we're at it, I'm going to get my own legal advice on this. Once an ASIC investigator, always a bloody one,' he added, looking directly at me. I was sure he was throwing imaginary daggers in my direction.

To be honest, I would have been pleased if Winston had obtained legal advice to his liking. As the so-called moral conscience of the company, I had no problems presenting a conservative view. Also, if a contrary opinion were proven to be wrong, Winston would have someone else to blame. But to the best of my knowledge, Winston never did seek external legal advice. More disturbingly, as future events would demonstrate, Martin failed to liaise with our insurance broker. There would be no changes to Middle Kingdom's D&O liability insurance policy.

Chapter Twenty-Nine
The Emotions

I was at Crown Casino having beers with an old ASC colleague when I saw him. He looked a little more aged and worn, but there was no mistaking the boyish grin. There was James Powell, right next to a roulette wheel, with an arm around the neck of some unfortunate punter. So, he was still gambling, I thought. I must have stared for a good half hour or so as he moved between the gaming tables and the poker machines. He was too preoccupied to see me.

I always believed that gambling was a lonely addiction. No one ever seemed to say very much to each other. Despite the fact the soulless slot machines were lined up alongside one another, the vast majority of punters remained fixated by the screen in front of them. Interaction with the persons next to them was minimal. Although, as I observed, James was notably different. For some reason, he seemed to have a fascination with other people. James was continually approaching what appeared to be random punters, talking and laughing with them as though they were old friends. There was also an unhealthy degree of physical contact. I lost count of the times I saw him with his arm around some poor addict. The more I looked, the more I believed there could only be one explanation. James was trying to fleece some poor sucker.

I don't know whether it was the beers, my macho conversation with my former colleague, or the mere realisation that James Powell was still up to his old tricks. Whatever it was, I had had enough. As I watched, the anger inside of me bubbled like a volcano about to explode. I excused myself from my drinking companion, briskly walked over to gaming machines and tapped James on the shoulder.

'You're still a prick!' I said as he turned around, landing a right hook squarely on his nose.

As blood vessels burst, all hell broke loose. A sharp, massive pain shot up my right arm. I had never punched anyone in anger before. Schoolyard scraps were the limit of my boxing ambitions. Even the hurt of breaking an ankle in a school football match did not measure up to the pain I felt as my clenched fist slammed into the bridge of my victim's nose.

I cannot fully remember the subsequent chain of events, but I do recall hitting the ground. I hit the ground hard, and it was not by choice. I also recollect being hoisted from the floor by a big, burly security guard and ejected from Crown Casino headfirst out of a side door. Somewhere along the line, I incurred a perforated eardrum and split lip. Although I must have been a sorry sight as I nursed my fist, ear, and mouth, I felt particularly buoyant. In fact, I was elated. I had got one back on a thieving bastard, and that was no more than he deserved. As it turned out, I would never see James Powell again.

As my injuries healed, I began to reflect on the incident in a more rational manner. My behaviour may well have been alcohol-induced, but it was deplorable. My initial sense of elation was soon replaced by guilt. I had gained a perverse sense of satisfaction through physical violence. However, in the cold light of day, I knew that I had acted both illegally and immorally. No matter what harm James had done and what fraud he attempted to commit, I shouldn't have inflicted violent retribution.

Further, I experienced an unease that I could not quite describe. I felt that somehow the events at Crown Casino would come back in full force to haunt me. Little did I realise that those feelings would be just a sideshow to the emotional rollercoaster ride that I would endure a few days later.

For many, the love of money is a deadly sin. For Alfred, the love of money was just plain deadly. One humid summer morning, I arrived at the office deliberately late. The air conditioners would only operate after 8:30 am. I arrived at 9:15 am when the office temperature was comfortable. Yet, the atmosphere was not; Martin was on a couch, quietly muttering incoherently, the receptionist was blubbering into her silk handkerchief, and even Winston was subdued. With his elbows on his desk, resting his jaw in his hands, Winston was pale and spent. I didn't need a psychologist to reason he had been crying.

I asked a colleague what was going on. Why was everyone upset?

'Mr Lee. Alfred. He's dead. Had a heart attack while doing his paper round.'

I felt my legs go weak and immediately sat down. The news was monumental. I could not think of a worse nightmare for the family, the office, and even Melbourne's Chinese community. I must have sat for a least an hour coming to grips with the enormity of Alfred Lee's passing. Others were doing the same. It would be many weeks before the sound of laughter would fill those Collins Street offices.

It was some hours later before I truly reflected on my colleague's brief words, 'He's dead. Had a heart attack while doing his paper round.' Paper round? I thought. What the hell are they talking about? That was just utterly absurd. What would a multi-millionaire be doing a paper round for? A paper round would not pay more than a few bucks an hour. Martin had by then come over to sit next to me. I asked him for an explanation.

'His doctor told him he was a walking time bomb. His blood pressure had been through the roof for years. You see, Greg, he had to start eating properly and do some exercise.'

'But what's that got to do with a paper round?'

'Don't you see, Greg? That was his idea of exercise. You know what he was like. He simply couldn't take an hour off during the day to do something non-financially productive. Sure, it was exercise, but it was also paid work. How much he was paid was irrelevant.'

I got it. Martin's explanation made sense. All of Alfred's waking moments had been geared to either the creation of wealth or philanthropy. It was a simple conviction, which in the end would kill him.

As I walked past the CEO's office, I gave Winston a polite nod and simply said, 'I'm truly sorry.'

'Thanks, Greg,' was the quiet response. 'He was sixty-six. Sixty-six years, six-months, and twenty-five days. Too young.' As I walked away, I saw the tears rolling down my CEO's face.

Later that day, I forced myself away from the office to one of the many Chinese take-away eateries around Little Bourke Street. I wasn't hungry, but I knew I should eat something. I was not even aware what cafe I entered. I didn't know its name and had no recollection of ever being there before. My thoughts were with Alfred.

'One small sweet-and-sour pork, please,' I quietly said to the elderly shop assistant.

'Ah,' was the initial response. 'One gwai lo yuk!'

Surely, I had never met the shop assistant before, let alone spoken to her. I looked at her in utter amazement.

'What did you say?'

'One gwai lo yuk,' she repeated. 'Isn't that what your Mr Lee called sweet-and-sour pork? He was a good man, a real good man. We will all miss him.'

Chapter Thirty
The Bridge

It was about a month after my ear and split lip had healed that I heard news about James Powell. I think one of the older client advisers must have told me first.

'Remember James Powell?'

'Yes, of course,' I said.

'He's dead. Topped himself yesterday. Weren't you a good mate of his?'

I sat at my desk, dumbfounded. News that my arch nemesis was dead was bad enough, but the revelation immediately invoked an overpowering suspicion that I was to blame. It had only been a few weeks since I had physically assaulted him. The timing was just too short to be coincidental. Yet suicide, I thought to myself, does not make sense. James had everything to live for. I knew that Lucy and the boys were devoted to him. Then again, I reasoned, perhaps the gambling had got the better of him.

I read somewhere that problem gamblers were likely to suffer from low self-esteem, develop stress-related disorders, become anxious, and suffer from depression. Of course, if James had been experiencing a mental illness, then my assault and battery would hardly have been therapeutic. At the very least, it would have tipped him over the edge. *Oh my God,* I suddenly thought, *what have I done?*

Later, I discovered that James had failed to return home one evening. Apparently, he had driven to the top of the West Gate Bridge, parked his car, climbed over the steel barrier, and disappeared over the edge. No one had stopped. No one on that bridge reported what had happened. By the time James was found, he had been deceased for at least six hours. There was no note, but he had, in what was left of him, a high blood alcohol content.

No newspaper reported the suicide. The press never does. Fifty a year jumped off that bridge until retaining barriers were installed a few months after James's final leap.

Lucy phoned.

'He was really upset about something,' I deciphered, between her sobs. 'I think he got in a fight as he came home with a bloody nose one night from the casino. He had done so much good there, working as a volunteer for gamblers. He was so committed to their plight. We even established a family foundation to help addicts. Did you know part of his salary was directly debited to the foundation?'

Of course, I knew about the foundation, but not for one moment had I made a connection between the Powell Family Foundation and an anti-gambling crusade. On the contrary, I had relied on the grapevine and dismissed James as a hopeless addict. I was almost stunned into silence. My mind was in a whirl. After all, he had never mentioned his charitable deeds before.

'Lucy, he never told me about his work with addicts. He never said anything, not once.'

'Oh, Greg, he was so secretive. He couldn't bear to let people know. His father was a chronic punter, from the dogs at London's White City and Littlewood football pools, to the Newmarket horses. Too many to mention. James felt he had no choice but to get involved. He felt a sense of duty. It was not something he felt he could talk about.'

'I'm sorry...I had no idea. No idea at all.' By then, I was choking on my words.

'It took him years to tell me about his father's problems. When I first met him, he was a young, angry, and depressed boy. When his father took his own life, he left his mother and James with less than twenty quid.'

I had no idea, I thought to myself.

'It was the mid-seventies, Greg,' Lucy continued. 'Twenty quid was nothing, and it hurt. James always claimed his mother died from the grief. She loved James's father, but the gambling stood between then. No wonder James ran away as soon as his mother passed on.'

Oh my God, I said to myself, *I have completely messed up.*

'James also loved his job,' Lucy continued. 'I know there was something between you just before he left the Lee family. You said something and he panicked. He wasn't straight with you. What was it, Greg? What did James say?' *'You take this further, then it's you and me both,'* I immediately recalled his voice in my head. Once again, I said nothing.

'I would often find him crying. I wanted him to contact you, but he never would. You know he left the Lee family because of you?'

Again, no answer, but by then water was streaming down my face. Lucy pressed on.

'He didn't have a job to go to, at least not immediately, and lied so he'd get gardening leave. He just couldn't bear the looks you gave him. I know he must have hurt you, but he loved you. He really did.'

At some stage, I must have blurted out words to the effect that I loved him too. Although my mind was in a dreadful spin, I knew I had to do something.

'Are you all okay for money?' was the best I could come up with.

'What do you mean, Greg? I have a job and we're okay, at least financially.'

'But what about the mortgage?' I said. 'Can I help?'

I heard the makings of a very faint chuckle at the end of the phone. 'Thanks, Greg. I haven't had a smile in a long time. There is no mortgage, we're fine.'

'But how do you know?' I blurted back. How could Lucy's claim be true? Of course, there was a mortgage. James had used Lucy's power of attorney to borrow $65,000 from the bank to pay back Stephen Powell, and a mortgage secured it. James had told me that. I knew he didn't want Lucy to know what he had done, but Lucy would have taken control of all his finances as executor of his will.

She quickly provided the answer.

'Greg, you're a lawyer. You know about certificates of title. Well, I have the duplicate title sitting in my safe right next to me, where it's been for a decade or more. The mortgage was paid off years ago. Gee, you are sweet. Oh, would you please give the eulogy?'

So, James never did borrow $65,000 or, if he did, the sum was never secured by a mortgage. In other words, James lied to me. I never did work out what really happened, although our payroll officer confirmed that a significant part of James's salary had been directly debited to the Powell Family Foundation. Maybe the $65,000 was just a mistake. Perhaps a payment form had been inadvertently completed with the wrong payee. There could even have been a misreading of the acronyms 'PFF' for the Powell Family Foundation, rather than 'PPF' for the Powell Pride Foundation. Why did I not check the payment request form? I did not even know for sure that James had authorised the payment.

I never did manage to rationalise why James lied to me. He hadn't used Lucy's power of attorney to obtain finance, as he claimed. Indeed, he had blatantly lied when he told me that Lucy knew nothing about the Powell Family Foundation. She clearly knew a lot. James would rather I thought of him as a thief than a philanthropist. He must have been in a very dark place.

Still, James's mental state could not possibly excuse my behaviour. Even without the violence, my conduct had been reprehensible. I had flown off in a rage based on a simple ASIC extract. I was so preoccupied with the notion that the Lee Fund could be manipulated without collusion that I hadn't even bothered to conduct a basic investigation into the missing monies. What kind of friend does that?

I did deliver the eulogy, thankfully among several others, although embarrassment prevents me from repeating the content. Needless to say, it was full of tears and bucket loads of hypocrisy. At the end, in a whisper, I told James, or rather told his coffin, that I was sorry. I was sorry for the violent assault, sorry that I signed the power of attorney, sorry I never did check the payments request form, and sorry it was not me in that box.

Years ago, I had been surprised by the Catholic Church's decision to provide a funeral and burial for my mother. I had been told the church sought to fulfil the wish of Christ that all be saved, and that it would not be proper for the church to pass judgment on the spiritual state of others, even lapsed Catholics. Mother would have been appalled if she had known she would be buried with full Catholic honours. However, I suspect my father's spiritual state had more to do with Mother's funeral arrangements than her own.

I also suspect that James's funeral and interment had more to do with Lucy's beliefs than her late husband's. James had never shown any interest in religion. In fact, he mentioned that it was Lucy's decision to send the boys to Xavier College, Melbourne's prestige Catholic boys' school. I was also surprised, given the circumstances of James's passing, that the church would allow a funeral mass and burial in a Catholic cemetery.

Suicide, so the church taught, was a grave offence against life and the fifth commandment—a mortal sin. It was, therefore, a surprise to learn that the church had recently recognised the plight of those suffering from depression or mental illness and had accepted that a person with psychological issues may not be in full control of their faculties. In such circumstances, their suicide could not be judged as a mortal sin. I wondered if, in formulating its views, the Catholic Church had recognised its own role as a cause of widespread depression and mental illness, especially among young boys in its care. I was quietly relieved that I never did have a religious calling. I had done enough damage to one human being. God knows what I would have done if I had joined the clergy.

The funeral, in a suburban Catholic church, was a small affair. Of course, Lucy and her boys took centre stage. In addition to a few mourners from his last employer and a couple of Responsible Gaming Advisers from Crown Casino, only a handful of his former Lee Family Office colleagues turned up. It was, therefore, hard to avoid Lucy.

Lucy was mentally strong, but her resilience that day was tested to the limit. At the graveside, and at the small Malvern bar where we later gathered to remember James, she had sought me out. I was her shoulder to cry on. I held her hand. I clasped her waist and wiped the ocean of tears from her eyes. Aside from her children, I was her nearest thing to family. Of course, if she had known the truth, I would have been the last person she would have turned to.

One of the hardest moments was when Lucy asked me to join the board of the Powell Family Foundation.

'James would be so honoured.'

After all I had done, that was too much. I made up some bullshit story about not fully understanding addiction and that there were more worthy people to continue James's mission than me. Yet, both of those claims were undoubtedly true. I also feared that my role in James's suicide would not remain hidden for long and that Lucy would soon know the truth. Indeed, I waited for that dreaded day when the Coroners Court would call me. Of course, there was an investigation. Suicide was the verdict. I was, however, reassured by the fact that I was never approached in the case; my conscience grew a little lighter and I could sleep a little easier at night. Maybe the CCTV at Crown had not been working that fateful night. Perhaps the investigators never connected the events at Crown Casino with James's leap into oblivion a month later. My secret was safe.

I did see Lucy several times after the funeral, but I always found it hard to look her straight in the eye. When in town she would call and invite me for a coffee. I accepted on a few occasions, but gradually the invitations diminished. We never did say goodbye, although, by the time Middle Kingdom had hit the proverbial fan, we had stopped all contact.

Chapter Thirty-One
The Deathblow

Mei Jing Moore was the daughter of a successful Australian hedge fund manager and Singaporean television presenter. Known mainly as 'M.J.', from all accounts she was an inquisitive, loveable child who, for some inexplicable reason, had a fascination with ducks, particularly the ones with the loudest quacks.

Coincidentally, a raft of the Mallard variety happened to reside in the creek at the park next to the White Horse Early Learning Centre. In truth, it was more a small stream than a creek. When it rained, the water would swell to half a metre or so. When it was dry, the depth receded to no more than ten centimetres. One still, sunny afternoon, with not a rain cloud in the sky, M.J. Moore drowned in that creek. She should have been safely in the care of the early learning centre.

The office was sombre. We had lost Alfred and now a child whose only crime was her love of ducks. Martin wept for the lost child. He felt personally responsible even though he had no direct control or sway over the centre.

'Alfred and now a child. Who's next?' asked Martin. 'You know, bad news always comes in packages of three.'

I said nothing. Martin hadn't been that close to James Powell, and I was eager to avoid any discussions on his suicide. I was keen to focus the conversation back to Box Hill.

'What the hell happened? How did that poor kid get out?'

'Pretty much like the last time, Greg,' explained Martin. 'It wasn't a door but an open window. The problems with the foyer had just been fixed, but the painters had been in to finish it off. The window was open for fresh air, and the side gate was ajar because workmen were in and out of the centre.'

'What an awful coincidence,' remarked Winston. 'Who would have thought that correcting a safety snag would have led to this?'

'Now that is irony,' I quietly muttered to Martin. 'The one time he could legitimately use the word "ironic" he chooses not to.'

'Come on, Greg, focus!' snapped Martin. 'I think we have more pressing issues to consider than Winston's use of the English language.'

Martin's assessment failed to convince me. I had a strong feeling that Winston's problem announcement to the ASX would now be of considerable interest to the regulators. Nevertheless, it was not an appropriate time to raise the issue.

'You're right,' I said. 'He's got other things on his mind.'

Following M.J.'s death, or rather the media's coverage of M.J.'s death, Winston certainly did have other things on his mind. The *Herald Sun* ran a full two-page exposé of Middle Kingdom's 'shocking' governance practices and facilities, complete with a couple of charming images of M.J. Moore. Channel 7 had a crew and one of its transmission vans parked outside the centre for a couple of days.

The Age not only covered the tragic events but questioned the integrity of the Lee family and their suitability as care providers. *The Age* reporters were especially resourceful, running several articles on the history and development of the Lee family's business activities. One editorial was particularly disturbing. The piece strongly suggested that no one should be surprised by the irresponsible practices of a family dedicated to the cultivation of the opium trade. Another article drew comparisons with ABC Learning that had collapsed years earlier. Profits, so it was argued, had been built on low staff wages, cost cuts, and childcare tax rebates.

The press was consistent and relentless in their vilification of Middle Kingdom and the Lee family. Thankfully, Alfred was no longer around to read the criticism. As a result, the Middle Kingdom share price not only fell, it plummeted. The Lee Family Office received a barrage of hate mail, and much of Winston's time was spent appeasing disgruntled Lee Family Office clients. There was even talk of a class action by Middle Kingdom shareholders, although thankfully that did not materialise. Yet, in the space of little more than a week, the family's proud reputation of philanthropy and community service had been severely tarnished.

Winston and the Lee family's resolve to continue Middle Kingdom as a significant operating business had been dealt a hammer blow. The legal firm, DLA Piper, was appointed to delist the company from the ASX, and KPMG was charged with disposing of company assets. The Lee Family Office covered all employee entitlements and paid all outstanding trade creditors. Where a lease could not be assigned, the Lee Family Office paid all rent for the remainder of the term. Overall, the Lee Family

Office tipped in several million dollars. We would have paid anything to avoid voluntary administration and further criticism. In the end, only shareholders suffered financially, and all early learning centres, other than the one in Footscray, were closed. Alfred would have turned in his grave if that centre had been shut down.

'It is ironic,' I said to Martin one day. 'We spent all this time worrying about financial risks. Yet, insolvency was not an extreme or even moderate risk. We never were going to cut funding so that insolvency was a real possibility.'

'Mm,' muttered Martin. 'Yes. In hindsight you're right, but also in hindsight, I am worried about the risk review. Once that gets in the hands of the regulators, they'll know that Box Hill's safety problems weren't fixed up when they should have been.'

Martin was right that we had no grounds for refusing to hand over the risk review by the very fact it was not a privileged document. This time, the inevitable DEECD prosecution would just be the tip of the law enforcement iceberg.

In the immediate aftermath of M.J.'s death, the White Horse Early Learning Centre was literally swamped with regulators and law enforcement officers. In addition to DEECD authorised officers, there were police, representatives of the Coroners Court, and WorkSafe investigators. Although the police ultimately prepared a coronial brief focussed on the cause of M.J. Moore's death, it was WorkSafe that conducted the bulk of the investigation into the tragic circumstances surrounding the toddler's demise. In response, our first tasks were to notify our insurance broker and to instruct a leading law firm to take carriage of Middle Kingdom's insurance claim. A senior partner and a couple of senior associates were assigned to the matter.

They would soon be joined by a seasoned barrister, Ms J. Benson or 'Benni' as she preferred to be called.

Within days, ASIC commenced a separate investigation. While one regulator focussed on matters of safety, the other regulator would concern itself with the extent and quality of market disclosure and potential breaches of directors' duties.

In what became a long and painstaking process, my role was mainly one of liaison and coordination with the law firm and Middle Kingdom directors. I was responsible for reviewing all relevant documentation and populating a virtual data room. I organised interviews for the law firm with Middle Kingdom directors and staff, as well as countless special board meetings. Throughout, I was mindful of the need to maintain strict confidentiality, particularly as I had provided privileged legal advice to Middle Kingdom directors on their personal liability. I drafted and oversaw an internal communications policy so that access to pertinent information was on a strictly need to know basis. Without such measures, privilege would be lost.

Of course, it was harmful enough that the safety problem had not been fixed up before the risk review. The damage could only be further compounded if the regulator knew that the directors had received germane legal advice. My advice was evidence that directors were aware of the flawed layout of the White Horse Early Learning Centre and had failed to both rectify the problem and inform the ASX in a timely fashion.

The week or so following the tragedy was intensely emotional. All of us, Winston included, were shocked to be implicated in an incident that had claimed a young life. Yet, at the same time, and with the weight of the regulators and media bearing down on us, we had to look after ourselves. Initially, I was worried that Middle Kingdom itself would be prosecuted but, with ASIC's involvement, I became convinced that Middle Kingdom directors, especially Winston, would be charged with Corporations Act offences. Nevertheless, I had no reason to fear I would be in the firing line. Unfortunately, my absence of fear was misplaced.

The investigation powers of WorkSafe and ASIC were similar. Both regulators had powers to require the production of documents, to inspect books and records, require disclosure of information, compel assistance and answers to questions, and apply for search warrants. Yet, it must be noted that because the regulators had different aims, their use and timing of such powers varied. Indeed, in the immediate aftermath of the tragedy, WorkSafe relied heavily on its powers of entry, inspection, and workplace examination. The ability to enter the White Horse Early Learning Centre without a warrant was the single main difference between WorkSafe's and ASIC's investigation powers.

WorkSafe's initial focus was on the foyer, especially the open window and the side gate. Photographs and measurements were taken, plans were drawn, and interviews with staff were conducted. Records were reviewed and copies of staff and child attendance registers were demanded. In those first few hours, the White Horse Early Learning Centre manager had been interviewed along with all on-duty staff. With the help of the police, who had interviewed M.J. Moore's parents, and a witness who had seen a small unaccompanied child heading towards the Box Hill creek, Worksafe investigators had quickly determined the factual events leading to M.J. Moore's death.

Only later would WorkSafe demand more comprehensive records in the form of work, health and safety policies and procedures, hazard and risk assessments, incident records and reports, board and committee papers and minutes. Winston and managing director Danny Chan would be compelled to answer questions, and a more comprehensive interview with the centre manager would be conducted.

Even to Winston, the aim of WorkSafe's enquiries was self-evident. The regulator was slowly and methodically building an irrefutable case that Middle Kingdom had failed to reasonably provide and maintain a working environment that was safe and without risks to health. M.J. Moore's death was not merely an accident. Rather, it was an accident waiting to happen.

ASIC investigators did not attend the White Horse Early Learning Centre or the creek. They had no reason to. ASIC would just review Middle Kingdom's books and records and interrogate the firm's directors and officers. ASIC's involvement commenced with a notice to produce relevant documents. Unsurprisingly, the notice focussed on Middle Kingdom's continuous disclosure obligations. It would not have taken an ASIC genius to establish that Middle Kingdom had put out an announcement just weeks before M.J. Moore's death, claiming that all safety problems at the White Horse Early Learning Centre had been addressed. The odds were though, that the ASX compliance team had made the link and reported through to the regulator.

ASIC's initial production notice was limited in its scope. The notice required board papers and minutes, along with all correspondence with the ASX. Surprisingly, the notice did not extend to audit and risk committee matters. Yet, it was clear from the outset that ASIC would not go away easily. There would be no internal directive to close the file. ASIC was fully aware of the connections between Middle Kingdom and the Lee family. It was the regulator's chance to put the family in its place. Perhaps ASIC was concerned that the enforceable undertaking had not shaped behavioural change and that firmer enforcement action was required.

I cannot recall whether it was a WorkSafe or ASIC notice to produce relevant books and records. Over the following months, we received multiple notices from both regulators. Of these, one particular notice was broad enough to cover both my risk review and legal advice to directors. My subsequent discussions with Benni the barrister did not go well. Indeed, they were distressing. Benni was of the firm view that my legal advice was not privileged and should be handed up to the regulator. Her comments left me gobsmacked.

'Look, the idea that you can wear separate hats or can divide responsibilities into compartments is just plain wrong. The scope of a company secretary's role is not always limited to administrative tasks. Rather, what responsibilities you or any officer has is a question of fact. By your own admission, you were an active and influential participant in the corporate decision-making process. You can't turn round and say that you did something as company secretary, then something as a risk manager, and then something else as a lawyer. They're all part of the same package.'

'But,' I interjected. 'I was careful to show I was acting in an independent professional capacity...' It was Benni's turn to interrupt.

'I'm sorry, but you were the company secretary, a member of the executive leadership team, head of a comprehensive operational risk review and took charge of dealings with the regulator. You weren't functioning with the professional attachment essential to attract privilege. Your involvement was not limited to providing legal advice. You need to look at Shafron's case. If we fight this, we lose.'

I was vaguely aware that Peter Shafron had been general counsel to James Hardie Limited and that there had been outrage over the manufacturer's compensation foundation for victims of asbestos-related activities, but I had no idea of what Mr Shafron's particular legal issues were. I made a mental note to read *Shafron v ASIC* but never got around to it. I was more concerned about my inevitable meeting with Winston. It would be one I would care to forget.

'What do you mean, it's not privileged?' Winston exclaimed. 'I have the advice right here. Right at the top, it's marked confidential and subject to privilege. In any case, you're our lawyer, right? That's what we pay you for.'

I started to remind Winston that I was paid to do a lot of things and many of them were only vaguely legally related. The main issue, though, was the unprivileged nature of my advice.

'Winston, I really thought that I had done everything to ensure the advice was privileged, but the High Court has considered circumstances similar to ours...'

Winston cut me off in a tone that was distinctly devoid of compassion.

'My God, that's it. Can't you get anything right?' He was on a heated roll. 'We're still seething over that bloody ASIC enforceable undertaking that you got us, and now this. You're supposed to know this stuff. I know plenty of lawyers that could have easily provided the advice, and now we're in the shit because you didn't check the basics.'

I started to apologise, but at the same time mentioned that, as far as in-house counsel was concerned, the law on privilege was far from settled. Winston, however, was in no mood to hear my plea in mitigation.

'If the law is not settled, as you call it, then any decent lawyer would have pointed that out from the outset. Why didn't you brief out? God knows, over the years, I've lost count of the times you hand-balled stuff to your legal mates. Why not now?' It was a rhetorical question. 'Right, as far as I'm concerned, that's it, you're off the matter. I don't want you involved. If I had my way, you would be out of the door right now. Mason, you're on notice.'

I immediately felt an enormous sense of injustice. This was not my fault. Crucify me for killing James Powell, I thought, but not for this. On second thought, do not. What I had done was far worse than what I was then unjustly accused of. I kept quiet; after all, I suspected Winston had been looking for an excuse to get rid of me for a long time. Unlike Alfred, he never liked or appreciated me. Now that his father was no longer around, he could call the shots.

Chapter Thirty-Two
The Endings

A couple of weeks later, Winston was true to his word. I would be permitted to continue as the Lee Family Office financial services compliance officer. It was not long though before my time as Middle Kingdom's company secretary and Lee Family Office's legal counsel came to an abrupt end. Martin would take over what was left of Middle Kingdom's company secretarial duties, and Winston's twenty-something cousin, Jason Lee, would be appointed as the Lee Family Office's new in-house lawyer. Jason held a practising certificate. He had recently completed his supervised legal training at a suburban law firm, specialising in conveyancing.

Winston Lee announced the 'restructure' at a staff morning tea.

'As you are aware, this has been a difficult time for us all, particularly given the unfortunate incident in Box Hill. Every day we're responding to WorkSafe or ASIC. It's been a nightmare, and Greg has been working tirelessly to ensure the best outcomes. However, it's time to share the burden. From next Monday, Martin will take over as Middle Kingdom company secretary. Also, Greg will move to the role of "special adviser," working with the independent expert to ensure our financial compliance procedures are tip-top. This is a challenging role, so please join with me in thanking Greg for accepting the position.'

A polite clap of hands followed, although it was obvious to many staff that 'special adviser' was just a euphemism for 'dead man walking.' Neither Martin nor Eileen joined in the applause. Martin appeared sullen while Eileen looked like she was about to explode. They knew I had been pushed aside. Winston continued in the same nauseating vein.

'I am delighted to announce that Jason Lee will soon be joining us. Many of you know Jason as a client, but he is also an accomplished lawyer. We are very lucky to have secured his services. He will be taking over as legal counsel. Please make Jason very welcome.'

Following the announcement, Winston called Martin to one side. From Martin's reaction, I figured Winston had forgotten to inform him previously that he was about to inherit more company secretarial duties. Martin was visibly unimpressed. I couldn't hear what was said, but Martin turned his back on Winston and walked away. Later, Martin confided that he was angry with Winston for sidelining me and for the blatant display of nepotism. The knowledge that he was about to be appointed Middle Kingdom's company secretary was just the tipping point.

Eileen, who had never aspired to Martin's standards of professionalism, was far more scathing in her criticism of Winston.

'Brilliant!' she began sarcastically. 'He's just a fucking insecure narcissist, looking to blame others for his miserable failings. So now he's hired a little adolescent upstart with about as much corporate knowledge as my cocker spaniel. Don't worry, Greg, he'll come running back to you once the pubescent fucks up.'

I was not at all convinced that Eileen's prophecy would come to fruition, although I valued her support. Of course, I was gutted by the turn of events, but Eileen's humour lifted my sombre mood. I did, however, have another reason to smile. I knew that ASIC, in particular, would be poring over Winston's failings as a director. I would take immense pleasure if Winston were prosecuted. Yet, of course, one should be careful about what one wishes for.

The production of books and records in response to ASIC's initial notice gave rise to a whole series of compulsory examinations. Ultimately, ASIC's primary concern was the company announcement to the ASX. Both Winston and I found our way again to ASIC's Victorian Regional Office, although I would not make the same mistake twice. On this occasion, I readily accepted legal representation. Also, Danny Chan and the White Horse Early Learning Centre manager were called to give evidence. I suspect that their examinations were similar in substance to my own.

After the usual preliminary formalities, the ASIC inspectors asked a series of questions relating to Middle Kingdom and its governance structure, focusing on the circumstances surrounding the announcement to the ASX. They were keen to know that Winston had drafted the document, that I had checked specific facts with Martin and Winston himself, convened a directors' meeting, taken the minutes of that meeting, and faxed the announcement to the ASX.

Thankfully, much of the questioning focussed squarely on factual matters. The ASIC inspectors were polite and respectful. There would be no repeat of the derogatory remarks I had received during the Project Olive Oil examination. Yet, I felt decidedly uneasy, particularly when the questions addressed my review of the announcement.

'So, you only spoke with Mr Chan and Mr Lee. You did not engage or contact the builder who repaired the service door or anyone at the early learning centre?' asked the lead inspector.

'Privilege. Correct. I was being asked to provide a legal sign-off. I considered it appropriate to follow up with Mr Chan and, more importantly, Winston Lee.'

Unfortunately, my unease only deepened when the questioning moved to the risk review and my legal advice. In particular, the ASIC inspectors were interested in the timeline of events. They wanted to know when I became aware that the foyer had not been repaired. Again, there were questions on who I spoke to and my communications with directors.

'When did you first know that the foyer had not been refurbished?'

'Privilege. During the risk review for the audit and risk committee. A colleague and I visited the centre.'

'Who did you inform and when?'

'Privilege. I let Winston and the committee know when we completed the risk review. That was a few weeks later.'

'Exactly, when was that?'

'Privilege. I would have to check my notes, but it would have been a week before the next committee meeting. That said, Winston and the committee chairman got the draft papers at least a few days before that.'

'Thank you. You also mentioned that your legal advice was provided to the audit and risk committee at its next meeting. Was your advice provided to the board as a whole? If so, when?'

'Privilege. Yes, it was, immediately following the committee meeting. The chairman of the committee asked me to circulate to the board.

My evidence would have provided the ASIC inspectors with all the ammunition they needed. They had clarified that not all of KPMG recommendations concerning the layout of the White Horse Early Learning Centre had been implemented before the release of the announcement to the ASX. I had disclosed that I had become aware of that fact during the subsequent risk review and had later reported to the audit and risk committee. Further, all directors were fully aware of their personal liability for continuous disclosure, yet we had not corrected the problem announcement to the ASX prior to M.J. Moore's death.

While Winston and Danny were ASIC's primary targets, the non-executive directors were also in the firing line. At an information session to the board, Benni, the barrister, reasoned that ASIC would believe that the non-executives knew, or ought to have known, that the announcement would influence the market.

I was surprised that my attendance at Benni's briefing was required. After all, I had been removed as company secretary and effectively excluded from all matters relating to Middle Kingdom. I did not have to wait long for an explanation. When that explanation did arrive, it hit me as hard as a casino bouncer's clenched fist. I was literally stunned into silence as Benni explained that I could be pursued for various breaches of the Corporations Act.

This cannot be happening, I immediately thought. I felt my chest tighten and the contents of my liquid lunch rose up my oesophagus. I barely heard or registered the remainder of Benni's presentation aside from her referring to the offences of misleading and deceptive conduct that I previously addressed in my legal advice. Benni focussed on the fact that each director and the company secretary, in other words, me, had breached their duty of care and diligence by failing to ensure that the statements to the ASX were accurately worded. She referred to the monetary penalties and commented that we could all be banned from managing companies. I can't be sure of the finer points of the briefing; I was in no state to listen attentively. I was panicked into silence.

At the end of the session, I took a couple of large breaths and approached Benni. I needed an explanation as to why I could be potentially singled out.

'Benni, I was merely acting as legal counsel when I reviewed the draft announcement. I was giving legal advice. I wasn't acting as an officer. Yes, I know as company secretary I'm an officer, but all I did as secretary was fax the document to the stock exchange.'

Benni calmly but awkwardly stared me in the face. She must have stood silent for at least ten seconds as she tried to formulate a polite yet honest response.

'Alas, Greg, you still don't get it. As I explained to you before, you've actively participated in decision-making that affected the core business operations of Middle Kingdom, and the courts won't entertain a divisibility of roles. You can't wear two hats unless you're two-faced. Unfortunately, and I mean this in the nicest possible way, you're not two-faced. Everything you did was in the role of a company officer.'

'But many in-house lawyers are company secretaries. Many of them are on an executive leadership team or have responsibilities that affect a substantial part of business operations. How can they give privileged advice? How can they do anything that won't be seen as part of an officer's responsibilities?'

'With great difficulty, Greg; and the fact you're a legally qualified company secretary raises the bar. The courts expect more from us lawyers.'

I came to the realisation that I had failed to act with due care and diligence. I had, in Benni's words, fallen short of my duty to protect Middle Kingdom from legal risk.

'So that's it,' I said in a despondent tone. 'I'm going to be criminally prosecuted as an officer when all I was doing was giving legal advice. You know, Benni, I was so concerned about the wording of the announcement that I even talked to Winston about it. I guess though I should have conducted my own checks or even fixed the problems myself. I had the delegated authority.' What's more, I thought to myself, I could have told the board when I first knew the foyer and side gate had not been repaired, instead of waiting to the end of the risk review.

I felt sick. My head was spinning enough as it was, but my conversation with Benni took an immediate twist. It was the words 'criminally prosecuted' that did it.

'Christ, if there are any criminal charges, we will be defending them,' responded Benni. 'I'm sorry if I haven't been clear, but I would be shocked if ASIC took any criminal action. I am expecting civil penalties and banning orders, but not a criminal prosecution, or at least not by ASIC. I'm sure, in due course, WorkSafe will lay criminal charges against Middle Kingdom, but that's it.'

'Yes, I understand the civil penalty regime,' I replied. 'The regime provides for criminal prosecution and the offence of providing false information to the ASX has a maximum two-year jail term. I'm sorry, but I am worried I'll get a criminal record out of this.'

'Okay, it's possible criminal charges may be laid, but where's the proof of intent in all of this? Look at the legislation,' Benni said, pointing to her copy of the Corporations Act. 'Yes, you could, in theory, get two years for providing false information, but look, it clearly states it's a "fault-based offence." In other words, the prosecution needs to prove intent.'

As I listened to Benni, it slowly started to dawn on me that my past was returning to haunt me.

'Okay, there are a couple of possible offences, but additional ingredients have to be present to establish a criminal case. A good example is the offence of failing to act in good faith in the best interests of the company. The prosecution needs to prove you acted recklessly or dishonestly. Similarly, if it were argued you misused your position or company information, they would still have to prove you were intentionally dishonest.'

'Sure,' I responded as an image of an indignant Marcus Stein came quickly to mind. 'But somewhere I thought with regulatory offences you don't always have to prove a guilty mind. I remember some cases from about twenty-five years ago. The courts held that directors could be criminally liable without the need to prove subjective dishonesty.'

'Oh, I don't recall any criminal cases like that. Sure you're not thinking of civil cases or just minor statutory offences? Anyway, if there was anything like that back then, that's all been sorted out.'

As she spoke, Benni flipped the pages of the Corporations Act and pointed to the relevant sections. It was clear that the legislation only provided for civil action where a director thought he was acting for a proper purpose.

'Come on, Greg, why are you looking so glum? You weren't deliberately or recklessly dishonest. Go back to your law school days and the basic presumption that *mens rea* is required for statutory offences. I accept the principle is not universal, particularly for minor offences, but these Corporations Act matters are hardly minor. You're fortunate we don't live in a police state.'

Yes, I was fortunate, I thought to myself, but not in the way Benni meant. I said nothing, as the words of a lawyer from times past returned with full vengeance—*'You were lucky!'*

I was lucky, I thought, and Marcus Stein was unlucky enough to encounter an investigator swayed by dubious notions of criminal responsibility. You might well assume that the said investigator should have realised the errors of his way. After all, criminal law is an essential subject of any law degree, and twenty plus years of legal practice is a long time. But the sad truth was that until my conversation with Benni, I had never once thought to entertain the idea that my prosecution of Marcus Stein was a miscarriage of justice.

As it was, Benni was right on all counts. ASIC did launch Federal Court proceedings against Middle Kingdom for misleading and deceptive conduct, and for breaching the continuous disclosure obligations. Further, ASIC sought civil penalties and banning orders against each of the directors and myself for failing in our duty of care and diligence. ASIC claimed that we each had a duty to be satisfied that the announcement to the ASX was correct in all respects; instead, we all knew, or ought to have known, that the announcement was materially false.

It was rumoured that Winston was initially outraged and adamant that we should all rigorously defend the action. However, Benni's wiser head prevailed, and we all quietly rolled over and accepted our punishment. By that time, we had collectively exhausted the sub-limit of our D&O insurance for civil penalty orders and were dipping into our own pockets. Besides, none of us would relish the public opprobrium that would invariably accompany contested proceedings.

In the end, both Winston and Danny were banned from managing companies for seven years and fined $60,000. Five non-executive directors each received three-year bans and fines of $30,000. My punishment, along with the audit and risk committee members, was slap bang in the middle. Each of us was banned from management for five years and fined $45,000. By the time all the legal bills came through, my total debt was more than double the fine. It was a small comfort that our punishments would have been a lot more but for Benni's involvement.

Of course, if I had spoken up when I had the opportunity, that civil penalty order sub-limit of $250,000 could have been raised, and our D&O insurance would have responded to all claims against individual officers. My unhealthy disdain for indemnities and my secret desire to see Winston hurt had returned to bite me. I figured that Winston would have owed about $150,000 all up. In a couple of weeks, he would receive a Lee Family Office dividend for more than five times that amount. I would struggle financially for years.

Months later, Middle Kingdom, by then just an unlisted public company with a different name and few assets, would itself be prosecuted for the death of M.J. Moore under occupational, health and safety legislation. Looking back, the company officers, myself included, were lucky not to be prosecuted individually for failing to exercise due diligence over Middle Kingdom's health and safety duties. I suspect that we have Benni again to thank for that.

By the time of the WorkSafe prosecution, I was gone. Shortly before my fifty-ninth birthday, I was called into Winston's office. At that time, Winston was portrayed as a consultant, although in practice he continued to behave as chief executive officer. It was one of the rare occasions that we were civil. There were no tantrums, no accusatory outbursts. Indeed, neither of us needed to say much. I knew why I had been called in. It had been evident for a long while that my days at the Lee Family Office were numbered. I can't even remember if I formally resigned or if I was fired. It does not now matter. While I was hardly jumping for joy, there was a sense of relief that my days with Winston Lee were finally over.

On my way out of Winston's office, I passed Martin and Eileen in deep conversation. It was clear from the look on the faces that they knew my departure was imminent. Eileen attempted to lighten the sombre mood.

'Remember to send us a postcard from Copacabana Beach.'

I attempted a smile, but it was little more than a grimace. I was in no mood for gags, particularly those that were based on ripping off the Lee Fund. Martin, whose sense of humour was limited at the best of times, didn't get the joke. He just gave me a sad, thoughtful look.

'Take care, mate, and go easy on the grog.'

I did go easy on the grog, at least for the next half an hour—the time it took me to pack up my office and walk to The Oxford

Scholar Hotel. I am not sure why I chose that pub, other than the fact that Winston would not be seen dead there. It would have been twenty years since my last visit. The décor itself looked remarkably untouched, which was more than you could say about me.

As I sat by the pub window looking at the young faces of the students milling around RMIT, I became increasingly morose. I once had their bright and cheerful disposition. How many of them, I thought, would end up halfway around the world and alone? The sense of calm that served as a shield during my final meeting with Winston evaporated.

If only I had listened to the ASC lawyers or Tich Allen I would have probably kept a decent job with the public service. The joy I experienced as a corporate investigator hardly compensated for the stress of being investigated and prosecuted. If I had spent less time in the pub than at home with Lena, I might also have had a wife and family to turn to. If only I had done some basic administrative checks, James Powell would still be a living friend and not a dead memory. Yes, I had been hung out to dry by that shit Winston Lee, but my behaviour had hardly been exemplary.

Happy Birthday. I muttered to myself. *You have absolutely nothing except a civil penalty to pay, a heap of legal costs, and a tarnished reputation.* I returned home that night with a desperate need for more alcohol. I was out of beer, but a cheap bottle of scotch, the stuff you should only drink with cola or soda, sat enticingly on a kitchen shelf. I was tense, angry, and confused, all in one. I had lost everything. Straight from that bottle, I swallowed a huge mouthful of neat whisky and followed that up with two or three more.

I switched on the radio. I don't know why I craved music at that moment. Perhaps, I thought, it would have a calming effect, as the whisky had only exacerbated my misery. I was counting on the power of music to transport me, even if briefly, from my troubles. I'm not sure what I was thinking, although I vividly recall what happened next. For the second time in my life, something in me flipped. For a split second, I was aggressively physical, although thankfully not towards any human presence. I turned the radio dial to Gold 104.3.

'Coming up next is Alanis Morissette,' announced the presenter in a sickly-sweet voice.

'Not in my house she's fucking not,' I snapped, as Winston's face came prominently to mind.

I grabbed the whisky bottle and hurled it with attitude at the radio. The bottle literally exploded on impact. The radio would never recover and the carpet would require steam cleaning. Weeks later, I would still find slivers of glass or plastic and bits of metal that had once lived and worked inside that radio.

If I'm honest with myself, that smashed radio was an apt metaphor for a broken legal career—a career founded by unrealistic expectations, raised on misconceptions, and destroyed through negligence. Along the journey I had encountered friends and enemies; those that helped me and those who hindered. Still, in the final wash-up, there really was only one person to blame for my misfortune. It's that fellow I see each day in the mirror.

Postscript

I often bumped into Greg Mason, mainly at those professional development courses that lawyers dutifully attend. We had a lot in common as we were both immigrants who had worked for the corporate regulator before switching to corporate law later in life. Further, we also enjoyed a beer or two and relished swapping yarns of life as an in-house lawyer. There, though, the similarities ceased. I never shared his anxieties and frustrations; and I was fortunate enough to escape the ignominy of enforceable undertakings and civil penalty orders.

Still, the old proverb 'there but for the Grace of God go I,' stuck in my head. Maybe, I had been lucky. My CEOs were true professionals, my colleagues were well-trained and collegiate, and our clients were generally courteous and accommodating. Perhaps, Greg had just been unlucky to encounter the likes of Tich Allen and Winston Lee. But, either way, I had this gnawing feeling that he had been hard on himself. Was Greg really responsible for James Powell's suicide? Was Lena Kostakidis genuinely the angel he made her out to be? The trials and tribulations of the Lee Family Office appeared to be more Winston Lee's doing than Greg's. Sadly, I could not provide him with solace, but, by God, I tried.

The Melbourne legal fraternity is small, and the body of its in-house corporate lawyers is even smaller. I heard gossip that Greg had departed the Lee Family Office, but the details were sketchy. I assumed he had taken up a legal position elsewhere. As our relationship had been limited to chance meetings, I never expected to hear from him again. Yet, months later, and out of the blue, I received a telephone call from him. He had drafted a manuscript of his life story and asked if I could edit it. He needed an editor that could empathise with his 'lot in life,' as he called it. It was an unusual favour, but I readily accepted. After all, our previous encounters, however merry, were characterised by an underlying knowingness of the peculiar world we shared. Without hesitation, I looked forward to taking on the project and renewing the friendship.

As it turned out, the man I once knew had irreparably changed. Over the next few months, we met regularly, mostly in pubs. Invariably, those occasions caused considerable damage to both my liver and wallet. That was no surprise. After all, it was common knowledge he drank like a fish. I'm sorry to report that the light and laughter that had characterised our earlier encounters was missing. He was too far wracked with self-doubt and pity.

Even before reading Greg's manuscript, I was aware of the fact that his fortunes had declined rapidly. His trendy Fitzroy abode had been exchanged for decidedly mundane rented accommodation in a lower socioeconomic part of Melbourne's western suburbs. It was Greg's only path to clear his legal debts and finance his twenty-plus pot a day drinking habit. His world was small and barely extended beyond the distance from his unit to the local hotel. To the casual observer, it was a superficial existence. Yet, the reality was that the strong kinships forged at the bar formed the foundation of Greg's supportive social network; his fellow patrons and drinking mates were family. In no small part, the pub was his refuge.

Greg admitted to me that he could never step inside Nauru House again, and quickly lost contact with the Lee family and staff. The one exception was Eileen, whom he briefly continued to see. It was through Eileen that Greg learnt that Martin had resigned a few months after his own departure. It didn't shock Greg in the least that Martin had grown tired of babysitting the new legal counsel. Familiar with Martin's high moral standards, Greg was not surprised that his tolerance for working under a banned director was short-lived. Besides, Greg explained, Martin didn't need the Lee Family Office; his skills were in high demand, and as such, he had no problem landing a partnership with one of the 'big four' accounting firms.

According to Greg, Eileen had not even bothered to wait a few months. Word had got around that she had told Winston to 'stick his job,' leaving Eileen feeling thoroughly disgruntled that anyone could believe she was that polite. While she did use the words 'stick' and 'job' in her resignation speech, they were accompanied by an assortment of colourful expletives. Despite his morose demeanour, Greg chuckled as he imaged Eileen's departure. He was sure she did not leave quietly.

No doubt, Greg would have continued to enjoy Eileen's company. After all, Eileen was particularly forthcoming with her collection of Winston Lee insults. Unfortunately for Greg, she was also quick with jokes about fraud and extravagant Brazilian holidays at the Lee family's expense. Such humour merely brought back bad memories. James Powell would be etched in

Greg's mind forever and a day. Thus, his reunions with Eileen ultimately fizzled out.

Greg never applied for a new legal position and let his practising certificate lapse. A barrister acquaintance advised that he ought to make full disclosure of his civil penalty and banning orders to the Legal Services Board as part of the annual renewal process. In truth, it is doubtful that the Federal Court orders would have adversely affected Greg's chances of renewal. The number of practising lawyers with far worse condemnations than Greg's is too many to mention.

Lamentably, the fact remained that Greg's will and ambition had deserted him. Whether or not the Legal Services Board would question his suitability to continue as a solicitor was not the issue. He no longer considered himself sufficiently fit and proper to hold himself out as a provider of legal services.

My attempts to present a different reality fell on deaf ears. I subtly argued that if Winston had displayed some rudimentary professionalism, Martin and Eileen would still be employed by the Lee Family Office. I suggested that I could draft his manuscript to more objectively highlight the failings of others. Regrettably, he would hear none of it. It was evident that he neither needed nor desired more than basic editorial feedback. He allowed me to fix up a few typographical errors and insert a few Oxford commas. That was the sum of my contribution. Errors of fact and opinion have remained. Greg was adamant that he was the true villain in the piece and that his memoir should reflect that view.

'I should have listened to Tich Allen,' he said. 'You know, Pete, I still hear him in my dreams. *Heh, you laddie, you will never make a lawyer. I told you so!*'

Other than myself, Greg would resolutely avoid the legal fraternity. The Melbourne legal profession is a tight-knit community, and word quickly gets around when one of its own messes up. Therefore, Greg was careful to avoid the Williams Street end of Lonsdale Street. Before he moved house, he unceremoniously dumped his collection of Law Institute journals and twenty years' worth of legal memorabilia into a large yellow recycling bin.

I asked Greg if writing the manuscript had itself unnecessarily rekindled bad memories of Tich Allen and his experiences at the Lee Family Office. He smiled contemplatively into the distance, remarking that putting his life story down on paper was the only way he knew how to make peace with himself.

In truth, I doubted whether this autobiographical narrative had the power to deliver the cathartic comfort he craved. Time is a fickle mistress, and for some, like Greg, she never lets go. Throughout our renewed friendship, it became increasingly clear that there was only one person who could provide him with salvation, yet the cruelties of life and death robbed Greg of that opportunity.

The last time I saw Greg was in the Royal Melbourne Hospital, just a few days before his ailing body succumbed to cirrhosis and diabetes. By then, he was just a shadow of his former self. His eyes were dark and sunken, and his hands continually shook due to delirium tremens. As I turned to exit the ward, I noticed Greg gingerly lift a framed photograph from his bedside table; a faded, black and white snap from his bygone days. He never saw me leave, let alone utter a goodbye. The tears on his cheeks and his steadfast determination to keep the framed image still, told their own story. Greg's thoughts were far from the present. Perhaps he was recalling his long-lost idyllic youth or just overcome with melancholy. I know not which, but I swear I caught a glimpse of a smile; one that radiated love and affection. His eyes were firmly fixed on that photograph, while a young woman with a contented smile beamed back.

Peter Fairchild

About the Author

Peter Fairchild has pursued a four-decade career in law and law enforcement, and holds a Master's degree in criminology. With various roles in Asia and Australia, his experience includes twenty-odd years as a corporate lawyer. Now happily retired, Peter lives in Melbourne with his wife and cocker spaniel.